JEREMIAH

KRIS MICHAELS

KMRW LLC

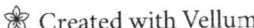 Created with Vellum

CHAPTER 1

S *everal years ago:*

The cold, hollow sound of a cell door clanging shut no longer sent a chill of dread down Dr. Jeremiah Wheeler's spine. He'd grown accustomed to the sights, sounds, and smells of the penitentiary in the past three years. Working with the inmates of the supermax facility had hardened his senses to the now-familiar drill of entering and exiting the prison. He'd deposited his wallet, cell phone, and all contents of his pockets into his locker prior to entering the first of the many secure gates and holding points he had to work his way through to reach his office and group therapy room. His small piece of real estate sat crammed into the far corner of the medical wing. It was the last office before the main exit for the doctors and nurses who worked with the inmates. The space they allotted him was precious and far too small for his needs, but with the overcrowding that was systemic in all prisons, they had scaled everything back to make more room to accommodate more prisoners. He made it work.

The first order of business was an inspection of the room they used for the group. He searched it morning and night. A knifing when he first started working at the prison initiated the practice. The shiv left for the inmate was tucked under one of the old chairs he'd acquired to make the sessions a little more bearable. Now he had metal chairs bolted to the concrete floor, but he always checked. With a glance at the clock, he sat down at the drab gray metal desk and turned on his old computer. The thing wheezed and sputtered, but the tech people at the prison had kept it on life support. He wasn't allowed to bring in his own laptop, so he waited for the dinosaur from the1980s to belch and hiccup its way to life.

Grabbing yesterday's paper coffee cup, he navigated through another secure door and waved to the guard in the bird's nest. The overwatch for this area was normally a senior guard that was winding down toward retirement. Today, Eddie Fastal was in the bird's nest. He lifted his coffee cup and Eddie nodded with a thumbs up. Jeremiah smiled and headed for the coffee machine. He filled two new paper cups after tossing yesterday's worn-out cup into the recycle bin. He detoured to the nest on the way back and Eddie buzzed him in.

"Damn, thanks, man. I've been jonesing for a cup for the last hour, but we're short-manned again today."

"That's getting to be an everyday occurrence, isn't it?" Since the state had outsourced the manning at the facility, the staffing had diminished.

"Eh, today it's because Harper's old lady had her kid. Thomas is still out with pneumonia. We're at minimum manning. We go down anymore and there will be gaps in coverage, but we can handle everything right now."

Jeremiah sat down and kicked up his feet on the long console of monitors and camera feeds. "How's the wife and kids?"

"Doing good. The youngest just got accepted to State on a full ride. So damn proud of that kid. He struggled there for a while, but he got himself together. Wants to be an engineer. He's a wiz with math. The oldest is doing good. She called last week and told us she was pregnant with number two. Good thing her husband works from home. Two under two is going to be a rough go for a while."

Jeremiah laughed. "Did Louisa ever tell Shelly what causes babies?"

Eddie snorted as he took a sip of his coffee and the guard coughed so hard Jeremiah reached over and patted him on the back. "Damn, Doc, you got to warn me before you say shit like that. And the answer is I don't know, and I don't care. I taught Eddie Jr. to wrap it up tight and that no means no, period. What the women discussed between themselves isn't my business."

"That's a tad old-fashioned, isn't it?" He took a sip of his coffee before an escort on the monitor caught his eye. "What's going on?"

"That's Macmillan."

Jeremiah sat up. "Shit."

"My sentiments exactly. That monster isn't supposed to come out of solitary, but he's been throwing up and had blood in his piss. They're bringing him up for Doc Freeman to examine."

"Make sure they keep him locked up." Jeremiah rubbed his chin. That man was the reason he pumped iron and had started mixed martial arts training. Jeremiah watched the shackled man hobble between two guards with another acting as overwatch from the rear.

Eddie's eyes snapped his direction. "Damn, that's right, he damn near got you when you first started, didn't he?"

"Yeah. He saw a newb, and he went after me."

"Well, thank goodness he didn't kill you. You've been doing good here, Doc."

"For some." He'd acknowledge he made a difference to those who weren't so jaded that they wouldn't ask for help. "I need to get back. I've got two one-on-one sessions before group. Tell Louisa I said hi and Eddie Jr. that I'm happy for him. Congrats on grandbaby number two!"

"Will do, and I'm too young to be a grandpa. I keep telling everyone that, but nobody listens."

Jeremiah turned after the door to the nest shut and held his hand to his ear and said, "What? I can't hear you?"

Eddie flipped him the bird before they both laughed. Jeremiah meandered back to his office, not really seeing the drab gray hallways, rather thinking of his one and only experience with Macmillan. A convicted serial killer with seventeen confirmed kills. The police believed Macmillan had killed many more and were constantly requesting time to question him about his crimes or others that were similar to his. The man was the clinical definition of ASPD, antisocial personality disorder. Macmillan ticked all the boxes. He was a textbook example of egocentrism as he acted to appease his own sense of self-gratification, not at all bothered with inconsequential things like the law or societal norms. The man lacked empathy or remorse, breathed hostility and deceitfulness, was manipulative and callous—and he was a psychopath. Not all people with ASPD were psychopaths, but Macmillan doubled down. Ted Bundy had nothing on this guy when it came to the charming department. Cyrus Macmillan had a captivating way of talking that was magnetic and engaging. Many people had underestimated the evil that thrived under that pleasant exterior. Jeremiah had, and it had almost cost him his life.

When he first took on the job here at the penitentiary, he'd accompanied two FBI agents to one of Cyrus' interviews. He observed and took notes, completely enthralled by the way that Cyrus played with the agents. With regal aplomb, Cyrus ended the interview and stood up, shuffling toward the door where the guard waited. Only leaving wasn't on his mind. Jeremiah, busy writing his notes, failed to see the man lunge. The pen in his hand became Cyrus' weapon. He stabbed one agent in the chest and grabbed Jeremiah, using his shackles as the means to attempt to choke him to death.

The other FBI agent and the guard hauled Cyrus off him, but it was a close thing. Another fraction of a second and Macmillan would have killed him.

It took a week after that close call to build the nerve to come back to the penitentiary. He started bodybuilding and took self-defense classes, resolving to never be defenseless or intimidated by another human. Yet that caution—no, fear—had always stayed with him. Years later and he wasn't sure he'd processed the event. Perhaps he never would, but today he knew how to protect himself, how to deal with inmates, and how not to put himself at a disadvantage.

His first one-on-one session was forty minutes of instruction on how to live inside the pen, although, being honest, Jeremiah knew the young man he was seeing shortly wouldn't last in here. He was young, pretty, and stupid, a triple strike. He'd be someone's bitch before long or join a gang hoping to prevent it from happening, only to be used by the inmates of the gang. The kid shouldn't be here; hell, two out of ten of the people who walked through that door shouldn't be here, but this young man killed a family of five on the interstate by driving the wrong way while stoned out of his mind.

The second session was one of his regulars. Chuck Dawson had robbed a store, and the shop-keeper had pulled out a shotgun. Chuck used the knife he was wielding and sliced the guy's arm wide open. Caught as he was leaving, Chuck was doing time for robbery and attempted murder. The man was trying to pay for his wife's cancer treatments. There was no insurance and no way to pay, so he'd tried to steal the money. His wife died a year ago, after three years in remission. Chuck admitted his crimes and was a model prisoner, but when his wife died, his remorse had turned to hatred of the police and the system that he now blamed for taking him from his wife's side. Was his sentence too harsh? Perhaps. But there was nothing Jeremiah could do about sentencing, much to many of his one-and-done session participants' dismay.

He annotated Chuck's file in the ancient computer and glanced up at the clock that rested in a cage of metal wire. He had time to slip down for another cup of coffee before his first group session. Perfect.

"Hey, Remi. How you been?" Kyle Snyder, a nurse

in the medical ward, greeted him as he exited his office.

"Hey, man. Doing well. Heading for more coffee. What about you?"

They meandered down the hall. "I'm grabbing a soda, but caffeine is caffeine, right?" He slid his ID through the slot and deactivated the lock. Jeremiah let the man go through and let the door shut because he had to process through via his ID so the guards had an accounting of where people were. He slipped his ID into the slot and frowned. He tried it again, but the light flashed red.

"What the--" A loud, sharp alarm blared throughout the medical block. Red lights flashed and in one instant all the doors that opened with identification cards sealed, locking everyone where they were. Both he and Kyle turned to the bird's nest. Eddie was behind the glass, yelling into the phone as he turned and saw them. The fear in the guard's eyes said more than his words ever would.

"Get somewhere and hide," Jeremiah yelled at Kyle, who nodded and sprinted toward the back of the hall. Jeremiah hesitated for just a second. If asked why he'd never be able to explain, but he turned back to where Kyle had run.

Macmillan was in the hallway.

Blood drenched the man's orange and white striped inmate uniform.

The serial killer smiled at Jeremiah and entered the room where Kyle had ducked. Jeremiah slammed against the door and screamed at Eddie to let him in. The only thought in his mind was to help Kyle. After years of training, he was strong enough now. He had the skill to kick that murderer's ass. A blood-curdling scream filled the hall on the other side of the locked door as Macmillan dragged two people, Kyle and one of the secretaries, from the room. He threw Kyle against the wall and grabbed the woman.

"Stop! Don't do this!" Jeremiah screamed and beat on the door. "Leave her alone!" Macmillan sent him another smile and then laughed as he shoved his hand in the woman's mouth, wrenching down, breaking her jaw. It flopped against her throat, attached only by skin. Macmillan held her up when she passed out from pain. He let her drop to the ground after using his fingers to slap the woman's jaw, sending it flapping back and forth.

Jeremiah pounded on the door. He turned and looked up to beg Eddie to let him in. What he saw sent horror through him. There were three inmates in the bird's nest. Blood and brain matter splattered against the window.

He turned his attention back to Macmillan, who now stood directly in front of him at the door.

"Let me out or they both die."

"I can't. The door is locked." He shoved his ID into the slot over and over, letting the man see what he said was the truth.

"Too bad." Cyrus shrugged and turned, making his way back to his two victims at a leisurely stroll.

Jeremiah dashed back to his office and picked up the phone. "Come on! Damn it!" When it connected, he yelled, "This is Doctor Jeremiah Wheeler. Macmillan and three inmates are loose in the medical wing. Three inmates are in the bird's nest and Macmillan is in Medical Hallway B4."

"Are you safe?" a disjointed voice asked.

"For now. Once those assholes figure out how to open doors, I'll be dead."

"We've taken the controls offline. They shouldn't be able to unlock anything. We've got our Rapid Response Team gearing up and the locals are sending their SWAT team and hostage negotiators." He heard the guard over the phone. "Doc Wheeler, can you see the inmates or any staff?"

"Hold on." He pulled the old phone as far as the cord would allow and then stretched out the door.

"I see two inmates in the bird's nest. There is a lot

of blood spattered on the window. I don't think Eddie made it." He turned his head and met Macmillan's eyes as he stood in the hallway with a phone against his ear. "Cyrus pulled one of the secretaries' jaw off. I don't know what her status is. She passed out because of the pain or is shocked out."

"Which secretary, Doc? We're trying to account for as many people as we can."

"The one that works over near HR, brown hair, about fifty. Kyle Snyder is unconscious in the hall. Wait, Cyrus is talking to someone on the phone."

"That would be us. He says he wants to talk to you. They're going to patch him through, but we'll have people on monitoring the calls. You need to stall him, Doc. There are guards down all over the place and a full-on riot in Cell Block C. I'm thinking this wasn't a coordinated effort, but Macmillan capitalized on it, just like the other two in the bird's nest. The techs are ready to patch you through now."

"What am I supposed to say?" Jeremiah stared down the hall, making eye contact with Macmillan.

"Do your doctor thing, man. Just keep him talking as long as you can." The line clicked several times, and he knew the second someone connected him to Macmillan. He could hear heavy breathing across the connection.

"You wanted to talk to me?" He held the phone to his ear as he stared at Cyrus.

"What a very fortunate turn of events for you, Doctor." Cyrus' head cocked to the side and his eyes narrowed. "You know, I thought you'd left the penitentiary. We haven't visited in years."

"I learned my lesson, and you satisfied my curiosity." Jeremiah glanced up at the clock, noting the time. How the fuck long did they want him to stall this man?

"Which is particularly interesting because you did nothing but tweak *my* curiosity. In fact, over these past years, I have done nothing more than run that scene in the interview room through my head. The mistakes I made, such a shame. You should be dead. I should have snapped your neck instead of trying to strangle you." Macmillan cocked his head. "Did the FBI agent die?"

Jeremiah leaned against the door jamb. "You know the answer to that. If he had, they would have charged you with another death."

Cyrus laughed, "Oh, Doctor, what difference would it make? I have only one life to serve and seventeen life sentences. Executions are on hold in this state. They'd bang the gavel and then march me back to my box to live in solitude. It's a shame, you know. FBI Agent Docker and you, Doctor Jeremiah Wheeler, are the only two victims I tried to kill who are still alive."

Jeremiah blinked at the man's words. Docker, yes, that was the man's name, but Cyrus would have only heard it once when they were all introduced as he entered the interview room. "Sorry to disrupt your plans."

Cyrus smiled at him. "Disrupted? No. Delayed? Perhaps. That depends on what happens here today, doesn't it? I'm bored. The woman is going to be my distraction. I want you to watch. If you don't, it will be so much worse for her and the man."

"You don't want to do this." His hand shook as he held the phone tight to his ear.

"Oh, but I do. I assure you I do," Cyrus chuckled. "If the morons who run this establishment hurry, she will not have to suffer long. Ten or twelve hours if they take their time. I have coffee and snacks. I'll be fine." He held up the metal door guard of the vending machine. "Sharp stuff, but dull, too. It will make jagged cuts. Don't you love jagged cuts? I do, but not as much as the sharp straight ones that bleed freely. I wonder if I can strip her skin from her. Strange, I've never tried that, and I have plenty of time. Remember now, you will watch. If I see you aren't, I'll move on to the man and torture them both. Your choice, Doctor. Eyes wide open." Macmillan dropped the receiver and moved back to the woman.

"Please tell me you have someone coming in."

"Doc, we're trying," the guard's voice echoed in his ear. "We have cameras on him."

Jeremiah held his breath as Cyrus stripped the woman. He flipped her onto her stomach and...

She lasted nine hours. Cyrus drew pictures on the wall with her blood. Jeremiah dropped the phone three hours into the ordeal and tried to watch but not see. It was impossible. The screams, the pleading, and then finally Cyrus' soft singing as she died haunted him.

Kyle fought when Cyrus pulled him from the closet where the nurse had been shoved while he was unconscious. Cyrus laughed and used the metal sheet to slice through Kyle's Achilles tendons. Macmillan flipped Kyle onto his stomach and began the process again.

Startling him, he heard a loud whistle from the phone. Still staring at the bastard, he picked it up and listened. "Doc, we're ready to breach. Distract him."

Jeremiah stood away from the wall and walked to the door. He knocked on the window.

Cyrus popped up from his work and looked over his shoulder. He smiled widely. "Doctor! How wonderful of you to join me!" Cyrus stood and looked down at the blood that soaked his body. "A glorious day, isn't it?"

Jeremiah crooked his finger in a beckoning motion. Cyrus damn near skipped to the door. "Do you want to see better? Should I pull him down here?"

Jeremiah shook his head.

Cyrus frowned in confusion. "What do you want then? I'm a busy man."

"Nothing." He spoke for the first time in ten hours, and the word grated as if the insignificance of its utterance lived at a cellular level.

The back hall door blew off its hinges and a storm of armored men flooded the hall. Cyrus gave them a cursory look before he turned around and stared directly at Jeremiah. "I didn't want these two, but I want you and Agent Docker. You will be mine, Doctor. Remember what you see, what you will feel when I peel the skin off your body. I will bathe in your blood. Then I will pull your intestines out and choke you with them."

Jeremiah watched as they hauled Cyrus through the flow of blood. The heavy doors muffled his maniacal laughter, but Jeremiah heard it. Several men swarmed in and placed Kyle and the woman on stretchers. A guard jogged to the door. "We've got to clear two more areas, Doc. We'll be back for you."

He nodded and turned around, going back to his office. With care, he picked up his phone and put the receiver back on the cradle and placed it on his desk. A sense of detachment settled on him. He sat down in his chair with the distinct purpose of looking up the woman's name. Ellen Daily. He'd never forget her name or any of her screams. If he lived a thousand years, he'd be able to recall in finite detail what that bastard had done to her and to Kyle. He pulled out a few pages of paper and wrote exactly what had transpired. Every detail. When a guard knocked on his door, he lifted his eyes.

"Doc, we got to get you out of here now."

Jeremiah nodded and lifted the paper. The first ten pages were his account of what happened. The last was his resignation. He signed them both. "You okay, Doc?" The guard asked as he approached his door.

Jeremiah blinked at the young man. "No. I am not." Exiting his office, he and the guard walked to the main door which worked when he presented his ID. A police officer stopped him. Without missing a beat, he handed the ten-page statement to the officer along with his business card. "My contact information if you have any further questions."

His boss, the deputy warden, rushed toward him. "Jeremiah, I don't know how to apologize—"

He held up his hand, a weird sense of displacement still driving his actions. "I tender my resignation." He handed the stunned woman his letter, ending his contract with the penitentiary.

"I'm not accepting it. Not right now. Call me in a few weeks. Take some time to consider this. Please."

Jeremiah stared at the woman and nodded because he wasn't capable of higher thinking. Now that he was out of his office, his one and only goal was leaving the prison and never, ever setting foot inside one again. He went through the motions of gathering his gear before he turned and handed his badge to the security checkpoint. "I won't be needing these any longer." He dropped his badges off and walked out of the door. The slap of hot air replaced the smell of the prison. The sound of an ambulance siren turned his head. He watched as not one but two ambulances tore out of the parking lot. How many had died or been injured today? What caused the riot? How had Cyrus roamed the prison without chains or shackles? Jeremiah's eyes swept the thirty-foot fences and the strands of Constantia wire, the guard towers, and massive security surrounding Cyrus that kept humanity on the outside safe.

It wasn't enough.

Not nearly enough.

CHAPTER 2

"About time you answer your damn phone. I was afraid I'd have to waddle my fat ass onto a plane and come out there," Doctor Jamison Fredrick's gruff old voice snapped across the connection before Jeremiah could even speak.

"Well hello to you, too, Jamison. How have you been? Good? How's the job, the wife?" His monotone and flat response sucked because he was happy to hear his mentor's voice, but he couldn't get past the lack of sleep and nightmares he'd been having every time he closed his eyes.

"Everything and everyone here are fine. I'm worried about you, however."

"You heard?"

"No, I saw. The whole damn thing."

"How?"

"Guardian is investigating the company to whom the state turned over responsibility."

Jeremiah pushed up off the couch and ran his hand through his hair. "For what?"

"Can't disclose that, I'm afraid. Unless you want to come to work for us."

It was a running joke. Jamison thought the sun rose and set with his damn Guardian. But Jeremiah had a different career path. He was going to spend his life taking care of those society had forgotten. He closed his eyes and sighed. Not any longer. Never again.

"Remi, how are you holding up?"

He dropped back against the couch and stared at the dark ceiling. "Not good."

"Nightmares?"

"Daymares, too."

"I can understand why. We are going to get you through this, but I want you to do something for me." Jamison's voice held the confidence of a lifetime of psychiatric practice.

"What's that?"

"Leave."

"I did. I handed in my resignation. I left." Jeremiah glanced at his tiny little apartment. Normally, he was out and about doing things, meeting with friends, going to the gym. This tiny efficiency apartment was just a place to hang his clothes. He had three pictures of family and the rest was here when he'd rented the place. The walls of the small apartment had been creeping closer to each other since he'd left the facility. Day by day, they inched in, getting tighter.

"They're idiots if they took it while you were under duress, and that's not what I meant. Pick up and move away from there for a leave of absence, or you will always see something that reminds you of working in that place. I want you to give yourself a break. You need to find neutral ground. Someplace that you've never been, a quiet place where the pace of life is slower, gentler."

"I'm not ready for a fucking rocking chair, Jamison. Besides, the deputy warden said she wouldn't accept my resignation. She wants me to give it a couple weeks,"

"Did I say anything about a rocking chair? No. But you and I both know you went through a major trauma two days ago. You need to get away so you can pull this shit out and look at it—memory by memory."

He sighed. Jamison was right. What he had to do

22

was obvious, but fuck him, he didn't want to pull out each agonizing memory and deal with it.

"Can you go home?" Jamison prompted.

A chuff of humorless laughter escaped him. "I thought you said slower and gentler. I've told you about my mother, right?"

Jamison chuckled. "Ah, that's right. The pageant-mom-slash-socialite, how could I forget? Your father still has political aspirations even dealing with his wife's tendencies?"

"If you ever met her you wouldn't forget her, and yes, my father is going to be Governor of Alabama one day. Home isn't what I need now, J."

"What about your sister?"

"Genevieve moved away from Alabama. She found a little restaurant in a backwater South Dakota town that she fell in love with."

"Do you still have your motorcycle?"

Jeremiah's eyes popped open. "I do." He had a custom Harley he'd paid dearly for and babied like most would care for a beloved pet.

"How about a road trip?"

"To where?" It was an honest question. Where could someone go to slow down and maybe relax while he worked through a fuck-ton of baggage the incident had dumped in his mental closets?

"South Dakota."

Jeremiah blinked. "Why in the hell would Genevieve want me there?"

"Because she's family, she loves you, and you need to get away from where you are, even for just a little bit. We can have our sessions in private via video chat or the phone. It would give you time to heal."

"Sessions? Who said I was going to hire you as my couch, J?"

"Who else do you trust?" Jamison batted the question back at him.

He grunted. "Few people, that's for sure."

"We'll work on that, too," Jamison added. "Take care of things out there and then get your ass on that motorcycle. I'll talk with you next Monday. Don't make me call twice. I'll charge you double."

"Heaven forbid," Jeremiah drawled, but he laughed for the first time since... He snapped his attention back to the conversation, not allowing his mind to travel down that road again. "Hey, Jamison. Thank you."

"You'd be there for me."

"I would." Jamison was a good friend; he'd move heaven and earth to make sure the man had what he needed.

"If you get to a point where you need to talk, if shit gets heavy…"

Jeremiah sighed. "I'm not suicidal. Did what Macmillan do fuck with me? Yeah, but that isn't a road I'm going down. I don't even see the signposts for it."

"Cyrus Macmillan." Jamison spat the name.

"Yeah."

"How in the hell did he end up without restraints or without a guard?"

"They had him up in the medical wing to run some tests. From what I've learned, his doctor and three nurses are dead. He was wandering the halls when the riot broke out and initiated a lockdown. If the alarms hadn't activated, I would have walked right into him."

"You have a guardian angel, my friend."

He shook his head even though Jamison couldn't see him. "What I have are nightmares and probably PTSD." He swallowed hard. Even though Cyrus was locked away in a supermax facility, there wasn't enough distance in the world to tamp down the memories of that madman or what he'd done.

"Put in for a leave of absence. If you decide not to go back, you can send in your resignation. Then hop on that deathtrap of yours and head to see your sister."

Jeremiah leaned back and cast his gaze around the tiny apartment. Why not? At a minimum, it would be a break and he'd get to see Genevieve. He had some things to clear up first. He drew a deeper breath and felt some weight fall from his shoulders. "I'll do that."

"We talk once a week, or I'll damn sure come find you."

"I can do that."

CHAPTER 3

J eremiah pulled into the parking lot of the Bit and Spur Bar which sat on the junction of the road a few hundred feet before the town of Hollister, South Dakota. He turned his bike off and put the kickstand down. After pulling off his helmet, he sat for just a moment. No movement, no roar of his engine, just the distant sound of music coming from inside the small bar. He'd traveled through vast empty expanses, just him and the road. The time to think was a blessing and a burden. There were times he could forget the recent events, but the lingering fear persisted. No, the sensation was more akin to a hyperintense saturation of everything he saw and heard, almost as if his body was in a constant fight or flight response.

He hung his helmet from his handlebar and stretched as he un-assed his bike. With several slaps of his gloves, he blasted the road from his leather pants and jacket. He rolled his shoulders and pushed his fingers through his hair. A scuffle at the door to the bar drew his attention.

Jeremiah ambled toward the building, holding back until whatever was happening settled. He saw two men stagger out of the door. A third followed them out and yelled, "Get the hell out of here and don't come back, even when you get sober. I'm sick of you Klingler boys. I've called the deputy. If you don't want to land in--"

The smaller man in a baseball cap twisted suddenly. Years of watching inmates had honed his instinct. Jeremiah sprinted forward. Baseball cap thrust forward with a knife and shoved the damn thing into the man throwing them out. The third man laughed and kicked him when he hit his knees.

Jeremiah ran through the smaller man, knocking him to the gravel. Mr. Laughing-Like-a-Loon got a right hook to the jaw and dropped like a bag of cement. As the first man got to his knees, Jeremiah kicked him in the ribs, sending him to his side, curled into a ball. The distinct sound of ribs cracking would keep the fucker down for a while.

The man who'd been stabbed held the knife in his hands.

"Hey, no, no, no. Dude, you don't want to pull that out. Come on, let's get you settled. Did you call the deputy?"

The guy looked at him, his eyes glazed over, whether from the pain or the shock Jeremiah didn't know, but he needed answers. "Dude, what's your name?" He helped the man down and removed his hands from the knife. "Okay, we're looking good here." He examined where the blade had entered the man. "But we aren't pulling this sucker out until you're at a hospital."

"Declan." The man licked his lips. "Declan Howard."

"Nice to meet you, Declan. Did you call the cops?"

The smaller blonde man tried to get up but ended up crawling like an inchworm through the gravel. The lonely sound of a siren in the distance answered Jeremiah's question at the same time as Declan nodded. "Damn Klingler kids. They started shit inside. Broke some stuff. I tossed them."

Jeremiah lifted the man's t-shirt from around the knife and examined the wound with the small pocketknife still protruding from the entry point. "Yeah, I was walking up when I heard you throwing them out. You're going to be okay; this isn't as bad as it looks." Declan winced. "Or feels. Seriously, you lucked out."

A set of cowboy boots appeared at the doorway. Jeremiah looked up at the old cowboy. "The police are on their way."

He nodded at the leather-skinned old man. "If you have an ambulance service or a medic in the area, you need to get them heading this way."

The old guy nodded and headed back inside the bar. The siren grew louder, and more cowboy boots exited the facility.

"Declan, did this guy stab you?" A heavy hand fell on his shoulder. He shrugged it off and cursed under his breath.

"No. He helped me." Declan's statement seemed to help put an end to the aggression he was feeling from the crowd.

A police car skidded into the parking lot, spraying gravel and dust as he slid to a stop.

"Get the fuck out of my way!" A deep baritone voice split the crowd. Jeremiah glanced up. Of course. A big man wearing blue jeans and a plaid shirt with a gun belt strapped to his waist and a badge on his chest stepped through the crowd, a double-barrel shotgun pointed right at Jeremiah. The deputy scanned the crowd as he asked, "Declan, what happened?"

His patient opened his eyes. "Those damn assholes were fighting in the bar. I threw them out and then Carl Klingler turned on me with a knife, sticking me before I had a chance to react. Biker dude here was walking up to the door and put both him and Curt down real hard and fast. Then he had someone call the ambulance."

The deputy nodded toward Jeremiah. "Who are you and what were you doing here?"

Jeremiah held the knife still with his hand. "Just a man who is stopping in to visit his sister and then I'm heading out." He glanced up and nodded toward the shotgun. "Dude, I promise, I am not the bad guy. Want to point that toward the heavens?"

The deputy cocked his head and arched his eyebrow as he tilted the shotgun skyward. "Medic?"

Jeremiah shook his head. "Doctor."

"You good here while I tend to those assholes?" The deputy motioned with his shotgun toward the two Jeremiah had dropped earlier.

"Yeah. The smaller one might have a couple

cracked ribs. I haven't seen the other one stir. One punch to the jaw." Jeremiah grabbed Declan's shoulder when the man tried to move. "I know it hurts, but I guarantee if you move it will only make it worse."

"Ken, here comes Eden." The crowd split again, and a woman ran directly up to where he and his patient were. "Damn it, Declan, I thought we agreed after I stitched you up last time you wouldn't start leaking for at least a year." She dropped her bag beside her and glanced over at Jeremiah. "I'm a nurse practitioner, I've got this now. Thank you."

"He's a doctor." Declan groaned the comment. "A pushy one, too. Won't let me move."

"Then he's a smart pushy doctor." The woman moved away. "What do we have?"

"Here comes Doc!" Jeremiah lifted and watched as a man pushed his way through the crowd.

The deputy headed over and knelt down beside Declan. "Those two aren't going anywhere except jail."

The man he assumed was the doctor dropped beside him, setting his medical bag beside the woman's. The deputy sniggered, "Damn, Doc, thought you were just around the corner. What in the hell took so long?"

Zeke threw him a glaring look, "Believe it or not, for the first time in two days I was sleeping, Ken. What have we got?" He addressed the question to the blonde.

Jeremiah knew it was time to turn over the patient, so he rattled off his assessment, "Strong pulse, his pupils are equal and reactive, the knife needs to be stabilized. He is conscious, and unless I miss my guess, he is one lucky son of a bitch. The blade appears to have gone through the subcutaneous tissue but didn't puncture the abdominal wall. We've been here for over ten minutes and it doesn't seem it has compromised the cavity. No swelling from any obvious internal bleeding although with movement of the knife we have oozing. The color and amount are wrong for an arterial bleed."

The man blinked at him. "Doctor Ezekiel Johnson, and you are...?"

Jeremiah nodded and returned his attention to the knife he was holding. "Doctor Jeremiah Wheeler."

"Well, if we are introducing ourselves, y'all, I'm Eden Wade." The woman handed Doctor Johnson a roll of gauze. "Let's stabilize this knife."

Jeremiah held the knife as the other two worked

to stabilize the blade. He could hear the sound of a siren over the mumbled conversation around them.

The deputy lifted and in a clear, level voice stated, "All right, the bar is closed for the night. If you owe Declan for your drinks, either write it down for him or go put your money on the bar. If any of you have had too much to drink, you call for a ride. I don't want to scrape any of you off the gravel when I get back from Belle Fourche."

Remi lifted his eyes and chuckled as the cowboys dispersed, several reaching for their wallets and heading back inside, others meandering to the line of pickups in the parking lot.

He lifted away and rolled his shoulders as the local doctor took over and made his own assessment of the patient. The nurse moved out of the way when the ambulance pulled into the lot.

The EMTs hurried to the patient. With practiced ease, the driver lowered the gurney beside Declan and commented, "Damn, Zeke, you need to stop coming up here. Every time you show up, we have a run."

"Well, stop having tornados, fights, and stabbings. Besides, I'm moving up here next month. The county finally decided this area needs a full-time doc." Jeremiah, the deputy, the nurse, Eden, and

Zeke worked as a team to help the EMTs move Declan to the gurney and then transport him through the deep gravel of the parking lot to the bus. The doctor climbed in the back. He looked at the woman. "Eden, can you pick me up from Belle? I'll let you know if they transfer him to Rapid City."

"Sure, but it won't be until after my morning appointments." The woman grimaced a bit when she answered.

"I can bring you back, Doc. I'll have to go down tomorrow morning bright and early to finish my reports on these assholes," the deputy said as he shut one of the ambulance doors.

"Perfect." The doctor sighed and looked down at Declan. "Let's get you taken care of."

Jeremiah shut the other door and hit the side of the bus twice. The ambulance pulled a wide U-turn and headed back the way it had come.

"I'm going to need a statement from you." The deputy handed Jeremiah a card. "I'm Kendall Zorn. I'll need you to stick around or let me know where you'll be so I can get the paperwork from you."

"Jeremiah Wheeler. I'm here for a couple days, a surprise visit to my sister." He took the card and shook the man's hand.

"Yeah, who is that?" The man cocked his head and looked him square in the eyes.

"Genevieve Wheeler."

"Gen? No shit? You just missed her then. The last Saturday of the month after she closes, she makes a supply run down to Rapid City and spends the night. She'll be back tomorrow about midday."

Well, shit. That meant finding a hotel or pushing on, and he was too damn tired to do that. By the looks of the small town when he pulled through it to get to the bar, a hotel wasn't looking promising, either.

"Gotta tell you, I had you pegged for the bad guy on this one. Not many doctors around here dress in black leather and have a snake tattooed on their neck," the deputy chuckled. "That will teach me to judge a book by its cover. Eden, do you need a ride back to the clinic?"

"No, I'll walk back after I grab a beer from the bar. I'll pay for it and lock the door behind me."

The deputy thanked her before he dipped his head in Jeremiah's direction and headed toward his patrol car where the two men were sitting.

"He should have had the doc look at those two," Jeremiah mused as the patrol car turned around and followed the ambulance's path through town.

"Nah, those boys are from tough stock, although this is the first time they've resorted to weapons. Normally, it's just fistfights."

"Normally?" Jeremiah followed the woman into the bar. She lifted the hinged bartop and stepped behind it like she'd done it a million times. "What's your pleasure? I'm buying."

He lifted his bloodied hands. She nodded across the building. "Bulls are that way."

"Bulls?" Jeremiah blinked at her.

"Yup. Heifers are over here. I'll wash up, too." She laughed and headed to the bathroom. "You'll get used to it."

He shook his head and made his way to the restroom. Sure enough, there was a picture of a cartoon bull on the door. When he made his way back to the bar, the woman had two draft beers pulled. The outside of the glass was frosted, and it looked like freaking ambrosia.

"Thanks." He picked up the mug and drank three-quarters of the brew in one go. The sharp, cool drink flooded through his dehydrated body. Ambrosia wasn't a kind enough description for the thirst-quenching of this brew.

"Thirsty?" Eden hopped off her barstool and went around the bar again, topping off his beer.

"Yeah. I had a long day, pushed through until I got here rather than trying to find a place to camp out in the middle of nowhere, but it looks like the effort wasn't worth it. My sister is out of town." He took a drink of the fresh beer and sat down on the barstool.

She pulled her drink across to where she was standing. "Gen talks about you. She misses you. I can tell that." The woman laughed. "She didn't know you were on your way, did she?"

Jeremiah chuckled. "That would be a no. I was going to surprise her." He cocked his head. "Do I detect a southern accent?"

Eden laughed. "You do. Born and raised in Alabama."

Jeremiah almost choked on his drink. "No shit? Me too. Birmingham."

Eden nodded and then laughed. "Yeah, Gen told me where y'all had grown up. I'm from Selma."

"Damn, woman, what brings you to Hollister, South Dakota?" Jeremiah instantly wished he hadn't asked the question. The light behind those blue eyes dimmed.

"Long story," the woman chuckled and then shook her head. "Actually, it's not a long story. My husband died in a drive-by shooting outside the hospital in New Orleans where we both worked. I needed a change of pace, my friend knew of a company that placed nurse practitioners in areas that are underserved, and voila, here I am." She lifted her mug and saluted him before she took a drink.

"I'm sorry for your loss." There was nothing else he could say, was there?

"Thanks, it's been four years now. Little ole Hollister has been a balm to my soul. Don't let it fool you, though. For a tiny place, it has its share of drama."

"Like tonight?"

She laughed. "Not usually this kind. Fistfights when the hands come in happen, but drama comes in all shapes and sizes, and because it is a tiny little town, everyone knows everything about everyone and everything." She laughed and took another sip. "You'll see."

"I won't be staying that long." He took another drink of his beer.

"A long way to come for a quick visit, isn't it?"

His eyes flicked to her. "How would you know?"

She chuckled and lifted her arm. "Anywhere from here is a long way to come."

"What about you, are you planning on settling

down *way* out here?" Jeremiah drained the rest of his beer.

"I don't know. I'm playing it by ear. I'm sorry Gen isn't here."

"Yeah, but that reminds me, do you know of a spot where I can grab a room?"

She snorted. "That would be a no, but as Zeke has vacated my couch, you're more than welcome to sleep in my front room."

"I don't want to put you to any trouble." They'd only just met, and the invite should have been awkward, but it wasn't. The woman before him appeared confident in her abilities, was intellectually enticing, and obviously generous if she was offering a stray man a place to sleep for the night.

"No trouble. I'll move Zeke's stuff out of the way, and you can stretch out. My first patient isn't until nine-thirty. Do you have a motorcycle to go along with that get up or are you just a leather daddy looking for his little?"

Jeremiah threw back his head and laughed. "I have a bike, thanks. This isn't a kink."

She dropped a twenty on the bar and put the mugs in the sink. "I'm locking the door on the way out. We'll get your bike and head to the clinic."

"You live at the clinic?" He watched as she clicked

off the long row of lights and used an Allen wrench to unlock the push bar of the main door.

"Above it. Gen's restaurant is kitty-corner to the clinic. She lives above her shop, too." Eden slammed the door closed and tried the handle several times. Satisfied it was locked, she turned to him and asked, "Shall we?"

He chuckled. "You know, none of this would have ever happened in California."

"Yeah, that's right, you live in the Golden State. Nice place to live?"

He nodded as they walked to his bike. "It is. I have a practice out there."

"Ah, a doctor to the stars." She nodded and whistled when they turned the corner. "Oh, man, she's a beauty. Custom, and I love the paint job."

"You know bikes?" He smiled at his beauty, impressed that the woman recognized a custom bike when she saw one. The black to purple ombre formed the background for a white wolf on a snowy cliff. Visually stunning, he'd jumped on the artist's recommendation. His fenders had the same background, with white pinstriping and a wolf's eye on each.

"My brothers and father owned a service station. When the big chain gas stations moved in, they transitioned to an automobile and motorcycle repair shop. My older brother branched out into custom-built bikes."

"Back in Selma?" He stopped beside his motorcycle.

"That's right. Not as affluent as your folks in Birmingham, but they're getting by." She stopped him from getting on the bike. "If you start that thing up, you'll wake everyone in ten square miles. It isn't far. How about we just walk it?"

"All right." He grabbed his handlebars, righted the motorcycle, and lifted the kickstand. Pushing the heavy bike through the deep gravel wasn't fun, but once they hit the blacktop it was easier.

"You were telling me about your people?"

"Was I?" He glanced over at her and smiled.

"You were going to," she acknowledged.

He chuckled; the little blue-eyed blonde had spunk. "My mom and dad still live there. I'm sure you know Gen's story. I left as soon as I graduated high school, and except for mandatory appearances, I've avoided returning."

"Mandatory like weddings?" Eden glanced at him.

"Like funerals. My grandparents."

"Damn. Sorry."

"They lived a long, wonderful life. My grandfather was the one who encouraged me striking out on my own. He and my father."

"My mee-maw told me I needed to find a husband and have babies instead of going to school."

"Ah, a traditional."

"Nah, she just didn't think I had a brain in my head and thought my dad's money was better spent on a wedding."

Jeremiah barked out another laugh. "You know, I don't think I've ever talked to someone like you before."

"What? No other nosey women in your life?" She walked backward as he pushed his motorcycle.

"No. The only women in my life are my sister and my mother."

"Oh, dear. You're not damaged are you, Doctor?"

The humorless chuckle pinned him back in that hallway, but he pushed through the memory. "Actually, I'm a psychiatrist, and I can tell you we are all damaged to some degree."

"Ah, so not a doctor to the stars, rather a shrink to the stars." Eden pointed to a two-story building. "This is us. That's Gen. She parks behind her building where she has a nice yard, storage shed, and a huge smoker and barbeque. Bring your bike back here." She walked down a dark alley to the back of the building. He dropped his kickstand and settled his bike on the only patch of gravel not covered in weeds. "Up here." Eden trotted up a set of old wooden stairs. They creaked miserably when he climbed them.

"How old are these stairs?" He winced as one creaked loud enough that Eden turned around to look at him and then the steps.

"Probably as old as the building, so... ancient?"

"You should have the boards replaced." Another loud creak rent the air, confirming his assessment.

"I rarely use these steps. There is an interior set from my apartment to the clinic." She opened the screen door and then her apartment door.

"You didn't lock it when you left?" He grabbed the door handle and then stopped. There wasn't a deadbolt on the door. The only locking mechanism was the tiny latch that she could flip on the handle itself.

She turned on the light and marched through the kitchen. "There isn't a door in this community that's locked except the stores and the clinics, mine and Doc Macy's. He's the vet. We leave trucks running with the windows down and all our personal possessions inside. Welcome to Mayberry." He laughed at the old television reference. She grabbed a pillow from the couch and tossed it to the side along with a couple blankets. "Just a second." She headed to the back of the apartment.

Jeremiah walked around the small front room and glanced at the personal, intimate poses of Eden and another man, probably her late husband. A wedding picture on the shelf above the television confirmed it.

"Here you go. A new pillow and blankets. That couch is deadly. I fall asleep on it all the time. The bathroom is through there, first door on the right. Use the shower, towels and such are in there, use anything you need. I'm a heavy sleeper. I'll see you in the morning." She spun and headed down the hall. He heard a door shut and then silence.

The first thing he did was pad quietly back to the back door and lock it, though the racket the back stairs made when anyone walked up them was enough to wake him. God knew he wasn't going to sleep much. Still itching with nerves, he checked all the windows that he could find, even though they were on the second floor. He glanced at the front door. He opened it and turned on the light. The steep stairs led to another door. He carefully padded down the steps, checked the lock, and made his way back up the stairs. He turned the tiny lock on the door handle and wished like hell there was a lock with some substance in this place. No one shculd be this defenseless.

Pacing around the small, dark living room, he ran his hands through his hair and breathed deeply, pushing the panic down. This wasn't California. Cyrus wasn't here. Only that bastard *was* here. He was in his brain and fucking with him. Constantly. Jeremiah was exhausted, and that was probably feeding the anxiousness that marched under his skin like ants.

Glancing around, he realized he should have brought up clean clothes and his toiletry bag. The idea of walking down those stairs again in the dark didn't thrill him. No, he didn't want to drop to his death if one of those stairs croaked under him. So, he took a shower using her soap and shampoo and put his boxers back on after using his finger and her toothpaste to brush his teeth. Jeremiah pulled his phone from his jacket and laid down on the couch. He texted Jamison to let him know he'd arrived as he was the only person who knew he was traveling and dropped the phone face down on the sofa table. A tug crushed the pillow to his chest, and he rolled over onto his stomach and closed his eyes. For once, that damn hallway wasn't what he thought of before he fell asleep. Instead, it was the bright blue eyes of an irreverent blonde nurse practitioner who recognized and respected custom motorcycles. Maybe he'd catch more than a snatch of sleep between nightmares.

CHAPTER 4

Eden folded her jean-clad legs and leaned back in the overstuffed chair that sat in the corner of her kitchen. No doubt someone had placed it there for the cold winter days when the kitchen was the warmest room in the apartment. She'd kept it there because she loved sitting in it and drinking her first cup of coffee of the morning. Today, however, she barely noticed the coffee she was sipping. The man asleep on her couch held her attention. She'd heard him prowling the house at all hours of the night. The fact that her windows were shut and locked made her chuckle. There was something about trusting people this guy didn't get. But that was big city living for you. She'd opened her kitchen window before she sat down. The smell of morning was too enticing to forgo for the man's lock obsession.

It wasn't the right thing to do but she took her time as she relaxed in her chair and examined him. He'd draped his leathers over the arm of the chair, his combat boots standing beside them with his socks lying over the top. He wore a pair of purple plaid boxers that formed to his ass like a second skin. His heavily muscled legs were very long and tucked so he could fit in the confines of the sofa. She let her eyes travel up to his wide back and huge arms, one of which was flopped over the back of the sofa. A tattoo of a snake wound around his arm, up his shoulder, and rested on one side of his neck. He had dark brown hair that was currently wild, sticking up in various places. She smiled as she sipped her coffee. He must have fallen asleep when it was wet.

The sound of a truck driving down the street drew her eyes toward the kitchen window. This little town had been her salvation. When she arrived just over four years ago, she'd wanted nothing to do with anyone in the town. She wanted to lick her wounds and mourn what she'd lost, but Hollister had another idea. The first week she'd had visits from everyone who lived in town. They filled her kitchen with preserves, pies, and cookies. The following week the women from the ranches showed up. They were some of the strongest women she'd ever met, yet they, too, made the new female doc welcome. She'd repeated nurse practitioner so many times that first month that it became a running joke, and the people of the town still introduced her wrong but gave her a wink.

The little town had a flow of its own that balanced around the ranches and so did the injuries that she tended to. Broken limbs, deep cuts, concussions, and crushed feet. The first time she saw the damage a bull could do to a human foot she became a devoted town dweller. There was nothing on the ranches that she needed or wanted to see. Etched on each of her patients' faces was the evidence of a hard life, but the shock was these people loved what they did. They willingly cared for the stock and battled the elements that made the daily grind of ranching that much harder.

She smiled as the morning sun peeked into the window. The town would come to life shortly, but until then... She turned her attention back to the man on her couch. She leaned her head to the side. Zeke had used her couch frequently, but she'd never once ogled him the way she was admiring this dark stranger. Jeremiah Wheeler. His outside screamed bad boy and his demeanor countered that image. He was... exciting. She sighed. It had been years since she'd looked at a man the way she was looking at Jeremiah.

Her eyes lifted to her wedding picture on the shelf. Her husband, Riley, was a wonderful man. They were married for two years before he was killed. She'd lived double that time here in Hollister. The pace was slower, the people nice, and the prospect of a romantic relationship slim to none. At least, it was until Zeke started his practice after Doctor Coogan retired. Zeke made it obvious he wanted more than a friendship, but while it flattered her, she wasn't excited. His touch didn't set her on fire. She wished it had because Zeke was nice, but there was no spark for her.

She took another sip of her coffee and watched Jeremiah's ribs expand and contract. The relief of his muscles under his skin was beautiful in a physical sense and unnerving in others. That the sculpted body attracted her to him answered several questions she'd been pondering. Had the desire she felt with Riley been a fluke? Her eyes traveled down the long, muscled body of the sleeping man. No. She thought Jeremiah, the dark-haired, green-eyed bad boy, was attractive, and she admitted she felt a pull toward him but not toward Zeke. Zeke was an attractive man, tall, broad shoulders, blond hair, and blue eyes. Her friend Allison Sanderson swooned every time Zeke showed up. Eden chuckled quietly. Allison swooned every time any unattached man showed up. She'd fallen head over heels in love with at least twenty different men in the last three years without them ever speaking to her.

That hadn't been the case for Eden, and until recently, that was okay. She'd healed. She hadn't forgotten Riley, but the pain of losing him dulled, or rather muted. The awful ache that lived with her had turned into a sensation that she cherished instead of hated. Her short time with him had changed her and made her a better person. The time here in Hollister had allowed her to let him go yet still hold him close, something she didn't think she'd ever be able to do, but the fact was she was lonely and was ready for another relationship.

Zeke and she had gone out several times, and the town probably had them married already, especially since he slept on her couch whenever he was in town late. But Allison had set the ladies of the Catholic-Protestant Sewing circle on their ears when one of them dared to intimate that they were living in sin. It was nice that her friend had defended her honor, but she didn't care about gossip. Although this dark, sexy bad boy who had his Harley parked in her backyard would light up the gossip mongers for weeks. She smiled at the thought.

Jeremiah groaned and rolled onto his back, adjusting his length to the shorter couch. She glanced at his morning erection and almost choked on her last sip of coffee. The doctor had been blessed with… Eden jerked her eyes away from the man and stood up, heading for the coffee pot near the kitchen window. Dear Lord, she'd been ogling the man and sizing him up for… for what? It wasn't like he was sticking around. She poured a cup and moved over to the window looking out on Main Street. It had been a long, long while since she wanted sex, and now wasn't the best time for that urge to raise its head.

"Good morning."

She jumped at Jeremiah's deep voice behind her. He'd pulled on his leathers and a t-shirt while she'd been daydreaming. "Hey, would you like a cup of coffee? I'm going to fry a couple eggs for myself, and I have plenty if you'd like some breakfast."

He smiled at her. "Coffee and eggs sound wonderful." He grabbed a cup off the small shelf beside the machine. "That couch is comfortable. Thank you."

"Are you sure? You were pacing about quite a bit last night." And he didn't look rested. She doubted he got much sleep at all.

"Yeah, strange places do that to me. I hope I didn't wake you."

"Not for more than a moment." She shook her head.

"I do appreciate you letting me crash here," he smiled as he spoke.

"Anytime. Zeke sleeps there when he's here late. He says the couch is comfortable."

Jeremiah grabbed a kitchen chair and turned it around, straddling it as he faced her. "I'm not stepping on any toes by being here, am I?"

She blinked at him, trying to decode his question. "Toes?"

He lifted his coffee to his lips and blew across the top of the liquid before he spoke. "Do you and Zeke have something going on?" She watched transfixed as he took a sip. "Damn, that's good."

"Thanks, and no. I've gone out with Zeke twice. Both times as a friend, and he sleeps on the couch." She grabbed a frying pan from inside the oven and put it on the burner.

Jeremiah's eyebrows lifted. "Ouch, that must be a punch to the man's pride."

She turned and frowned. "Why would you say that?"

Jeremiah shrugged and stood up. He opened the refrigerator and took out the carton of eggs, handing it to her. "Well, from a masculine point of view, if I got up the nerve to ask a lady like you out and after two dates I was still on the couch, I'd be wondering what I'd done wrong."

Eden snorted. "Dear Lord, you think highly of yourself, don't you? Did you miss the part where I said friend?"

Jeremiah laughed and rubbed the back of his neck as his cheeks colored. "Well, no, but..."

"Not buying it." She nodded to the refrigerator. "Grab me that small coffee can in the fridge, would you?"

"Sure." He dipped in and handed it to her. "Is that the secret to your fantastic coffee? Cold grounds?" Eden lifted the lid and showed him the inside. His eyes drew together. "What in God's name is that?"

"Bacon grease. Everything's better with bacon." She shrugged. "I can use something else for your eggs, but you'd be missing out."

Her guest's eyes popped wide, and he jerked around before he asked, "Did you hear that?"

Concerned, Eden stopped and listened. There was nothing but the normal sounds of the old building and the town waking. "No, what did you hear?"

"The entire state of California just gasped. I can feel the oxygen suck from here."

Laughing, she plopped a spoonful of grease into the pan and started the burner. "I have bacon-fried eggs once a week, all the health nuts in California can rest assured I'm not single-handedly waging war against cardiovascular health. All things in moderation, and is that a yes or a no?" She cocked her head and waited.

"That's a hell yes. I'll make the toast if you direct me to the bread." Jeremiah took another sip of his coffee as he waited for her to point to the small pantry where the bread was. "Is this homemade?"

"Yep. Sourdough. Rumor has it the starter for that bread began when the original Mrs. Hollister came across in a covered wagon. Allison's mom bakes every other day and sells it at the market. There is a serrated knife in the butcher block."

"Allison?"

"Huh? Oh, sorry. Allison Sanderson, a friend. You'll meet her if you're here more than a day."

"How's that?" Jeremiah sliced the bread with the precision of a surgeon.

A low, rumbling knock on the front door stopped her from cracking the first two eggs into the frying pan. She handed the unbroken eggs to her guest. "Here's your breakfast. It sounds like I have a drop-by and the ones that show up first thing in the morning are the ones that have tried to mend themselves and failed. I'll be back up when I finish."

She slipped her feet into a pair of sneakers and opened the door to the inside stairwell. At the bottom, she unlocked the door and pushed it open. Zeke stood on the sidewalk with his hands shoved into his pockets.

A smile hit his face. "Caught a ride back up with the ambulance crew. They needed to wait for a restock so it worked out. Did I miss breakfast?"

Well, okay. Zeke's enthusiasm for eggs seemed a bit weird, she thought, but whatever. "Ah, no. Come on in. How is Declan?"

She headed back up the stairs.

"The biker doc saved him further complications. If he'd tried to pull that knife out, it would have done some damage. Strange that he just turned up like——"

"Like this?" Jeremiah stood at the top of the stairs, barefoot, holding two eggs in one hand and the frying pan in the other.

Eden laughed and stepped past him, grabbing the frying pan as she moved by. "Yep, just like that. Why aren't you frying those eggs?"

"I wanted to make sure you didn't need any help." She sat the pan back on the range and turned around to find the two men staring at each other. "Zeke, this is Jeremiah, Jeremiah, this is Zeke."

They both turned to her with confused looks on their faces. "Well, you were staring at each other, I figured you'd forgotten you'd already met." She extended her hand for the eggs. "Add some more toast, Jeremiah. Zeke, you set the table." She took the eggs and turned back to the effort of making breakfast.

"Do you want me to do that while you get dressed?" Zeke's question spun her around.

Jeremiah laughed. "No, I can manage both. How's the bar owner?"

"He'll live. Thanks to you," she heard Zeke speak as the plates rattled. "Where do you work and live?"

"I'm on hiatus out here to visit family. I'll be

staying a while." Jeremiah answered the question but avoided answering anything Zeke had actually asked.

"Hiatus? Do doctors get rich in... where was it you were from again?" Zeke placed the plates beside her, and she gave him a side-eye. He shrugged and reached for the silverware drawer.

"Rich? No, I was rich *before* I started my practice. Old money, you know, but we don't do what we do to get rich, do we?" Jeremiah chuckled. "I'm a psychiatrist and work at a federal penitentiary in California."

Eden glanced at Jeremiah, pausing her routine of spooning the hot bacon grease over the egg yolks to cook the surrounding whites without having to flip the eggs.

Zeke snorted. "So, you work with the criminally insane. Why bother, they're lost causes aren't they?"

Jeremiah straightened and rolled his shoulders. Eden saw her new friend tense, but Zeke wasn't watching; he was digging in the fridge for something.

"I work with incarcerated men. Those who are there for a short time and those that are there for the rest of their lives. And by the way, I haven't checked recently, but when I went through my fellowship, 'criminally insane' wasn't an entry in the Diagnostic and Statistical Manual of Mental Disorders. No matter the location, everyone—and I mean *everyone* —deserves the right to talk to someone, to find professional help when the darkness becomes too much to bear. Just because they are behind bars doesn't make them less of a person." Jeremiah sat the plate of toasted and buttered bread on the table. "I'm no longer hungry. I'll gather my stuff and see myself out."

"Zeke." Eden's growled warning or the fact that Zeke realized he was being an ass had the guy moving. She took the pan off the burner and watched Jeremiah move into the living room.

"Dude, man... I'm sorry. It has to be the lack of sleep. I didn't mean to put down what you do." Zeke stopped on the far side of the kitchen table and watched as Jeremiah grabbed his boots.

Jeremiah threw a glance his direction. "Yeah, you did. You were preening in front of the woman you have your sights on. I get it, man." He sat down on the chair and pulled on his socks and boots.

Zeke opened his mouth and then snapped it shut. "Damn." He scrubbed his face and glanced at her. "I'm sorry."

Zeke said the words to her and not to Jeremiah.

She frowned at him and shook her head. "Jeremiah, I know you are staying for a couple days. Please, leave your things here. When you and Gen meet up you can stop by and pick them up."

Jeremiah slung his leather jacket over his shoulder and smiled at her. It was the type of smile that would melt any woman's heart and warm her blood. "Thank you for your hospitality, Eden, but everything I need is in my saddlebags. I'll find the deputy and give him my statement while I'm waiting for Gen to get home." He headed to the back stairwell. "Johnson, it's been real." The door shut quietly after him.

Eden spun on her heel and slammed her hands onto her hips. Zeke blinked at her sudden turn and put his hands in the air in supplication, but the action didn't stop her. She shook her head and narrowed her eyes. "Ezekiel Johnson, what on earth was that?"

Zeke linked his hands behind his neck and stared at her. "He was right. I was showboating to put him down and impress you. He knows Gen?"

"She's his sister, and newsflash, Zeke, that shit doesn't work, and why in the heck would you want to do that?"

"Are you kidding?" Zeke's jaw slackened.

"Do you see laughter in this expression?" she countered, pointing at her face.

"Eden, I don't know how much plainer I need to make it. I want a relationship with you, and you've kept me at arm's length. What was I supposed to do, watch him come in here and sweep you off your feet?"

She opened her mouth and then snapped it shut, trying to compose the things she wanted to say, but the swirling miasma of 'oh shit' that was floating around in her gray matter would not be settled, not with a pause. She drew a deep breath. "First, Zeke, I like you--as a friend."

Zeke groaned and dropped his head back, staring at the ceiling. Finally, he looked at her. "You friend-zoned me? Because of him?"

Eden frowned and shook her head. "Because of Jeremiah? No. Absolutely not. Because I don't feel anything more for you than a friend? Yes."

Zeke stepped forward. "Give me a chance, Eden. I know I could be the man you want me to be."

She smiled; her anger floated away with his words. "Don't you see? Changing for me should tell you I'm not the one for you."

"Nothing, huh?" He took her hand in his and stared down at it.

"Friendship isn't nothing, Zeke, it is precious." She squeezed his hand and then slipped from his grasp. "Do you want eggs? They're tough as rubber by now." She tried to right the environment in the room by moving the conversation back to the mundane.

"You know, I'm not hungry either. I'm going to go grab my truck and head down to my office. Call if you need me for anything."

"I will." She watched as he hesitated at the front steps. He dipped his head and opened the door, closing it behind him.

Eden spun and grabbed the sink, staring out the window. She'd tried to let him down gently; the conversation was overdue, but still, saying the words and hurting a friend was never easy. How in the world had her morning gone from bliss to this? She turned to look at the eggs and groaned. No amount of bacon fat was going to make what just happened between her and Zeke better. Hopefully, time and perspective would mend the distance she'd just put between them. Until then, she'd do what she'd done for the last four years: heal and move on.

CHAPTER 5

J eremiah fired up his motorcycle, put on his helmet, and pulled out of the alley behind the clinic. In the day's light, he drove down the small street and took in the tiny town. A small hardware store was next to the clinic, across the way was Gen's restaurant, and there was a blondish-brown sandstone church at one end of the town, a dark red brick church at the other. Gen's place was flanked by a small gas station and a market across from another church. This one was red brick with a steeple and bell tower. He sped up as he left the town and headed south.

It took a couple hours of traveling before he wandered through the highways that traversed through the depths of the Black Hills. As he rounded a curve, a large, beautiful lake came into view. The sign he passed called it Pactola. The surface glimmered into fractures of a million points of light. He drove on for another hour or so before he pulled off on an access road and drove back on a bumpy gravel lane that led to a small clearing. Taking off his helmet, he soaked in the beautiful day and the sounds of nature. The chirping of birds in the high pine trees along with the scampering of red squirrels were lulled by the sounds of the wind gently blowing through the pine boughs. Closing his eyes, he pulled the fragrant air into his lungs. God, if he could only bottle the peace of this place. He kicked the stand for his bike down and stretched after dismounting. There were several granite boulders the size of his motorcycle but twice as tall to the right. He scrambled onto one of the boulders and hefted himself up to the top. The view was amazing. He glanced at his watch. He had time for a nap, and he fucking needed one. The sun-warmed rock under him soaked through his tired muscles. He closed his eyes and let himself drift.

. . .

Jeremiah?

He snapped his head up. Gen's voice turned him around. She laughed and ran toward him. He stood up and walked toward her. Just as he reached her, she gasped, her body jerked, and her mouth opened in a silent, bloody scream. He looked down. A piece of jagged metal protruded through her chest.

Gen fell into his arms and Cyrus stood behind her in his prison uniform, smiling, covered in blood. "Everyone you love will be my projects."

He gasped and bolted upright. Sweat dripped from his brow. He covered his mouth with his hands and stared at the nature around him. Nothing as vile as Macmillan should ever be in this area, not even in his dreams. He laid back down and stared up at the blue skies and billowing white clouds above him as he concentrated on breathing and getting his heart rate down. His watch's alarm went off and he silenced it. The contrived noise violated the quiet that surrounded him, but he had an obligation and a promise to keep. Pulling his cell from his coat pocket, he balled the coat up again and propped it under his head. Lying on his back, he kicked one ankle over his propped-up knee and shook off the last of the dream.

If it has reception, I'll call. If not... oh, well. He lifted his phone and grimaced. Was he hoping that he wouldn't have reception? Hell yeah, but with three bars, he punched in the numbers he needed to call.

"Damn it, Remi, it's been too long." He smiled at Jamison's voice.

"What? I talked to you two weeks ago."

"And I've worried every day, thinking you wouldn't leave California. How is South Dakota?"

"Believe it or not, I'm lying on top of a ten-foot-high boulder watching a hawk circle overhead while listening to the sounds of nature in the Black Hills. It's almost like I've been transported to the 1800s. I don't even hear any cars."

Jamison hummed before he asked, "I thought you were going to stay with your sister?"

"I am. She's out of town and will be back later this afternoon. I'm enjoying nature. Quit being such a killjoy, dude." God, he hoped his fake-as-shit playing tone passed Jamison's bullshit meter.

"Sorry, my idea of nature is my landscaped back-yard with my mosquito zapper working and a fan aimed at me, running at full blast."

That did make him snort a laugh. "Anyone ever tell you you're getting old?"

"My wife," Jamison chortled. His friend waited for a moment before he asked, "How are you doing?"

Remi sighed and stared at the hawk that circled above him. "I'm managing, but the memories are... Fuck, in all honesty, Jamison, I've read cases and studied people who were capable of such atrocities, but seeing it, hearing Ellen and Kyle beg and scream and knowing there was nothing I could do..." He let the words trail off. His mind was back in that fucking hall... When Cyrus stared at him, making sure he was watching, his gut rolled, and he gulped back the putrid wave of bile that rose in his stomach.

"I watched the tapes of the event again."

Jeremiah's eyes snapped to his boots although he wasn't actually looking at them. "The event? Is that what we're calling it now?"

"What would you prefer to call it?" Jamison bounced the comment back to him.

"Hell? Is there a better word?" It was worse than any soundless video could ever convey. "I'll hear their screams for the rest of my life." He pushed his hands through his hair. They were shaking, and he would not stop the reaction.

"What was the worst part?" Jamison's voice was calm and low.

Jeremiah stared past his boots for a long time before he spoke. "Not being able to help."

Jamison hummed an acknowledgement. "There was a locked door between you and Cyrus."

"The guards could have opened it." He shoved his hand through his hair. "I could have switched places with one of them." Jeremiah closed his eyes and drew a deep breath. His mind had him right back at that fucking door. The *locked* door.

"You've read Cyrus' file. You know as well as I do he would have killed all of you."

"He still wants to kill me, Jamison. What difference would it make?"

Jamison's voice grew concerned. "Explain that?"

"Cyrus. He wants to kill both me and that FBI agent, the one he tried to kill when he went after me. He didn't finish what he started, and he's fixated on both of us."

"When did he tell you this?"

Jeremiah clenched his fists. "Before they could pull him out. After they stormed the hall."

"Baseless threats. He wanted to get into your head."

"He did." Jeremiah opened his eyes again.

"How are you sleeping?" Jamison asked.

Jeremiah sighed. "Doctor one-oh-one? I slept last night, altogether about two hours."

"How many nights has that happened?"

He lifted his eyes to the tops of the pine trees. "Counting last night? All of them."

Jamison sighed. "I thought so. What happened last night?"

"Well, besides breaking up a fight, saving the local bar owner's life, and sleeping on Hollister's nurse practitioner's couch? Nothing."

Jamison choked and coughed and then mumbled a curse about coffee stains before he ordered, "Stop being elusive and tell me what happened."

Jeremiah smiled at the grumbling demand and explained the events of last night, leaving out the fact that the little nurse was sexy as hell and damn fun to be around.

"So, you were in control of the situation."

"From the beginning to the end," he acknowledged.

"A good feeling," Jamison prompted.

Jeremiah searched the sky and lifted his eyebrows. "A damn good feeling."

"You showed yourself that you were in fact capable. That Cyrus hadn't taken that away from you, didn't you?"

He nodded, although Jamison couldn't see him. "I did."

"Do you need any meds to help you sleep?"

Jeremiah shook his head. "No. I'm not starting down that path, nor do I need anything to level my moods or defray my anxiety."

"Doctor, would you at least let me ask the questions?" Jamison tried to sound put out.

"Maybe next time," Jeremiah conceded.

"You'll call again?" Jamison asked, surprised.

"I'm not an idiot. I need to work through what happened. How long are you willing to help?"

"I'll be here as long as I need to be, whenever you need me to be, Remi, for as long as it takes."

"Thank you." They were small words, but he needed to acknowledge his friend's help.

"Then we'll talk the same time next week, or if you need me sooner, just call."

Remi chuckled, "You got it, Doc."

He could hear Jamison's eyes roll. The man hated that moniker. "Keep it up, mister, and I'll charge you triple."

"Triple of zero is what exactly?"

"A case of whiskey and a box of cigars," Jamison snapped the reply along with a laugh.

"Only if I get to help you consume them."

"I look forward to it. Take care of yourself and call me if you need to." He could hear his friend's concern.

"I give you my word."

Jamison sighed, "Good. Very good. We'll talk soon."

"Until then." He disconnected and dropped the phone onto his chest. He'd soak up the warmth a bit more and then head back to Hollister. It would be good to see Gen again. Other than their infrequent calls and texts, they hadn't talked much since their grandfather's funeral.

The distinct rumble of a motorcycle pulled him into a sitting position. A Harley made its way down the trail. The rider, an older gentleman by the looks of the gray handlebar mustache and beard, came to a stop by his bike. The man glanced around until he saw Jeremiah. A wide smile exposed a mouth full of silver teeth, almost like the character out of one of the Bond movies. Jeremiah couldn't see the man's cut, but he was flying some motorcycle club colors for sure.

"Howdy," the man said as soon as he turned off his bike.

"Great day for a ride, isn't it?" Jeremiah asked as he slid down the face of the boulder and landed on his feet in front of the man.

"Damn straight. Any day on my bike is a good day. Had to get away from the shop for a bit."

Remi nodded. "I know that feeling."

"You own a cut?"

He shook his head. "Independent and determined to stay that way." He glanced at the guy's cut. The word 'Prez' was embroidered across his left chest and the crest for the Hill's Hell Hounds was below it. He'd worked with gang members before. Treading in club territory if they thought you were the enemy was a surefire way to get dead.

"Little early for the rally." The guy pulled off his aviators. Those eyes were dark and watched him like a hawk, although he spent a few seconds admiring Jeremiah's bike.

"Rally?" Jeremiah frowned for a minute. "Oh, Sturgis? I doubt I'll still be in the area, but if I am, I may drop by."

The man stared at him and lifted an eyebrow. "You look like club material, but you don't talk much like it."

Jeremiah tossed back his head and laughed. "Do you allow psychiatrists in your club?"

The guy stared at him for a moment before a smile pulled at his lips. "Have a medic, but no doctor. Do you know how to patch up people?"

"Dude, you wouldn't want a shrink to work on your body. I've forgotten all that shit they crammed down my throat in med school." He made his way to his bike and picked up his helmet and looked at the other rider. "Name's Jeremiah."

"Tank." The other rider nodded. The name suited him; he was built like one. The biker nodded to Jeremiah's ride. "You going north or south?"

"North, heading back to see family. You?"

"I have a custom bike shop in Rapid. Just came out here to feel the quiet." Tank nodded at Jeremiah's ride. "That is quality work. That paint job must have cost a fortune. Get it done around here?"

"Nah, man, a small shop outside Santa Maria, California. Yours is outrageous." The metallic flames faded into a skull when you moved from one side to the other.

"My kid did that. He's the best around here." Tank reached in his pocket and handed Jeremiah a card. "We don't mind independents. Ever get the itch to ride with the group or you need something for that bike, here's the address."

"I'll pass on the ride, but I'll take you up on the maintenance. Hard to find people who would take care of this baby like I would." Jeremiah put on his helmet and stepped over his bike after securing the business card along with his cell phone.

Tank reached out a fist and bumped Jeremiah's. "Stop by, I'll show you some of my kid's work."

"I'd like that." He cranked his bike and gave Tank a salute before he pulled a U-turn and retraced his route back to Hollister.

CHAPTER 6

J eremiah rode his bike into the small town and was shocked when several people on the street lifted a hand in greeting. He couldn't remember the last time someone he didn't know had acknowledged him. Small towns had charm that way.

Instead of turning right and pulling behind the clinic, he veered left and drove to the back of the cafe. His sister, Genevieve, spun around from the cargo trailer that was opened behind her truck. The look of confusion on her face vanished and a smile as bright as the Alabama sun split her face.

"Remi!" She launched toward him and damn near knocked him and his motorcycle onto the gravel drive. He grabbed her and the bike, straddling the machine to keep from going over.

"Whoa, there. Give me a chance to get off my bike before you maul me." He laughed when she jumped back and hopped up and down on her toes.

"Hurry up! Oh, damn, have you bulked up or what?"

He placed the kickstand and swung his leg over just in time to catch her again. "It's so good to see you!" She hugged him and they swayed together for a bit, but she didn't let go, which was weird. He nudged her and whispered, "Hey, what's wrong?"

She released him and wiped at her eyes. "Nothing, I'm just being silly. Why didn't you call?"

He shrugged. "You know me, I didn't want you to put yourself out."

She tapped his helmet with her finger. "Hello? Since when is putting fresh linen on the guest bed a burden?"

He chuckled and took off his helmet. "Looks like you have a heck of a haul." He nodded to the trailer.

"I so do! I stock up for the month and flour in fifty-pound sacks aren't fun to move from point A to point B, let me tell you." Gen swiped a strand of her long black hair back and tucked it behind her ear.

"Let me get this put away. Come in and pour yourself a cup of coffee and we'll visit while I work."

"Like that would ever happen." He lifted a fifty-pound bag of flour and slung it over his shoulder, grabbing another in his right hand. "Lead the way."

She blinked and scrambled to the back door of the cafe. "Flour is to the right, bottom shelf in the storeroom." She pointed to the storeroom that was organized within an inch of its life. Each shelf was labeled with a small whiteboard that showed the product name and the date she placed it into storage.

"I see that degree in business management from Brown came in handy." He rested one bag against the door jamb and lowered the one he had on his shoulder into its place.

"Stop, I get that song and dance from Mom." Gen muscled over the other bag of flour and he lifted it up into its position.

"Ah, how is Mother?" He turned around as he spoke and saw her flinch. "Sorry, still a sore subject?"

Gen nodded. "How about we save that conversation for a glass of something adult and we'll make it extra strong?"

"Deal. What else do you need me to do?" He'd seen more supplies and headed back out to the small trailer.

"Remi, you don't have to do this." Gen jogged to catch up with him.

"Well, I am, so get over it." He hip-checked her, sending her to the right about five steps. She snorted a laugh and veered back to the trailer. They loaded up and headed back into the cafe.

"How long can you stay?" Gen asked the question as they placed tins of oil, cans of tomatoes, and every other pantry item imaginable into the storeroom.

"That's open-ended right now. I took a leave of absence from the prison." He turned to go back out to the trailer.

"Jeremiah, what aren't you telling me?" The soft question halted him in his tracks. He turned and looked at his sister. She was beautiful in the way of the old-fashioned movie stars. Classical features, deep blue eyes, and black hair had helped her win Miss Alabama and first runner-up in the national pageant. Of course, that hadn't been enough for their mom. "Remi?"

He dropped his head back and stared at the ceiling for a minute. "Remember that adult beverage we are going to have after we finish unpacking the warehouse store you bought out?"

She smiled and nodded. "Yeah, I remember that."

"You share your story and I'll share mine."

She slapped her hands together and moved toward the door. "Deal, but you're going first."

He chuckled and followed her out the door. They'd need a fifth to get through the afternoon.

"This is nice, Gen." He walked around the front of her cafe. There was a long counter with ten stools and a bank of booths that stretched across the front of the space. Clean, small, and everything she'd always talked about.

"Thanks. I opened with just the bar space and some little tables, but I ordered the booths, and I installed them two months ago. The ranch hands don't enjoy sitting at bistro tables, not really their scene."

"I can understand that." He glanced through the pass-through to the kitchen. It wasn't huge but was well-appointed according to the tour Gen had just given him. "You live upstairs?"

"I do. That is still a work in progress, but I'm almost done. Come on, I'll show you where you can unpack." Gen led him back through the kitchen and waited while he retrieved his belongings from his saddlebags.

He took two steps up her stairs and groaned as the wood squealed. "You need to replace these stairs." She snorted a dismissive sound and kept going up. He shook his head and prayed the stairs held him and his small bags. From the sound they were making, it was a close call. "I swear I don't know which set of steps is worse, yours or Eden's."

Gen stopped at the landing. "You know Eden?"

"Yeah, I met her last night at the bar fight."

"The *what*?" Her hand stilled on the door latch.

"The bar fight I broke up. Are we going to go in or are you hoping this landing will hold instead of dropping us to our deaths?"

She chuffed out a sound and opened her door. "Home sweet home." The door opened into her kitchen. It was twice the size of Eden's and had new countertops in a brown color that matched the floor and was a counterpoint to the white cabinets.

He whistled. "Nice."

"Thanks. Come this way. This, obviously, is the living room, through there is my bedroom and bathroom. Follow me." They turned and headed down a small hall. "This is your bathroom and here is your bedroom. I'll grab some fresh sheets and make up the bed."

He sat his kit down inside the room and glanced around. A queen-sized bed and dark wood headboard and dressers countered light blue walls and dark blue curtains and comforter. There was a rocking chair in the corner and an old table with an old-fashioned pitcher and wash basin on it. "Perfect. Thanks for letting me crash in on you." He shrugged off his jacket and laid it on the foot of the bed.

"Anytime, you know that. You get settled, I'll make us something for lunch and pour those adult beverages. I can't wait to hear why you're in South Dakota."

He watched her walk away and smiled. His sister and he had been damn close. Growing up, time and distance had loosened that connection to a degree. They didn't talk often now. They exchanged emails and a few texts rather than calls because her schedule and his never matched up. He stacked his clean clothes in the dresser and put his laundry bag in the corner. He'd ask to use her washer and dryer tomorrow.

A waft of a heavenly aroma snuck through the air and his stomach growled viciously. He hadn't eaten since lunch yesterday and his body was not happy with him. With that in mind, he made a beeline to the pots on the stove. "Red beans, sausage and rice, and a salad." Her voice came from behind him. "I figured it was too early to hit the hard stuff, so..." She opened the fridge and pulled out two beers.

"Perfect. Damn, I forgot what a fantastic cook

you are." He took his beer from her and twisted the top off.

"You haven't tasted it yet," she joked with him and pulled out two bowls, ladling in the rice and then the red beans and sausage. "Here you go. Have a seat."

He didn't need to be told twice, and although his stomach objected, he waited for her to sit down with her food before he took a bite. "Damn, Gen, that is so good." The beans were tender but not mushy; the spice from the sausage had mixed with the sauce and it had just the right heat level.

"Thanks. Grandma Wheeler's recipe, changed to fit South Dakota ingredients, although you'd be surprised at what you can find if you look hard enough." She took a bite of hers and tipped her head. "Speak."

He snorted and shoveled another spoonful in his mouth. "Did you hear about the riot at the supermax in California?"

She shook her head, her eyes widened. "I listen to the news on the radio when I'm cooking in the morning. National news coverage isn't the best. What happened?"

"There was a riot, and they locked the prison down. Unfortunately, at the same time, one of the worst offenders had escaped custody in the medical ward."

She put her spoon down. "That's where you work, right? Were you there?"

He nodded and stirred his food. "I was. I witnessed this man do unspeakable things to two people I knew. He killed one, maimed the other. I was behind a locked glass door and couldn't do a damn thing to help them." He left out the graphic details, but by the way she was staring at him, he understood she was filling in the gaps. He put his spoon down and leaned back. "It was bad, Gen. The man had attacked me before, he wanted to get to me, and because he couldn't do it--"

"He fucked with your mind," she finished for him.

His eyes darted up to her. "Such words from a lady." He repeated his mother's admonishment and lifted a corner of his mouth in a half-smile.

She groaned, "We'll get to that subject in a minute. You said you took a leave of absence?"

He nodded. "I tried to resign, but they wanted me to take time off before I made that decision."

"You're not considering going back, are you?" She reached her hand across the table and placed it on top of his.

"No. I'll take the time they asked that I take, but I

can't see me going back inside." The thought of being locked in that prison with Cyrus, no matter how well-guarded the murderer was, made him sick to his stomach.

"Then stay with me until you figure out what the next step for you is." Gen dipped down to look at him.

He drew a breath and realized he was subconsciously worried that she wouldn't want him to stay, but the offer slid that worry from his shoulder. "It will only be for a couple weeks, maybe a month."

"You could stay forever, and I'd be ecstatic. Now that we have that settled, eat your lunch or you'll hurt my feelings."

He picked up his spoon, but before he continued, he caught her attention. "Thank you, Gen."

She smiled at him and nodded. "We've always stood stronger together, haven't we?"

"Ah, yes, dear Mother. Tell me what's going on there?" He spooned another mouthful of the delicious food and rolled his eyes when the taste exploded on his tongue.

"Well, I told you that Avery and I broke up." She shrugged. "I didn't tell you I found him screwing Chelsea, in my condo and in my bed."

He stopped chewing and swallowed hard. "I'll kill that bastard."

She raised her eyes. "You're a doctor. I don't think they authorize killing under that medical credo you swore."

"The 'do no harm' vow will not keep this guy from getting a fist shoved through his face." He grumbled the words. "Chelsea as in...?"

"My ex-best friend since second grade? Yes." She nodded and took a bite of food. "It was an epic scene. Get me drunk sometime and I'll give you all the sordid details." She waved her spoon in the air. "So, at Dad's suggestion, I got in my car and I drove. I ended up about three miles south of town when my radiator decided it was time to spring a leak. I limped it to Phil's gas station. When I saw this cafe all boarded up and lonely, I knew I'd found a place to stop. I love it here. Nobody knows who we are. There are no expectations except being a good person. The weather is harsh, the land is unforgiving, the ranchers are stronger than you might imagine, and this little town serves a purpose."

Jeremiah considered her words for a moment. "First, I don't believe Dad would ever set you on a road trip with no destination, and that doesn't explain the greeting I got today. So, explain." He lifted his beer and drank, chasing the lingering heat of the meal.

"Well, he suggested I go on a holiday—the Med was his suggestion." She smiled and winked at him and then her face fell. "Mother has been at me nonstop. I haven't given her my number and she's blowing up my email."

He remembered that she'd changed her number when she started the business. He'd figured it was because of a carrier issue in the sparsely populated area. "You've banned our mother?"

"She has my email address. That's it. Dad swore he'd never tell her where I'm at."

Shit, things were worse than he'd imagined. "Because?"

"Because after I found out Avery had cheated on me, I called off the wedding. She was beside herself. How would this reflect on *her*. She ordered me to go back to Avery and to make everything right. *Demanded*, Remi. She didn't care how *I* felt, how his cheating had affected me." Tears swelled in her big blue eyes. "She is still insisting that I need to apologize for overreacting and get over myself."

"Son of a bitch."

"Yes, yes you are," Gen laughed and sobbed at the

same time. She dabbed at her eyes and sniffed before she shook her head. "Sorry, bad joke."

"But it would appear in this case, it's the truth." He didn't like his mother on good days, although as her child he'd always love her, just not the same way he loved his father. Theirs was "a house divided" personified. Celest's rooms were away from theirs; his father's rooms were next to his and Gen's. Celest and his father hadn't shared rooms for as long as he could remember. There was a mutual respect but no love between the two of them, and he often wondered what kept his father in a loveless marriage. Celest's drive to parade both Gen and him around at pageants, her need to be in the limelight and be the center of attention, her incessant need to have the latest and best of everything had a handful of clinical diagnoses, all of which gave him an empathy for his mother. "Why would she insist you get back together with that cheating asshole?"

"Dad thinks it's because of Avery's family."

"The Montagues? I'm not sure I understand."

Gen stood up and took his bowl—which he realized was empty—and filled it again. "The Montagues are an old family. They don't have money like Dad, but they have status. A status that Celest couldn't obtain even if Dad becomes Governor someday."

He thanked her for the second helping and leaned forward. "How much pressure is she putting on you?"

Gen lifted a finger and went to the counter to get her phone. She opened her mail and handed the cell to him. He scrolled… and scrolled… and scrolled. "Wow." The implications of the obsessive emails concerned him. He cleared his throat. "Okay, so this is what we're going to do. I'm going to call Dad and have a talk with him. He needs to know the extent of this situation. Then I'm going to ask you to consider —just consider—giving her an inch. Maybe reach out to her on a pay-as-you-go phone."

Gen sighed and took her cell back. "She's mental. If I give her an inch, she'll take a mile."

"That is an astute diagnosis. What manual did you get it from, Doctor Wheeler?" He lifted an eyebrow and Gen laughed.

"Well, she is, and you know it."

He agreed, but the assessment wasn't as clinical as he was thinking. The manic behavior needed to be addressed. "I'll talk to Dad."

"Thank you. I'm not going to give her my number. Not yet. If she's this obsessive with emails, I couldn't imagine what she'd do with a telephone number."

He nodded. Gen's relationship with their mom had been more turbulent than his. He'd tried to intervene and provide a cushion for his little sister, but once he grew and was no longer a cute little boy but a gangly adolescent, Celest lost interest in him. Thank God for the time they spent with Grandma and Grandpa Wheeler. They showed both Gen and him what a normal and loving relationship looked like.

"Want another beer?" Gen asked.

"I do. Thank you." He finished his second bowl of food and leaned back in his chair. "I plan on earning my keep. Let me help you downstairs and do some things around the place, like replace those damn stairs." For both her and Eden. The thought of them crashing through the rotted wood would make that his first project.

Gen handed him a drink. "You know, you don't have to do that, but sometimes it is crazy busy and things like the stairs get overlooked. This little town is bigger than you'd think." She stopped. "Hey, you never told me about the bar fight."

Jeremiah chuckled and walked his dirty dishes over to the sink. He regaled her with the previous night's activity and him ending up on Eden's couch while he did the dishes and she dried.

"Oh, dang, I bet Zeke was fit to be tied this morning. He has his eyes on Eden."

"Yeah, I got that loud and clear." And he'd walked away from it. No matter how attractive he found the petite blonde to be, he wasn't here for long and she didn't strike him as the type of woman who did short-term arrangements. He rinsed out the sink after the last pan; for that matter, he wasn't that type of a person either.

Gen leaned against his arm and sighed. "It sure is good to have you here."

He pulled her into a hug. "It's good to be here. Don't worry, we'll figure out whatever is under Mom's bonnet and give it a good swat."

Gen laughed, "I call dibs on the first whack."

After Gen went to bed at way too early of an hour, Jeremiah pulled out his phone and hit the number for his father. The phone rang four times, and he was just about to hang up when his father answered. He could hear a large gathering as he spoke, "Jeremiah, I've been trying to be patient. I saw about the riot at the prison. I knew you'd let me know if there was any reason to worry, but dang it, give this old man's heart a break, will you?"

He sighed. Fuck, yeah, he should have called his dad before this. "Sorry, Dad. It was brutal."

"Were you... involved?" The background noise dimmed, and Jeremiah heard a door shut.

"Indirectly. There was an inmate that escaped and murdered some of the staff. I saw it happen."

"Damn it. You know I wish you'd move closer to home. With you in California and Gen in South Dakota, I feel like my family has abandoned me." His father chuckled and he heard ice drop into a glass.

"Actually, I'm up in South Dakota with Gen, visiting for a bit. Are you aware that Celest is bombarding Gen with countless emails telling her that the affair was her fault and she needs to come back and make things right?"

He heard his father's deep sigh. "Damn it. No, I wasn't aware. Gen made me promise not to give Celest her number, but I had no idea she'd gone overboard with the emails."

"Overboard is an understatement, Dad. I saw at least four or five hundred. Is Celest still seeing her therapist?"

"I'm sad to say that I don't know, but I will find out. She has already pulled this family apart. I know that you and Gen would have stayed closer if it wasn't for your mother's… tenacity."

Jeremiah rolled his eyes. "Dad, I'm going to be completely honest with you. Celest has issues that need to be addressed now, not later. I'm very worried about her. I have colleagues in the area that I can recommend. People who can help, but you're going to have to sit down with her and draw the line, one she can't cross, one that will motivate her to get better. Hands-off is not what she needs. She's literally terrorizing Gen. Something has to be done." In retrospect, his father's hands-off approach was never what she needed, but that was a realization after years of training and seeing patients.

His father was silent for a moment. "You're right. All right. I'll work on this and get a handle on the situation. Send me those names."

"I'll text the contacts to you as soon as we hang up."

"How are you, son? You don't take random vacations. You're a workaholic like your old man."

"The situation at the supermax messed with me. There was a need to distance myself from what was going on in California, so I jumped on my bike and came out here to South Dakota. Have you seen Gen's little place?"

"No, unfortunately, I haven't. I'll have to make time to do that. Is she happy?" He heard his father take a drink of whatever he'd poured.

"I think she would be happy if you could get Mom under control. The cafe is something she's very proud of, Dad. I think it would mean a lot to her if you'd come up even for just a day or two."

"I'll talk to Henry and get that put on my schedule."

"Henry? I thought your secretary was Opal?" He couldn't imagine his father without the sturdy Miss Opal at his side.

"Opal will be with me until we both shrivel up. Henry is my campaign manager."

"Making the run for Governor this year?"

"I am. I have a good chance."

"You'll make one hell of a Governor." His old man was amazing and not a radical. He could work with anyone, except, of course, Celest. But then again, who could?

"From your lips to God's ears. I need to get back out to the party. I am the man of the moment, after all."

"All right. Take care. Love you."

"I love you, too, and I will take care of the situation."

"Personally, Dad. No handlers."

"I promise. Good night, Jeremiah."

Jeremiah hung up the phone and forwarded three contact numbers to his dad's cell. At least he could mark that item off his list of things to worry about. When his father made a promise, he kept it.

He took off his boots and padded out into the apartment with the intent of shutting every window and locking every door. He was going to buy deadbolts for both Gen and Eden. There was no way they shouldn't have locks on their doors and use them. Damn it, didn't they realize there were monsters out there?

CHAPTER 7

Jeremiah ran as fast as he could. He could hear someone calling for him, begging for help. The halls he ran through were deserted. "Where are you?" He screamed the same thing over and over, trying to find the person who was calling him. He entered a room with hundreds of doors. The terrorized scream for help echoed from everywhere. He raced to a door and threw it open. There was nothing. Again and again, he pulled the doors open. At the last door, he paused. The screaming was louder. He reached for the door and hesitated before he opened it. The voice—he knew the voice. It was Ellen. She screamed again. Jeremiah backed up and swung around. The room had disappeared, there was only a small hallway with another door. He jogged to it and threw it *open. Cyrus Macmillan was behind the door and lifted a knife...*

He woke in a wash of sweat. The nightmare—hell, night terror—put any thoughts of sleep out of his mind. The spike of adrenaline from the dream tingled under his skin and had his heart pumping way too fast. He whipped the thin blanket off him and got out of bed. He ran his fingers through his hair. There was no going back to sleep tonight. Not after that. Hell, he wanted to go check on his sister. Wasn't that stupid? It was a dream. He rolled his shoulders. Wow, he needed to get out of the bedroom. It was too small and suddenly reminded him of a holding point at the prison.

Not wanting to wake Gen, he quietly padded into the kitchen. He jumped. "Shit!"

Gen spun around and dropped her shoes. "Did I wake you up? I'm so sorry!"

"Ah, no, but where are you going?" He blinked when she turned on the light.

"I have cinnamon rolls and biscuits to bake, coffee to brew, and breakfast to start." Gen sat down on one of the kitchen chairs and shoved her feet into her shoes.

He looked at the clock. "At four in the morning?"

She chuckled. "Every morning except Sunday. Go back to sleep, come down when you wake up, and I'll feed you."

"I'm wide awake. Let me grab a shower and I'll come down and help you." He would not sleep again tonight.

"Sure, I'm a one-person show, but you can keep me company." She stood up and headed to the back door, talking as she went, "I'll start the coffee first, it should be done by the time you —" A loud crack shattered the nighttime silence and Gen went to her knees.

Jeremiah bolted to the door, unsure of what happened. "Gen?"

She looked up at him and grimaced. "So maybe we need to move the stairs to a priority?"

He bent down. One of her feet had gone through the wooden slats. He held out a hand and she grabbed it. She extracted her leg from the hole. "Are you hurt?"

"I bruised my pride for sure. That wasn't exactly graceful." She lifted her jean leg and hissed at the scrape along her shin. "I'll go clean that up downstairs."

"All right. I'll be down in just a minute." He

watched her walk down the stairs and waited until he heard the cafe door shut before he examined the hole in the landing. It had been forever since he'd repaired anything, but he was up for the challenge. All he needed was lumber, nails, a power saw, and a measuring tape. How hard could that be?

Obviously, pretty damn hard. "I have to go where?"

"To Belle Fourche at a minimum. If the lumber yard there doesn't have the size you need for those steps, then you might have to drive into Rapid. I can sell you the nails, hammer, saw, and tape measure, but we don't stock lumber," Carson Schmidt, the manager of Hollister Hardware, explained. The man had introduced himself as soon as Jeremiah stepped through the door.

"All right, hook me up with that and a couple sawhorses, too." He rubbed his face and stared at the rows of tools and hardware. He could borrow Gen's truck to go get the stuff, but damn it, he didn't want to leave that hole she made when she dropped through the porch the way it was while he was gone. "You wouldn't have a sheet of plywood, would you? It's a safety issue."

Carson put the carton containing the circular saw on the counter. "I have a half a sheet left over from a project I've been working on."

"Man, I'll pay you double what you paid for it. Gen damn near fell through that landing this morning." Relief swamped him. He'd joked about that stairway being a death trap waiting to happen, but the cold, hard fact was the landing was now deadly.

"Gen Wheeler?" The man lifted his eyebrows.

"Yeah, she's my sister."

"Damn, you must be the guy that broke up the bar fight and saved Declan's bacon." The man shook his head. "You were the talk of the town yesterday. There was a heated debate about the motorcycle hellion who claimed to be a doctor and spent the night at Eden's place. The ladies of the church circles were burning up the telephones." Carson chuckled and started writing up a sales slip. "Gen is going to be very busy until everyone gets a good look at you."

Jeremiah blinked at the man. "Why?"

"Because they are going to want to see you for themselves."

He shifted and cocked his head. "Because?"

"Lordy, mister, if you don't know, you'll figure it out." Carson told him the total for his purchases, and he handed over his credit card. He gathered his new collection of repair materials on top of the four-by-four-foot sheet of plywood and walked them back to Gen's cafe. After he nailed the plywood over the hole in the landing, he made his way back into the cafe.

Eden was sitting in a booth and he smiled at her. She raised her coffee cup in his direction before Gen skittered to a stop in front of him. "What can I get you for breakfast?"

"Nothing, thanks. I'm going to need to borrow your truck to go get some lumber."

"Sure, keys are in the truck." She poured a cup of coffee and handed it to him. "But it's a long drive to wherever you're going, so sit down and I'll get you a sausage biscuit."

He took the cup and shook his head. "You left the keys in the truck?"

"Always. Everyone up here does." She shrugged. "You get used to it."

He shook his head and meandered over to Eden's booth. He leaned down and whispered, "If I sit down here will Zeke piss all over my leg?"

She rolled her eyes. "No. I took care of that once and for all yesterday."

Jeremiah sat down across from her. "Ouch."

She nodded. "For both of us. He's a good friend."

"Who wanted to be more." Jeremiah took a sip of

the coffee and glanced around the small cafe. Every stool and booth had people in them which, considering the size of the town, was surprising. "Is this crowd usual?"

Eden glanced around. "For this time of the morning, no. It would seem you caused a ripple in the community. They're probably here to check you out." She nodded discreetly to the back table. "Father Murphy and Reverend Olsen are regulars on Monday morning. Doc Macy is the vet and he's here most mornings. The ranchers come and go, but the older ladies are here to check you out. I haven't gotten the latest gossip from Allison, but something is making their tongues wag."

Gen did a drive-by and popped a plate with two sausage biscuits, jelly, and a small thermal pot of coffee on their table. "Eden, you need anything else?"

"No, I'm fine, go worry about them." She nodded to the women congregated a few booths down.

Gen plastered a fake smile on her face and headed that direction. Jeremiah watched his sister for several seconds before Eden spoke again. "What is on your agenda for today?"

He picked up a biscuit and spoke before he bit into it. "Measuring Gen's stairs and landing for lumber. She about fell through the landing this morning. If you want me to, I can get lumber for your stairway as well."

Eden leaned forward. "You have a thing about steps, don't you?" He hummed an affirmative and nodded, his mouth too full to state the obvious about deadly dry rot.

"It would be nice to get them fixed. Then maybe I could work on my yard and put in a little barbeque and some paver stones." She chuckled. "Maybe even some flowers that I couldn't kill."

Jeremiah swallowed his food. "You mean your weed and gravel patch?"

Eden tossed a crumpled-up paper napkin at him. "Tell me how much I owe for lumber and your time."

Jeremiah took another bite and closed one eye, squinting at her. "You couldn't afford me, so let's call it repayment for the kindness you showed a stranger."

She snorted into her coffee and muttered, "Right."

He leaned back and picked up his cup. "I was serious."

"You realize it is going to cost hundreds of dollars for the lumber and your time to build them, right?"

He nodded. Not like he had much else to do

while he was here. Gen wasn't joking when she said she was a one-person show. Her processes were economical and timed to the minute. Getting in her way only threw her off her game plan. That's why he'd been at the hardware store the second it opened at eight. Before that, they visited as she waited on the people who wandered in at six in the morning.

"Well, I'll pay for the lumber and your time or you can't work on them." Eden emptied her coffee cup and sighed. "I have a patient due in ten minutes. Do we have a deal?" She extended a hand to him.

He grasped her small hand and flicked his eyes to hers. Her soft but hurried pull of air told him she felt it too, the connection between their skin. He tightened his grip when she moved to pull away. Her face flushed a dark pink and she glanced around the small cafe. "Let's make it a trade. I love my sister, but I don't want to get in her way. Show me the Black Hills, introduce me to your town, make me eggs fried in bacon grease, or sit on your front porch with me and tell me stories about the people who walk down the street."

Eden tugged at her hand again and he released it. "Why?"

He shrugged. "I told you, I want to stay out of

Gen's hair, especially since I'll be staying longer than a week."

She stopped her slide to the edge of the bench. "When did you decide that?"

Just now. When I held your hand. "I'm not sure." He wasn't sure of anything at the moment except that her blue eyes were beautiful, and he had nowhere to go. They were reason enough to stay. For now.

She stared at him for a moment before she smiled. "I'll take that deal, but only if you allow me to pay for the lumber. Not negotiable."

"I can work with that. I'll be over to measure the stairs and landing before I head to Belle Fourche."

She stood and tugged down her scrub top. "Thank you. Beers on me tonight. That bench, about sundown." She nodded to the wooden bench outside her clinic.

"I'll be there." He watched her walk away, turning a bit to see how the scrubs clung to her pretty little ass. As he turned back to his biscuit, he met the stare of at least eight women who'd made no pretense at watching the interaction. He gave them a rakish smile and winked. Instantly, several huffed and turned around, but one with graying red hair and green eyes smiled at him and winked back. The lady sitting beside her placed a hand on his new friend's forearm and pulled her back into the hushed conversation.

He downed the biscuit in four bites, chased it with coffee, and took his dishes back to the wash station in the kitchen. Gen darted through to plate up an order, and he took the opportunity to let her know he was heading out.

Setting the GPS on his phone, he put it in a cup holder and headed south. A smile spread as he realized he had a date tonight. A beer with a pretty lady. The day was looking up.

CHAPTER 8

E den wiped down the exam room, cleaning up after her last patient. Ryan Conklin, the ranch foreman for the Hollister Ranch, had sliced his palm open. It was deeper than they felt they could patch up at the ranch, so they'd called, and she'd waited on them. She also updated his tetanus shot, which was a major victory in her book.

The front door jangled, and Jeremiah walked in. "Did I get the time wrong?" A teasing smile lingered on his face.

"No, I'm late. A rancher versus rusty metal incident."

"Nothing major, I hope?"

"Nope. Normal stuff. Give me a minute and I'll

head up and grab us a couple of beers." She gathered trash from the stainless steel table.

"How about you finish that, I'll pop up and grab those beers and meet you out on the bench?"

A sense of relief swept over her. She was very particular about cleaning and was thankful he wasn't rushing her. "That sounds perfect." She stepped on the pedal of the trashcan to lift the lid and threw away the wastepaper. By the time she finished, she could hear his boots on the stairs leading to her apartment.

After she washed her hands, Eden turned off the light and stepped outside. It was a beautiful spring evening. She turned on the bug light at the other end of the porch because the mosquitos at sunrise and sunset in South Dakota were big enough to be called vamp-quitos and wear a black cape. They'd drain your blood in a heartbeat. She sat down beside him. Once again, she acknowledged just how big this man was. He handed her a beer, and she took it and took a long drink.

"Bad day?" He leaned back on the bench, turning toward her, stretching his arm along the back of the seat.

She angled toward him and shrugged. "Busy, but

that isn't a bad thing. Keeping my visits up convinces the county to keep paying me."

"Is it possible that they'd stop?" His brows drew together.

"Always. Times are tough, but I see my regulars. Older patients, parents of my ranchers and of the people in town that are Medicare and Medicaid recipients. It brings in revenue and I've survived the chopping block so far." She wouldn't stress it. She'd be employable no matter where she went—*if* she went. The pace and people of Hollister fit her needs now. She sighed and leaned back; her shoulders brushed Remi's arm that stretched behind her.

"What speaks to you about this town?" He stared down the street, his eyes distant.

She sighed and thought for several minutes before she answered. "There's no pretense here, or should I say very little. This little town provides for so many even though it's a small speck built on a road junction. That way leads to Buffalo and that direction to Newell. Bottom line is it serves a purpose. There isn't any excess here. Just the essentials. It's like the world stripped this little town down to its best parts."

"I thought that, too. It's real."

The feel of Jeremiah's fingers playing with the ends of her hair should have coaxed her to move, but instead, she leaned on his arm. The sun was setting, and the small community had matriculated to their homes, the storefronts and clinics darkened for another night. There were massive cumulus clouds on the horizon blocking most of the grandeur of the sunset, but as they moved, rays of orange, red, and gold spilled to the ground, giving the horizon an unworldly feel. "It's beautiful." She stared at the sunset and sighed.

He made a noise of agreement. She took another sip of her beer. "Selma, Alabama is a small town. Compared to Hollister it is a metropolis, but I miss nothing."

"Nothing?" He took a swig from his beer and sent her a glance before his eyes strayed back to the setting sun.

She snapped her fingers. "Sushi."

He lifted an eyebrow. "Not much call for sushi restaurants up here?"

"Remarkably, no. I'm not sure Hollister could sustain two restaurants, and Gen has already won them over with her delicious southern offerings."

"She's always loved to cook," he agreed, still staring at the sunset.

She watched as the last light of the day faded. "Were you able to get all the lumber you needed?"

He snorted and shook his head. The long, dark brown strands settled but he pushed them back off his brow. "I had to special order the risers from a lumber yard in Rapid City. "I'll work on the landings tomorrow and go down to pick them up the next day. The wood under the landings is solid so I won't be replacing the framework, just the boards on the top that were exposed to the elements."

"Sounds like two extensive projects." She closed her eyes.

"That's just the tip of the iceberg. Gen has started a to-do list for me. Guess I'll be sticking around for a while."

"Yeah? What's on her list?" She opened her eyes and met his steady stare.

"A root cellar to use to store vegetables but also to use as a tornado shelter."

She shivered a bit. The tornadoes she'd seen since she'd moved here were huge and unforgiving. "Well, get that done and make it big enough for me, too."

"What? You don't want one of your own?"

"Nope, I'm good at mooching butt space. Besides, I have nothing to put in a root cellar. I shop over at the

KRIS MICHAELS

market for things like eggs, milk, and bread. I use this huge chest freezer that someone put in a small room beside the office in the clinic for meats and anything that I can freeze. Occasionally, I tag along with Gen and we spend the day in Rapid, get our hair done, eat out, and see a movie. Sometimes Allison comes with us."

"Girls weekend out?" His voice softened.

"Yes and no. The necessity of living far away from anything major. Did you know the town has a Facebook page?"

He squinted at her. "I'm not on social media much, so no."

"Well, we post there when we head south to make a run. If someone needs something we can pick it up for them." She shrugged. It wasn't an inconvenience most of the time.

"Quite the little community." His fingers still played with her hair when she heard a truck turn from the highway. It wasn't unusual for people to come into town on a Friday or Saturday night to hit up Declan's bar, but everyone knew the bar was closed by now. She recognized the truck. "Oh, crap, that's not good." She stood and handed Jeremiah her bottle.

"What?"

"That's Keelee Marshall's SUV." She turned and

opened her door, flicking on the light as the vehicle skidded to a stop in front of the clinic.

A tall, willowy blonde with a ponytail that danced down to the small of her back jumped from the driver's side door. "Eden, Danny got thrown and Dad thinks it dislocated his shoulder."

"Bring him in." Eden held the door open. Keelee jogged around to the other side of the SUV and opened the door. A big, bulky kid groaned as the tall blonde helped him up the step to the wood porch of the building.

Jeremiah stood and placed the bottles on the ground. "If you're going to relocate it, you'll need someone to hold him and someone to do the procedure."

The woman Eden had called Keelee flicked a distracted glance at him and then did a double-take.

"Keelee, this is Doctor Jeremiah Wheeler, Gen's brother."

The woman nodded and helped the young man into the clinic and then the exam room.

"Okay, Danny, tell me what happened."

"He got on Twister even after I told him not to do it."

"I'm never going to hear the end of this, am I?" Danny hissed as he sat on the exam table.

"Never." Keelee retorted, but there was no heat in the comment. "The horse turned into a corkscrew when a dog dashed out of the barn. Danny flew about fifteen feet and landed on his elbow."

Eden grabbed the scissors. "Danny, I'm afraid that shirt is toast." She didn't give him any further warning before she cut off the material. "The shoulder and upper arm are swollen. Any numbness or weakness in your fingers?" He nodded. "Hand, arm, neck?"

"No just the fingers and *damn it...*" The muscles in his shoulder spasmed and he groaned. When the spasm passed, he panted and apologized for his language.

"Nothing I haven't heard before, but thank you. Okay, I'm going to do an x-ray and make sure there isn't any other damage, but from what I'm seeing and what you're describing it looks like a dislocation." Eden lifted the back of the table so Danny could rest against it and looked at Jeremiah. "Please, make him comfortable. I need to go set up the machine. I don't want to move him any more than we have to before we position him for the shot."

Jeremiah nodded and she dashed into the x-ray room. She thanked God the county had received the grant for it right before she'd taken the position. Her machine wasn't digital, but she'd become a damn good rad tech in the last four years. She turned the head of the machine into the position it would need to be to take a shoulder and arm shot and then draped herself in the lead apron.

"Pain meds aren't a good idea until we know what we're dealing with." Jeremiah's comment stopped her at the door.

"Good, 'cause I'm not taking anything. We got too much work to do." Danny's jaw clenched against the pain.

"If Eden gives it to you, you'll take it even if I have to shove it down your throat. This isn't the time to be all John Wayne on me." Keelee's response was what Eden expected. That woman was a rancher all the way from the tips of her cowboy boots to the top of her head.

"Jeremiah, help him up, please?" Eden watched as Jeremiah instructed the man on what he was going to do. He used his strength to prop Danny into a sitting position so he didn't have to tighten his muscles, but still, the young man's face blanched to a dusty gray.

The trip to the x-ray room and positioning him left the poor guy sweating and the tears that ran down his cheeks wouldn't be mentioned by anyone, *that* Eden could guarantee. They positioned him, standing, against the specialized plate where the film and sensors were located. She lined the crosshairs of the camera, inserted the tray behind Danny, and looked at Jeremiah. "Okay, you need to leave."

He nodded and exited, shutting the door behind him. She slid the lead drape across the wall. The curtains already draped the other three walls and above and below the room, and she'd been assured panels were also installed. She walked into the protective alcove and readied the machine for the shot. "Danny, when I tell you, stop breathing. You need to be perfectly still for me. Okay?"

"Yeah," the grunted answer came back at her.

"On three. One, two, three, hold." She took the shot at the exposure she needed, and when the machine cycled through, she told the young man to breathe easy. They repeated the process for each angle needed to ensure there was no damage to the head of the humerus. Before she called Jeremiah in and went to get the pictures, she straightened his arm and took a shot of his elbow, which had a wicked bruise on it.

Eden turned on the light and pulled the curtain back. "I'll be just a minute. Let's not move him. If it is just a dislocation, we can do the closed reduction here." She nodded to the gurney at the side of the room.

"Sounds like a plan." Jeremiah sauntered over to the young man casually, but Eden knew it was to be there if the man needed support. "You know, motorcycles don't throw you to the ground and try to trample you."

Danny laughed and then groaned. "Doc, you're killing me here."

Jeremiah laughed, "Not my intent."

Eden smiled and hustled to the other room and waited for the film to develop. It didn't take long before she was back in the room and turning on the backlight to slide the image into the slot.

"Full," Jeremiah said from behind her.

She nodded. "I'm thinking local anesthetic and traction to put it into place."

"What's that mean?" Danny asked from over her other shoulder.

"See here," she pointed to the end of his arm. "This is your collarbone, here is your scapula or shoulder blade, and this is the upper arm, which is the humerus. At the top is the head." She cupped her other hand over a fist. "What happened when you fell is that it jarred this bone out of that joint." She separated her hands, showing how it happened.

"So, it's not broken or nothing like that?" Danny stepped in closer to look at the x-ray.

"Correct. I took a shot of your elbow, and I can't see any breaks, but here is the hitch in that giddy-up. I'm not a radiologist. What I'm seeing here looks like a full dislocation. I will send these x-rays to Belle Fourche tomorrow and have the radiologist down there read them, too."

"So, I'm stuck like this until then?" Danny sighed in resignation.

"No, I'm going to give you a local anesthetic and Doctor Wheeler and I are going to maneuver that bone back into place. Then I'm going to x-ray it again and make sure we have it in place. Those pictures will go to the doc first thing in the morning. If he sees something that I don't, you'll need to take a trip south."

Danny nodded. "How long will I be off a horse?"

"Two weeks, and that isn't just off a horse. You'll be in a sling and you will not use that arm. I'll also make sure Keelee is aware of your restrictions."

Danny snorted. "Between Keelee, Tori, and Aunt Betty, I'm sure I won't be allowed to do a thing. The boss is going to be... disappointed." Danny shook his head.

"Let's move over here and get you into position.

I'm going to go out and tell Keelee what's up." She helped as Danny got onto the gurney and Jeremiah lowered him down to a prone position. "Be right back."

She hung up her lead-lined cloak and dashed out to the exam room where Keelee was pacing.

"Frank was right, it is a dislocated shoulder. I'm sending the x-rays to Belle to the radiologist for confirmation. We're going to numb that shoulder and then put it back into place."

"We've got insurance and I'll pay any copay." Keelee handed her an insurance card.

"No worries. I'll take down that information while we're letting the numbing agents work. The county will bill the insurance company and let you know what isn't covered." She unlocked the medicine cabinet and withdrew what she needed. "Danny said your sister is back. I hadn't heard that."

Keelee sighed. "Yeah, she was in a big accident back East. Broken and battered, but she's getting stronger every day. Physically."

Eden hesitated at Keelee's last comment. "Mental trauma from the accident?"

"I think so. I hear her crying at night. The nightmares and such. I've talked to Dad and we're going to ask her to see someone, but damn, that would be a day's drive there and back. Whatever, we'll deal. We always do." The woman gave a closed-off, tight smile.

"Right. Let's get Danny patched up."

An hour and a half later, Eden turned off the light and followed Jeremiah out of the clinic. He went outside and picked up their two half-empty beer bottles. "Looks like we didn't get that drink." Jeremiah took them to the trash can at the corner of her clinic and deposited them.

"I'm sorry. Some weeks I can go days without a patient, and then there are days like this." She rubbed the back of her neck. Jeremiah stepped up to her and turned her around, placing his hands on her neck and rubbing. The heat and pressure about melted her into a puddle of ooze on the wooden platform in front of her clinic. It had been so long since someone had taken care of her. She sighed and relaxed under his skillful massage.

As he kneaded the tight muscles of her neck and shoulders, he leaned forward. "Coffee tomorrow? I'll bring it over here. We can watch the sun come up instead."

She turned around and stared up at him. So damn handsome. Even this soon, she couldn't deny the draw she felt to this man. He'd meshed into her life tonight. There wasn't a moment of awkwardness while she worked on Danny. His support was silent yet there. "I'd love to have coffee and watch the sun come up with you." She lifted onto her tiptoes and kissed his cheek. "Until then." Eden stepped backward as a fire ignited in his eyes. She smiled. She'd done that. She'd put that hunger there, and for the first time in four years, the possibility of what was to come excited her. Even if it was short-term. She turned and went into the clinic, locking the door behind her. If she hadn't been so tired, she'd have floated up the stairs; as it was, she pulled herself up with the handrail. A smile slid into place. She had a date at sunrise.

CHAPTER 9

"Take this, too." Gen handed him a small cardboard container as he filled the thermos she'd dug out from one of her closets upstairs.

Jeremiah opened the box and smiled. Gen had settled two warm cinnamon rolls into the box on small paper plates. She'd also snuggled napkins into the side, avoiding the frosting. "Thank you."

"Absolutely. I'm so happy you and Eden are talking. She's a great friend and a wonderful person." She took a tray of biscuits out of the oven and grabbed the melted butter to brush over the top.

"You realize this is nothing serious, right? I'm only here for a short time." He capped the thermos and grabbed two of her paper to-go cups with caps.

"Does she take sugar or cream?" He hadn't noticed yesterday.

"Cream, no sugar. Don't use those. There are thermal cups with caps in the pantry. Grab a couple from there. I didn't say anything about it being serious. I'd love it if it were, but you're both adults and she's a great person, good enough for my big brother."

He found the small white cups on the shelf and dropped them in the box's corner. "That is one hell of an endorsement." He grabbed the rolls, thermos, and coffee. "Are you sure you don't need any help?"

She nodded. "Positive. I've been doing this for the last six months all by myself. I can do it with my eyes closed."

"Well, I wouldn't condone that practice, just saying." Jeremiah laughed and ducked out of the way when she tossed a piece of crumpled-up tinfoil at him.

"Go away." She laughed and turned back to her business and he let himself out the front door.

He crossed the street and sat down on the small bench before he poured himself a cup of coffee. He'd been up since about three. Snatching more than a couple hours sleep was a blessing, and last night he'd slept for five hours before he woke. It wasn't from a bad dream this time, but no matter how much he tried, he couldn't go back to sleep. When Gen appeared in the kitchen, he was waiting for her and accompanied her downstairs. They'd visited and laughed. He was able to wrestle a couple of the massive sheet pans filled with biscuits, rolls, and bread for lunch from her and load them into the ovens. It was a minor victory, but he'd take it. His sister worked damn hard to make her business a success. He was more than proud of her; rather in awe, actually. She'd made a hell of a move coming to Hollister, but she wanted a clean break with her past, and Hollister gave her that opportunity. He leaned back and took a sip of his coffee. It seemed the little town had given Eden that chance, too.

The door to the clinic opened and the woman he was thinking of appeared. "Good morning." She smiled and sat down beside him.

"Good morning. Did you sleep well?" He handed her the to-go cup, and when she took it, he grabbed the thermos.

"I did. Yesterday was an anomaly for me. I haven't worked that hard since the tornado that ran past Buffalo a couple years ago. Thank God, it killed no one, but it tore up some buildings, and there were injuries from flying debris. They had a search party for a man who was missing, but come to find out he'd gone out to the Hollisters' ranch."

"The Hollisters? As in the town's name?"

"Yep. The same. They have the largest ranch hereabouts. The Marshall and Hollister ranches are generational, and they have hung on to all the land. Some of the mid-sized ranches have failed, but most of them are hanging on. Too many of the little ones haven't."

"Economy?"

She nodded and accepted the cinnamon roll he lifted out of the box. "Oh, nice. I love Gen's baking. Economy? I guess so. When it is a small family ranch, if the children leave and the parents get too old to work the ranch it is either sell or hire hands. Most can't afford to hire help, so they sell."

He handed her two small creamers. "Who buys?"

"Oh, perfect, thank you. The Hollisters and Marshalls." She shrugged and peeled the top off of one creamer and streamed it into her cup.

"So, the big get bigger." He'd seen that in businesses in California. The small mom-and-pop organizations didn't stand a chance against the larger companies that could sell at a lower price because of the volume of product they could sell.

"I guess, but they aren't putting these ranches out

of business. They are protecting the area from the co-ops that have taken over the eastern part of the state."

"Co-ops?"

"Big companies that swallow up land. East of the river is primarily farming. The co-ops have the money and the equipment, and they have most of the prime land. Independent farmers and ranchers are a dying breed." She pulled off a piece of the cinnamon roll and popped it in her mouth.

"You've embraced all of this, haven't you?"

She smiled and took a sip of her coffee, sighing with pleasure before she answered. "How can you not? I know my neighbors. I have coffee at sunrise with new friends, and there is a respect given here that is missing in most of the country."

"I've noticed that. I've always called it small-town charm." He took a bite of his roll and pointed down the street to the east. The first rays of the day lifted over the horizon. She smiled and sat back in the seat, leaning a bit toward him to see around the post holding the overhang up. He moved the box and motioned for her to scoot closer. She did and he put his roll back in the box. He extended his arm behind her on the bench, and she leaned back into the hollow of his arm. "Thank you for this. It's wonderful."

She glanced up at him and smiled. "It is, isn't it? We should do this while you're here."

He stared down at her. The happiness in her eyes made them sparkle and it pulled a contented feeling from deep inside him. He smiled back at her. "We should. A standing date."

"Sitting, actually," she quipped and broke a piece of her roll off, offering it to him.

He bent down and took the offered pastry, brushing his lips against her fingertips. Her eyes flicked to his lips before she offered a shy smile and broke off a piece for herself. She licked the frosting from her fingers, perhaps a bit longer than was necessary. He closed his eyes and repositioned as his interest expanded, and his jeans... Well, they didn't. She was flirting, and he was more than happy to receive her attention.

"What's on your agenda today?"

"Landings." He'd be able to replace both Gen's and hers today.

"Oh, that's right. Got any plans for dinner?"

"No, you?" He took another sip of his coffee.

"I know this great little place. Not far from here."

"Really? What type of cuisine?"

KRIS MICHAELS

"Well, the chef isn't Michelin-rated, but she's decent. Her specialties are comfort food. Fried chicken, potatoes, and corn are what's on the menu tonight. She buys one hell of a good blueberry pie that is produced locally. I can recommend it."

"Does that pie come with vanilla ice cream?"

"That option is always available."

"Sounds like a place I'd enjoy. Can I bring anything?"

She lifted a piece of roll to his mouth, and he took it, this time capturing her finger between his lips. Her mouth parted and her tongue darted out to wet her bottom lip. "Yes. A toothbrush."

He stared down at her and swallowed hard. "Are you sure?"

She moved the plate where the roll had sat and turned to face him. Her gaze traveled from his eyes to his lips. She lifted a bit and he dropped, consuming those soft, full lips in a gentle kiss.

Her tongue licked his lips. He sat up more and dropped his arm around her, pulling her in closer. Gone was the shy gentleness. It was replaced by a building hunger. They explored and teased, probed and played, and finally had to end the kiss or die of asphyxiation. She pushed away from his chest and looked up at him. "Oh, yeah, I'm positive."

"Whoa, me too." He leaned down again and swiped a gentle kiss across her swollen lips. "What time do you want me?"

"Now." The word came out as a breath and then she squeaked. "I do not believe I just said that." She sat up and her hands flew to her face.

He chuckled and put his coffee cup in the box at his feet. "Don't get embarrassed on me now."

"I'm not really, that just sounded… desperate." She sat her coffee cup, which had been in her hand the entire time, down in the box with his.

"A little bit of desperation is acceptable, even preferable." He took her hand in his. "But I have to remind you I'm not a permanent fixture. I'm only here for a couple of months."

She cocked her head and smiled. "A couple of months? That's up from a couple of weeks, and I understand temporary."

He nodded and pushed a strand of her blonde hair out of her face. "I don't want to hurt you."

"You can't if I don't let you." She smiled at him. "Don't overthink it, Remi. Just come to dinner." She stood up and offered him a hand.

He took it and rose, not releasing her hand but standing, still connected. "You never answered. What time?"

"Six-thirty."

"I'll be there." He dropped and brushed a kiss across her lips.

"Morning Eden. Doctor Wheeler," the call came from across the street.

Eden collapsed in giggles against him. She turned and waved. "Good morning Phil. Wonderful day, isn't it?"

"For you, I'd say it is," the older man chuckled and rolled up the only maintenance bay door to his filling station.

"Well, it looks like the entire town will know we're…" She stopped and a frown crossed her brow. "Dating? Phil is one of the biggest gossips in town."

He shrugged. "That doesn't bother me, and dating is a good word." He had dated no one since he was in college. Most of his adult relationships had been about mutual gratification and getting to know each other wasn't on the menu. Hell, he'd give dating another shot. What could it hurt?

CHAPTER 10

"Son of a bitch!" He jerked at the bite of pain and dropped his drill before he grabbed his hand. The board had splintered when he drove the wood screw into a hard knot of the treated board. A four-inch shard embedded itself in the side of his hand. About a half-inch of the wood was under his skin.

He dropped to his ass from his hands and knees where he'd been screwing down the last of Eden's landing. He had four to go and he'd be damned if a splinter was going to stop him. He carefully worked the big piece of wood out and wrapped his bandana around his hand. He'd clean out the entry point and fish out any shards left after he finished. Muttering curse words, he retracted the screw and moved over an inch, driving the four-inch wood screw through the plank he was installing, deep into the platform's supporting beams. With the last board in place, he stood up and let out a low groan as he straightened his back. His spine popped several times. It took another hour to affix the hand railing and wooden lattice work around the landing. The one he replaced didn't have the lattice, but he thought it finished off the space. Eden could put out a small table and chairs on the landing and enjoy the garden warmth of the sun without nosey neighbors having an all-access pass to what she was doing.

His t-shirt was drenched in sweat as the afternoon sun baked down on his back, but the feeling of accomplishment was extraordinary. He'd just finished putting away his tools in the heavy box he'd found at Gen's when the back door opened. Eden gasped. "Oh, my goodness, look at this! Thank you so much!" She stepped out onto the landing with him and jumped up and down on her toes. "This is so much better. I never realized how bad these stairs were until you said something." She reached out and touched the railing. "Oh, my. I'm going to paint this white and maybe put some plants out here. And a couple chairs. This is perfect. Thank you so much."

He chuckled and caught her when, in her exuberance, she hopped on her toes over to him. "You're welcome, but don't go down those stairs yet. I'll get the risers tomorrow and it will be a couple days before they'll be completely replaced." He lifted his hand and she caught it.

"What happened?"

He glanced at the bandana and shook his head. "Splinter. I pulled most of it out. I'll get the rest after I shower."

"I can do that for you. I'm a master splinter-remover." She nodded at the apartment. "That way you can go down the inside stairs." She glanced at the box holding his equipment. "Your weight and that box full of stuff, I'm not sure why they didn't collapse under you."

"Easy." He bent down and lifted a rope out of the box. "I tied it up, and after I made it to the top, I pulled the boards and the box up. I had to risk my life two more times to retrieve the handrails and lattice, but they weren't as heavy."

"Well, come in and we'll get that sliver taken care of."

He grimaced and shook his head. "I smell. Let me go take a shower. When I come back you can look at it."

She took a tentative step closer. "Thank you." She stood on her tiptoes and he leaned down for a kiss.

"It was my pleasure." He kept the kiss soft and intimate. The racing need he felt this morning wasn't gone. God, no. He wanted this woman, but he wasn't going to lose his self-control twice in one day.

Eden lowered from her tiptoes and broke the kiss. "Go so you can come back." The sexy-as-fuck look on her face would tempt him to walk over shards of glass with bare feet. He'd go—and he'd definitely be back.

Jeremiah knocked on the clinic door at six-thirty. The sleepy little town had rolled up its sidewalks for the night. Well, if Hollister *had* sidewalks, they'd be tucked away. The wood porches on the buildings constituted the majority of the walkways and a few paver stones through dirt-packed areas were randomly placed to aid a person from one building to another.

Eden opened the door. Damn. She'd changed into a summer dress and was wearing heels. He made a show of bending sideways to look at the three-inch platforms. She laughed, kissed him on the cheek since he was bent down, and twirled to go up the stairs, speaking as she moved. "Stop, my toes were getting a workout."

Watching her go up the stairs was a treat. The muscles of her trim legs led to those thighs that he wanted to discover with his tongue and fingertips. The thought of driving this woman crazy with need and then pushing her over the top and crashing with her had been vibrating under his skin since this morning.

When they got to the kitchen, she pointed at a chair. He glanced over and a sterile pad was spread across the table with a set of tweezers, a small scalpel, and butterfly bandages. He glanced at the red and festering wound where he'd pulled the wood from his skin. There was definitely something left in there. He dropped down into the seat and she took her place in front of him. Laying a sterile sheet on her lap, she positioned his hand so she could see better. She used the scalpel to lance a small piece of the skin that had been separated when the splinter punctured it. She removed the embedded shard in less than ten seconds. "There. May I suggest wearing gloves in the future?"

"Then I wouldn't get such personalized service." He leaned forward and pressed his lips against hers.

She broke off the kiss and shook her head slowly from side to side as a slow smile spread across her face. "You're going to be trouble, aren't you?"

He slid his hand behind her neck and pulled her back to him. "Not for you. Never for you." The slow heat he wanted to build smoldered, banked against the thrill of discovering every inch of her body. She placed both hands against his chest and pushed gently. He released her immediately.

"The food is going to be ruined if we don't eat soon." She stood up and handed him a butterfly bandage. "To keep that clean until it heals." She disposed of the rest of the implements and the sterile pad before she handed him a bottle of wine. "I don't know if you like white wine, but I thought it would go with the chicken. Would you mind opening it?"

"Of course." He wasn't much of a wine drinker, but the fact she'd gone out of her way to make the dinner nice fueled that little spark in his gut that knew this woman was special.

He opened the wine and sat it on the counter. "Do you want me to set the table?"

She glanced over at him from where she'd removed two plates full of fried chicken, mashed potatoes with gravy, and corn. "I've already done that."

He glanced at the kitchen table and back at her. She nodded to the back door. A smile flashed and she gave a self-conscious laugh. "It's only a card table and folding chairs, but I thought the idea of eating al fresco was too tempting to pass up, and now that I have a private area to do that, well, it was a no-brainer."

"Would you like me to carry those out?" He lifted his hands to help.

She shook her head. "I've got these. Would you bring the wine and open the door?" He snagged up the bottle and they made their way out to the landing he'd just finished. She'd put a bright yellow spread over the cloth with red napkins and white place settings. The total effect was attractive in a home-spun way. After she placed the food, he withdrew her seat and she blushed as he assisted her. Or perhaps the blush was fanned by the kiss that he placed on her cheek before he sat down.

"This looks amazing." He poured her a glass of wine and then himself. "When did you have time to cook this?"

"I didn't have any patients on the schedule today and Allison was the only one who stopped by in the morning and then Gen came over this afternoon to visit. She's so glad you're here. I think the tiff she and her mom are having is hard on her."

He used his knife and fork to cut the juicy meat from the bone. "My mother is a unique individual. I've talked to my father about her constant pressure on Gen."

"Did she tell you what that jerk did to her?"

He nodded and took a bite. He lifted a hand and chewed. "If I didn't know better, I'd say this is my Grandma Wheeler's recipe."

"It is, Gen gave it to me right after she moved in. We were having a community social, and I was volunteered to bring chicken. She made a massive pot of Jambalaya. It knocked everyone's socks off."

"I can only imagine." He chuckled and cut another bite and added a bit of homemade mashed potatoes and gravy. If it was physically possible for his eyes to roll into the back of his head, his would have. "You, my dear, are a fantastic cook. Your demure last night had me expecting boxed macaroni and cheese."

Her eyes popped open. "Yeah? You like it?"

He nodded again, bringing another bite to his lips. "Absolutely heaven after all the work today."

She took a bite and glanced around her. When she finished, she waved her hand. "This is like my own little haven. I researched hardy garden plants. Allison recommended lilac bushes. I think I'd like to plant one in each corner and then maybe have tulips and tiger lilies in between with grass everywhere else. I could lay out in the sun and not be self-conscious."

He set his fork down as he listened to her dream about the little yard below. "It sounds like a lovely vision for the space." He could imagine her in a bikini, but he'd like to take her to a tropical paradise and show her the magnificence of a Caribbean sunset. He picked up his fork when he realized the directions of his thoughts. Dreaming of a future wasn't healthy, not when he knew that this was a temporary relationship.

"Oh, I heard Declan was released today. Zeke said he'd be bringing him up either today or tomorrow."

His eyes flicked up to meet hers. "So, he's talking to you?"

She nodded. "We are the primary health providers for the county. Zeke has four counties for which he provides coverage, so me being here full time helps ease his patient load. The other counties don't have a practitioner, but they are more sparsely populated."

A slither of jealousy crept forward from some

unknown place and he slapped it back to whatever netherland it had sprouted from with a firm shove.

"How is Declan doing?"

"According to Zeke, he probably would be dead if you hadn't reacted so quickly." She looked over at him and winked. "I think that hurt him."

He chuckled. "Well, I can understand why. I have something he wants." He reached over and caressed her cheek.

She blushed wildly and reached for her wine. "Are you ready for dessert?"

He glanced down at his plate which he'd demolished in record time. He wiped his mouth and extended his hand. "I am, but I don't want pie."

She placed her hand in his and glanced back at the table. "I should clear this."

"It can wait." Jeremiah backed her into the side of the house and lowered to kiss her. Her arms wrapped around his neck and he took his time. His hands traveled over her small, tight body. The soft roundness of her breasts filled his palm and he wanted her out of that dress. Her hands had unbuttoned his shirt and spread it open to explore his chest. He broke away and growled. "Bed."

She nodded. "Yeah. Good idea." He released her only to get them inside. She opened the door and he

closed it after them. He waited until she opened her
bedroom door before spinning her and lifting her by
that pert little ass. Her legs wrapped around him as
did her arms. He opened one eye long enough to set
a trajectory and lowered her gently into the soft
cover of the queen-sized bed. He stood and toed off
his boots, stripped out of his shirt, and unhooked his
belt. He reached into his pocket and dropped a line
of condoms onto her bedside table, and yeah, he
wanted to use every last one of them.

Eden sat up in the bed and watched, and when he
stopped moving, she stood on her knees and slipped
the summer dress over her head. He swallowed hard.
Her body was beautiful. She wasn't skin and bones;
she had curves, ones that he wanted to know inti-
mately. Her breasts lifted with each of her breaths
and the tight, dark pink nipples were a siren's song.
He unfastened and unzipped his jeans, shucking
both them and his boxers in one shove.

She sucked an audible breath of air. "Wow."

He lifted an eyebrow and a smirk formed across
his face. He couldn't have prevented it if he'd tried.
She'd given him every man's dream compliment in
one word. He cupped his shaft and stroked it from
base to tip. He wasn't huge, but he wouldn't be
embarrassed in a locker room either. He kneed onto

the bed and she laid back, her legs spread to welcome him. He traced a finger up the inside of her leg and stopped at the lace panties that she still wore. "Do you like these?" he asked, and he put a finger under the thin elastic band that held them up.

"Wh—what?" She blinked up at him, obviously not tuned into his question, which, holy hell, made him harder if that was possible.

"These, they're very nice. Any sentimental attachment?" He lifted his finger a couple times, indicating the panties.

Her brow furrowed and she shook her head. "No, wh—"

He grasped both sides of the elastic and pulled, snapping the material and baring her. "Jeremiah!"

He dropped down on top of her and took her lips. Fuck him, he was acting like a caveman, but her moan against his mouth told him she didn't mind. He broke the kiss and started down her body. Her scent was fresh and floral, and her taste was delicious. He kissed and tongued down her neck and across her collarbone before he lowered to her breasts. Her softness was an aphrodisiac that fogged his senses and heightened every touch. He softly rolled the nipple of one breast as he kissed and tongued the other, swapping to give each the attention their beauty demanded. His free hand traveled lower, splitting her sex and delving into her slickness. Centering over her, he lifted to her lips again. Jeremiah reached out and grabbed the string of condoms. Tearing one off, he dropped the others next to them and made quick work of sheathing his hard-as-diamonds cock. He lowered over her and took her lips as he found her center. Carefully, he worked his way into her. She tilted her hips at each thrust, and they moved in concert until he buried himself deep within her. Reaching under her shoulders, he cupped them and held her in place as he used long, deep strokes to move them both closer to an orgasm. Her sex was slick and hot, confining and yet freeing. The way her body hugged his made him lose any will to be anywhere else but here with her. He felt her tremble and sped up.

Her fingernails dug into his biceps and her body tightened like a bow as she arched off the bed. Eden pushed out a guttural moan and her body rippled around his cock, clenching and tightening in waves before she dropped, spent and boneless.

He lowered his lips to her shoulder and kissed it gently before he moved inside her. Chasing his own release, he held her tightly to him and crashed through his orgasm. He tightened his jaw, yet still his

KRIS MICHAELS

growl of release echoed off her bedroom walls. He lifted a bit to give her air and to see her.

Her eyes were closed, her full lips partially open, and her face was flushed with a dark shade of rose. She blinked and opened her eyes. Her hands traveled up his biceps to his shoulders. "I think you broke me."

"Shit, sorry." He jolted and tried to move off her.

She grabbed him, stronger than he would have believed. "Not in a bad way. Believe me, not in a bad way."

He chuckled and kissed her shoulder. "I'll be right back, and then you can tell me how I broke you in a good way." He lifted off the bed and padded into the bathroom to dispose of the condom. He glanced at the mirror, and yeah, that look of satisfaction was one he hadn't seen in years.

She was laying on her side, her arm under her head when he returned. He slid on top of the soft cover with her and mimicked her position. "You were saying?" He leaned forward to kiss her on the nose.

Eden sighed and smiled at him. "I'm sure you get this a lot, but that was fantastic."

He shook his head. "It's you. You were the reason.

You have to be because it's never felt this... right before."

She lifted her eyes from where her fingers were twirling in his chest hair. "It does feel that way, doesn't it?" He nodded and she continued, "I was afraid that after four years, building up what Riley and I had in the past... I was afraid I wouldn't find this again, you know?"

"This?" he asked her as he pushed her hair from her cheek.

She closed her eyes. "Wanting someone. Needing someone."

He pulled her closer and held her, understanding that tonight she'd taken another step away from her dead husband. "I don't think he would have wanted you to be alone. Do you?"

She sniffed a bit and burrowed closer to him. "He wouldn't have."

He let her rest on his arm and held her close as she processed the events of the night. Finally, she arched her back and lifted an eyebrow.

He chuckled, "Yes?"

"You're being a doctor right now, aren't you?" She lifted up on her elbow and stared down at him.

"Maybe just a little bit." He lifted his hand and

made a pinching motion with his thumb and forefinger.

She smiled at him and pushed his long hair off his forehead. "Thank you, but I'd like the leather-clad biker dude back now."

He grabbed her and hefted her onto his chest as he rolled. "What can I do for you, wench?"

She laughed and slipped off the bed, grabbing his shirt. "You can bring me the dishes from the back landing." She put on his shirt and laughed as she buttoned it up. The tails came down to her knees, and man, it did things to him to see her in his shirt. She rolled up the sleeves while he put on his jeans, commando. He zipped them but didn't bother fastening them or the belt. "I'll wash, you get to dry." She stood on her tiptoes and pulled him down for a kiss. "Thank you."

He wrapped her up in his arms and returned the kiss. "I think I should be thanking you, but we'll worry about the manners portion of the night tomorrow morning. I have so much more in store for you tonight. I hope you don't have too many patients on the schedule." Kissing her one more time until they were both breathless, he let her go and headed out of the bedroom to gather the dishes. The sooner they were done with being responsible adults, the sooner they could use every one of the condoms he'd brought with him.

CHAPTER 11

E den filled the sink with hot, soapy water. The act of washing dishes morphed from drudgery to sexual foreplay. Jeremiah stood behind her, kissing her neck, roaming her body with his hands, and distracting her with long, passionate kisses between each pot and pan. She was wonderfully aroused by the time she sent him out to the landing to break down the card table and chairs. When he left, she grabbed a quart of vanilla ice cream, scooped a ton of whipped cream on top, and grabbed a spoon. She walked out onto the landing just as he was coming in.

"What is this?"

"Dessert." She put the ice cream on the railing and shimmied up to sit on top of it, too. "Here." She dipped down through the cream to the frozen bit and held the spoon out to him.

He stepped between her legs and pulled her against him. She wrapped her legs around him, still sitting on the railing. He opened his mouth and took the treat. She gave herself a bite and squealed when Jeremiah leaned forward for a kiss. The ice cream melted between both of their tongues and dribbled down her chin. She broke the kiss laughing and wiped at the mess. "That is the best dessert I've ever had. We should have more." He opened his mouth and she fed him a bite. He leaned in for another kiss. The erotic thrill of sitting almost naked outside while kissing this man as ice cream melted in their mouths was past anything she'd ever experienced. She'd had a satisfying sex life with Riley, but nothing she'd ever done had readied her for the incredible male currently authoring numerous fairytales, heavy on the sex, in her mind.

A thump from inside the apartment broke them apart. "What was that?" Jeremiah asked.

"I don't know." She let him help her off the rail. He held his hand out, indicating he was going first, and that was okay since she hadn't been expecting anyone. Quietly, they walked down the hall. Jeremiah stopped abruptly. She peeked out from behind him. "Zeke? What are you doing here?"

The man had taken off his cowboy boots and his overnight bag was on the chair. Zeke whipped around in shock. His stare went directly to Jeremiah. She stepped out from behind him. Zeke's eyes traveled to her and then back to Jeremiah. "Well, that didn't take long."

"Excuse me?"

"What the hell, dude?"

She and Jeremiah talked over each other. Zeke lifted his hand and shook his head. "Sorry, that was inappropriate. I'm sorry. It's no excuse, but I've had a hell of a day, and now it looks like I'm facing a long drive home."

A drip of melting ice cream fell onto her foot. She passed the ice cream bowl to Jeremiah and pointed to the kitchen. With another hostile look toward Zeke, he went into the kitchen. "How did you get in?"

"I have a key to the clinic. When you didn't answer the door or your cell phone, I assumed you were with Allison or Gen and let myself in. I'm sorry if that was impulsive, but you've never had a problem with me staying over."

"Until now." Jeremiah stood in the kitchen doorway.

Zeke nodded. "Until now."

"You're not driving back tonight; it is too far." She looked helplessly at Jeremiah. He narrowed his eyes at her as if trying to read her thoughts. She sighed, "You can sleep on the couch, Zeke. Remi, may I speak to you? In private?"

Jeremiah stalked across the living room as Zeke shook his head. "No, that's all right. I'll be fine."

"Zeke, plant your butt on that couch, you aren't driving south tonight. I will not let you fall asleep behind the wheel." She grabbed Jeremiah's hand and dragged him into the bedroom.

Jeremiah sat down on the bed and ran his hands through his hair. "This is awkward. I'm not going to lie. I don't want him here. Alone. With you."

Eden flopped down beside him and sighed, "He's harmless."

"Harmless, huh? I beg to differ. It appears he did one hell of a hack job on our plans for tonight." Jeremiah lifted her and turned her to face him before pulling her onto his lap. She felt tiny in his arms but safe and cared for.

She wrapped her arms around his neck. "But we

can do it all over again tomorrow." She leaned forward and kissed his lips softly, hopefully promising enough that the epic doctor-sized stop sign in the front room wouldn't deter him from coming back tomorrow.

"Is that so?" He damn near purred the words.

She smiled and nodded once. "I promise."

"Until tomorrow then." His kiss was branding-iron hot and there was no doubt in her mind he was acting possessive. There was no need to worry. None. Zeke didn't interest her, and she returned the passion he ignited.

When they broke, she stood up and started unbuttoning his shirt. He ran his finger from her collarbone between her breasts and let his hand drop. "I'm going to bring a shirt over for you. This look is sexy as hell."

She shrugged out of his shirt. "Sexier than this?" She held his shirt out to him and watched as his eyes darkened. He blinked several times and took a step back while grabbing his shirt. "I'm going to kill Zeke."

The agonized groan made her laugh. "No, you're not. I'll see you for coffee in the morning?" She went to her closet and pulled out her robe, wrapping herself up in it.

"I'll be there. Sunrise." He shrugged on his shirt

and buttoned it up, shoving the tails in his jeans. She watched him put on his socks and boots and stand again. Picking up his briefs, she smiled when he rolled his eyes. "I'll be back for them." He dipped down and gave her a kiss. "Sunrise."

She followed him out of the room and leaned on the wall as he passed through the living room, ignoring Zeke.

"I could have driven south." Zeke held his head in his hands and didn't look up at her.

She sat down on her small chair that was nestled in the corner of the conversation area. "No, you're exhausted, the baggage under your eyes is impressive."

"I need an office up here or maybe in Buffalo. The drive up plus a full day of driving all over the county and the drive back is a nineteen-hour day, minimum. I can do it two or three days in a row, after that, I'm toast."

"So, what's stopping you? You could petition the counties and the state for grant money. I think there is even a federal program for underserved areas." She tucked her legs under her, the soft terrycloth of the robe covering her.

He dropped back onto the overstuffed couch cushion. "I have that all in the works."

"Good. When will you be able to transition?"

"Not as soon as I would like. Before your boyfriend hit town I was going to ask if I could stay here and make the move up. Now? Hell, I'll figure something out."

"Let me look around for a room for you. I can ask Phil; he's plugged into everything."

He shook his head. "I can ask him. Thanks." He leveled his gaze on her and stared at her until she felt uncomfortable.

"What?"

"Seeing you with him, it drove your point home. You feel nothing for me."

"I told you, friendship isn't nothing. I've known you for two years, Zeke. I enjoy working with you and I want to keep that relationship." She reinforced her words from the last conversation they had on the topic.

He nodded. "Can I tell you a secret?"

"Sure."

"I'm not sorry I interrupted." A mischievous smile spread across his face.

She laughed and stood up. "Somehow, that doesn't surprise me. I'll get you bedding and a pillow." She padded down the hall and retrieved the items, setting him up for the night. "Night, Zeke."

"Night."

Eden tiptoed through the living room and headed down the front steps to the clinic entrance. She slipped out of the door and shut it quietly. Jeremiah hadn't arrived yet, but that was okay. She sat down on the bench and took a deep breath of the cool night air. It was getting hotter every day. Soon, temperatures in the high nineties would be the norm and they would put window air conditioning units back into sashes to keep everyone cool. There were a few houses that had central air but most used window units.

She loved this little town. It wasn't wealthy by any means. Everyone struggled to build a life, but it was home. She'd realized that about a year ago. She'd planted roots here. Few did. It was a hard life, but it was worth all the burdens. Home always was.

The sound of a door shutting turned her head. Jeremiah had two cups of coffee balanced on top of a small box. She was going to be spoiled by the time he left. She stood up and grabbed the coffee, lifting up for a kiss. He wrapped an arm around her and held her up as his tongue danced with hers. He relaxed his hold and ended the kiss with several smaller, softer kisses. "Good morning," he said before he released her.

"Good morning." She echoed the words and sat down with him. He opened the box and handed her a creamer. She gave him his cup and took the top off hers. "You're driving down to Rapid today?"

"I am. Want to come with me?" He handed her a sausage biscuit. "Gen said you liked sausage instead of bacon."

"I like them all, but her homemade sausage is amazing." She sat her coffee down and unwrapped the biscuit. "I can't go to Rapid today. I have two elderly patients coming in for routine screenings."

He nodded and they both took a bite of their food. She washed it down with a sip of coffee. "Maybe you could take me on a motorcycle ride in the Hills this weekend. I'm not required to be here every day and I don't schedule patients on the weekend."

He stopped chewing and looked at her. He swallowed hard and then asked, "You'd want to do that?"

"I'd love to. I told you, my brothers and father opened a motorcycle shop. I wanted one so badly and pestered them until they rebuilt a wrecked Royal Enfield. Only three hundred fifty cc's and I thought I was badass." She laughed and waved a hand. "It was the smallest motorcycle they could find so I could pick it up and manage the weight. I loved to ride with them."

He smiled at her. "Why don't you ride now?"

"Well, honestly, I don't have anyone to ride with. I don't think I'd enjoy it as much." She shrugged. "I guess being included and having something I could do with my family was a big part of the thrill."

"I'd love to have you ride with me. Saturday. We'll leave early and spend the day."

She eyed him and hesitated for a second before she suggested. "Why not spend the night, too?"

A wicked smile spread across his face. "No doctors to interrupt us."

She winked at him. "Exactly."

"It's a date." He leaned forward and she met him halfway. God, the man could kiss, and the tingling sensation of wanting more always surfaced around him. She was excited and terrified at the same time. Excited to be with a man again, terrified that keeping it casual would rip her heart out. In such a short time she'd developed feelings for him. Boy, she'd pegged it last night. He was going to be trouble and probably rip her heart out when he left, but there was no way she'd deny herself this happiness.

They finished their coffee while talking of child-hood memories of Alabama. "Did you ever go to the peanut festival?" he asked as he boxed up the remnants of their meal.

"Several times, that and the blueberry festivals. My mee-maw was a fantastic cook and she made blueberry preserves that were phenomenal." She drank the last of her coffee.

"I get that. My grandmother and grandfather were the best. They lived life in a different era, and I think that's why spending time with them was so special."

She nodded as they both stood. "I agree. Be careful driving, the bucks are in rut and they lose their minds."

Jeremiah pulled her into an embrace and rocked back and forth a bit as he looked down at her. "The bucks are not the only thing in rut. Lose the doctor. I'll be over when I get back."

She laughed and wrapped her arms around his neck. "I'll make sure he's gone or find him a bed to sleep in tonight. One that's not here."

Jeremiah bent down and kissed her. "Until then." She held his gaze until he smiled and headed back across the street. The wide V of his muscled shoul-ders and back narrowed at his hips and tapered through his long, muscular legs. She shivered as memories of their physical electricity zinged through her mind. Was she a fool? Probably. But she was unable to resist the pull of that man. Unable and unwilling. She'd never been so forward before, but then a lot of life had floated past her. She wasn't going to watch the river of life pass by her any longer. She was jumping in headfirst and seeing what was around the next bend. Eden leaned against the porch post and stared at the cafe until she heard Phil open his garage door. She stepped off the porch and headed that direction. It was time to get a place for Zeke to rent, and she was going to find it today.

CHAPTER 12

Remi turned off the radio in Gen's truck and rode in silence heading south. That damn Zeke had pissed him off last night, but once he had distance and time behind him, he'd admit the man looked wiped out. He'd fallen asleep thinking of Eden and awakened to a nightmare of Cyrus holding a knife to Eden's throat. He processed that dream now while he was alone and had time to think. In fact, he'd learned the psychoanalytic theories about dream interpretations. Freudian theories were a mandatory study, after all. Cyrus' presence was understandable. The traumatic events of the recent past were still being processed by his conscious and subconscious. And Eden? Well, his subconscious recognized that she was important to him. He lowered his window and let the air blow around him, resting his elbow on the door. Unobtrusive turnoffs to gravel roads punctuated the vast expanses of land.

Miles and miles of fence line dissolved into miles and miles of time to think and process. The trip to Hollister had been about *not* thinking about the incident, about pushing past it to make forward progress, to live his life, but the trauma stayed with him. Talking to Jamison once a week would help, but with his knowledge, sorting through the memories and pulling them out one by one was something he could do alone. If he ran across something that he couldn't work through, he'd bring it up to Jamison. So, he started with the thought that had been at the forefront for weeks now.

Why did Cyrus want to kill him?

Jeremiah glanced at the rearview mirror. There was no logical explanation for the way the man had fixated on himself and Agent Docker. But then again, when dealing with an antisocial personality disorder it wasn't always easy to peg the "whys." The man was a psychopath with a lack of empathy and remorse coupled with his manipulative callousness that were textbook examples of the diagnosis. Cyrus might not have a logical reason to fixate on him, yet he had done exactly that. The saving grace was the man was behind bars at a supermax facility. The last person to escape from that prison had done so on a medical transport. There was no way the facility managers would allow Cyrus to be transported—he prayed they wouldn't, not without shackles, cuffs, and chains. He was too dangerous to the world to be sent outside the prison walls for care.

He pulled at the feeling of anxiety, examining what was causing it. It took ten miles to figure it out. His anxiety over the fixation—and Cyrus in general —was due to the fact the man had escaped while in the medical wing and could have used any of the people in the facility to force the guards to open doors.

He shook his head. "They wouldn't have." He shifted in his seat. The guards locked down Cyrus during the riot and they would have kept the place locked down if he tried to escape, even with a hostage. Of course, the hostage would be dead, but Cyrus would rot in jail. Anxiety surrounding the belief the man would come after him, no matter how strong, had no foundation.

He drew a breath and then a deeper one. Time and distance helped with perspective. He needed this break, he needed to be away from the confines of the prison, and he needed to examine everything that had happened. One memory at a time, but he wouldn't push himself. Tomorrow, as he worked, he'd pull out another sliver of apprehension and turn it over and over until he understood where it came from and why he kept feeling the trepidation.

He stuck his hand out the window and felt the warm, buffeting winds try to push it back. The freedom was nothing like riding a motorcycle, but the feel of the air moving around him gave him a sense of peace.

His phone lit up and vibrated in the cupholder. Jamison. Why? He wasn't supposed to check in with his friend for another four days.

He swiped the face of his phone and answered. "Hello?"

"Where the hell are you?"

"Hold on." He hit the button and lifted the driver's side window and switched on the fan in the cab before he spoke again. "Driving to Rapid City to pick up some stair risers. What's up?"

Jamison was quiet for a few seconds. "Why?"

"Because Gen and Eden's stairs are a death trap and I needed something to do while I was here."

"Gen is your sister. Who is Eden?"

"Definitely not my sister," Jeremiah chuckled.

KRIS MICHAELS

"Well, that's an interesting turn of events. Are you thinking of staying longer?"

"Maybe. What's up? We aren't scheduled to talk for a couple days." He adjusted the cruise control up a couple miles per hour. There was no one for as far as he could see, and he could fly down these roads.

"I have a favor to ask," Jamison came straight out with it.

"What can I do for you?" He'd do anything he could for his friend.

"There is a young woman not too far from Hollister who is in a Post-Traumatic Stress recovery situation. Major mental and physical trauma. Would you be willing to work with her?"

Jeremiah chuffed out a sigh. "Dude, you know I am not licensed to work in South Dakota."

Jamison mocked him, "Dude, you know I work for Guardian, right?"

"Smartass," Jeremiah laughed at him.

"Always, but seriously, Guardian will handle everything. You'll have authorization to practice and prescribe within the week."

He blew out a lungful of air. "I don't have anywhere to see her."

"I checked. There is a county clinic in Hollister.

We can make inquiries and see if we can rent a room from them once a week."

"You've thought of everything."

"I have. The only thing I need is you saying yes." Jamison's smugness should have pissed him off, but it didn't.

"Let me work the clinic aspect. I've met the Nurse and Doctor that use the facility." He was pretty sure Eden would allow him to see the patient after hours, and hopefully, that would work for the woman.

"So, that's a yes?"

"That's a yes." He smiled at the whoop that came from his friend.

"You don't know how much this will mean to people in prominent places here at Guardian."

"Does she work for Guardian?"

"Ah…" There was a pause as if Jamison was trying to think of a way to answer that question. "Well, no. She was Agency I believe."

"Agency? Like FBI?"

Jamison chuckled. "No, for those of us who deal with the alphabet companies all the time, Agency is the CIA, the Bureau is the FBI. Then, of course, there is Homeland and ICE, all of which are self-explanatory."

"Thanks for the tutelage. What's this woman's name?"

"Victoria Marshall."

Jeremiah connected the dots. "As in the Marshall Ranch?"

"Exactly."

"Okay. Can you send me her records?"

"Nope. Agency won't release them. You'll have to do the intake and work up on your own."

"That puts us both at a disadvantage." He hated when providers were prevented from sharing information that would help their patients. "I could call her health care provider from the Agency to get a sense of what they've done with her in general terms."

Jamison sighed and cleared his throat. "Remi, the Agency is her biggest problem. They won't tell you anything."

"Damn. That sucks for her."

"It does, which is why I reached out to you, but…"

He looked at the phone. "Yes?"

"We'd want you under contract for at least six months at Hollister. We'd pay you, of course, and help you get your position back in California if the facility managers don't want to wait for you."

He pushed his hair off his face and glanced at the rearview mirror. "No, I'm sending in my resignation. I don't really know what I want to do, but I do know it isn't going back inside that prison."

"How are you doing?" Jamison asked, his voice softened when he spoke.

"I'm doing better. Sleeping more, dreaming less. Working at pulling out my emotions one at a time and looking at them."

"Doctor, heal thyself?" Jamison asked.

"No, more like Doctor, use your skills and work with Jamison to make sure you put this into the proper perspective."

"I knew I liked you." The approval in his mentor's voice was palpable.

"Because I'm awesome. Email me what you can as far as contact information for Ms. Marshall. I'll set up a place to see her and contact her to work out the time."

"I'll send the NDA you'll need to sign and our contract before I send that information," Jamison responded.

"We're still on for our call, right?" Remi asked.

"We are. You may be doing all the right things, but I'm going to make sure they stick."

Three and a half hours later, with Gen's truck filled to the top of the bed with wood and a few other items he decided to pick up last minute, he pulled into Tank's shop. The man who exited the garage didn't look exactly inviting, but in broad daylight on a busy street, there was little risk of a confrontation.

"Help you?"

"Is Tank here?" Jeremiah closed the truck door and locked it with the fob.

"Yeah, hold on." The man sauntered back into the shop and Jeremiah leaned against the truck to wait.

Tank ambled out of the office and the frown on his face turned into a smile. "Well, if it isn't the shrink. How you doing, man?"

Tank offered a hand, and he took it, giving a firm handshake. "Doing well. I was wondering if you had a Hoglet."

Tank belted out a laugh. "You're too damn big for that sized bike. You got a kid you're wanting to teach?"

"She's not a kid." Jeremiah leveled a direct stare.

"No shit, your old lady would rather have her own ride. You know that's what a bitch seat is for, right?"

"Not my old lady, but she's a feisty lady who knows motorcycles and loves to ride. She's about..." Jeremiah put his hand up to just below his pecs. "...this tall. She had a 350cc growing up, but she could handle a 500."

Tank rubbed the back of his neck with a shop rag. "I don't have any, but I have a Royal in the back. The thing's scratched to shit, but it runs. The owner laid it down when he was trying to pass a car up in the Hills. Lucky for the bastard he shot across the pavement to a lookout. Stupid fucker convinced himself the reason he went down was because his bike wasn't powerful enough."

"So, no one ever told him about controlling the bike?"

"Right? Like I said, he was a stupid fucker. Follow me."

Jeremiah chuckled as he walked into and through the shop with Tank. "What did you sell him?"

"Exactly what he wanted, way too much bike even for a man with his ego. He totaled that bike two days later and landed in the hospital with two broken legs and a broken arm." Tank shrugged. "I got paid, the dipshit is alive, and life goes on." He followed Tank to the back of the shop, past four maintenance bays, a paint booth, racks of parts, wheels, and tires. "It's out here."

He opened the back door and Jeremiah stepped into a small fenced-in area. Sure enough, the Royal leaned up against the fence. It needed a new seat, a paint job, and some chrome replaced. "How much to fix it up and get it ready?"

Tank tucked his cloth into his pocket and crossed his arms as his eyes traveled over the bike. "Most of it is cosmetic damage. Like I said, it runs. All prettied up, a grand."

"I'll take it." Jeremiah stuck out his hand. "When can you have it ready?"

Tank stroked his beard and then glanced back at the shop. "A month? We have a backlog right now. We'll have to sandblast the tank, prep it and paint it, order in additional parts. What color would you want the tank and fenders?"

"Sky blue," he said without hesitation. She'd look beautiful on it.

"Okay, maybe a pearl sheen?" Tank opened the door and let Jeremiah in first.

"As long as the base is sky blue, I'm good with whatever you do to it. She's a nurse, so no skulls and crossbones."

Tank slapped him on the back and laughed, "You got it, Doc."

Remi pulled his wallet out. "I'll pay for it now."

Tank shook his head. "Nope. Not how this shop works. The client has to love the job, or it doesn't go out the door and we don't get paid."

"Kind of hard to stay in business that way, isn't it?" Jeremiah shoved his wallet back down into his pocket.

"Doc, I'm giving you a bargain-basement price for a bike I don't like or want. Tell no one what you paid for that thing or my reputation as a high-priced motherfucker will go to shit."

"My lips are sealed. Doctor-biker confidentiality and all that." Jeremiah laughed when Tank let loose with a belly laugh so loud it rumbled the walls around them.

"Doc, you need to stick around. I kinda like you."

They exited the front of the store and he headed back to Gen's truck. He stopped and spun around. "Hey, any chance you know of a good sushi place?"

Tank narrowed his eyes and muttered, "I take it back."

CHAPTER 13

"Hey." Eden's greeting from the doorway caused him to look up from his notes. Jeremiah leaned back in his chair and smiled. He extended his arm and Eden walked into the small office she'd let him use to see Victoria Marshall. She ran her fingers through his hair, and he closed his eyes, enjoying the attention.

"Hard session?" she asked as she massaged his scalp.

He hummed an affirmation. His sessions with Victoria, or Tori as she preferred to be called, were a minefield of triggers, and the things she'd endured were at times beyond his comprehension. Tori Marshall was a fighter, and she was fighting against the depression and anxiety that the incident she was involved in stacked on her. It impressed him. She worked on the things he asked her to work on and was religious about their meetings. They'd met twice a week for the last three weeks.

"Are you ready for dinner? Gen isn't coming over tonight. Allison and she are playing cards with Allison's parents. Gen says they owe her over five dollars in lost poker revenue."

He laughed. "I feel sorry for them. She's tenacious when she's after something." They'd been alternating eating at Eden's or Gen's since he and Eden had started spending so much time together. He loved the easy comradery between his sister and Eden. All three of them gelled and he appreciated Eden letting Gen interrupt their alone time.

Eden dropped a kiss on his forehead, and he opened his eyes. "My sister works too hard."

"She does. It seems to be a family trait. Now, come up, dinner is almost ready."

"May I have dessert first?" Maybe he should have tried to suppress the leer that spread across his face, but the temptation of Eden was delectable.

She glanced up at the clock and smiled. "You have thirty-five minutes before we eat supper."

"Well, then, by all means, let us adjourn to someplace you can get naked."

She leaned down and kissed him. "Only if you get naked, too."

"Deal." He stood and locked up Tori's records in a locking desk drawer that Eden didn't use. They turned off the lights and made their way up to the small apartment. He swept her up and she wrapped her legs around him as he carried her to the bedroom. He'd had this woman every night, multiple times a night, for the last three weeks and he found he still couldn't satiate his hunger for her.

Jeremiah pushed open the bedroom door and set her down beside the bed. Not wanting to break the kiss, they performed an awkward dance to undress while still kissing. When she tipped sideways while taking off her jeans, he caught her and righted her. Gently, he pushed her back and pulled her jeans off. God, she was beautiful. Not a bit of makeup and her cheeks were pink with excitement. Her sky-blue eyes shone and the long blonde lashes framing them only enhanced their beauty.

He removed the rest of his clothes as did she. Eden shimmied into the middle of the bed and he followed her on his hands and knees. Feasting on her sweet flesh was his new favorite pastime. He'd traveled every inch of her body with his lips and fingers. She was like a hit of meth to an addict.

Mind-altering. Bigger, more, and once he had her, he had to have her again. Yes, he was hooked on Eden Wade, and in the last month, he'd fallen into a dangerous habit of thinking of her as his. As she opened her legs for him to settle between, he promised himself he'd stop doing that.

Tomorrow.

They knew each other and her hands traveled down his back to his ass. She gripped him tight and rocked her hips. He nuzzled her neck and whispered, "Want something?"

She made a small sound in the back of her throat and he chuckled. "In a minute. I want my dessert first." He kissed his way down to her core and spread her sex. Glistening and swollen, he took that first lick, and when she jumped, he dove in. God, he loved making her come this way. She was perfect against his lips and tongue. His fingers, slicked with her desire, stimulated her inside as he primed her with his attention. She grabbed his hair and pulled, but he wasn't budging, not until she climaxed. He doubled his efforts and was rewarded with her bucking her hips against his mouth. She stiffened and then bowed. Her legs shook and her insides contracted against his fingers. Her body released and he found the taste he'd wanted.

Eden gasped as he licked along the seam of her body. He kissed his way back up her body and stared at her when he reached her chin.

"Remi, please." She pushed against him with her hips as she pleaded. He captured her lips and reached over to the drawer where they now kept the condoms, patting around inside. Finally, frustrated by not finding what he was looking for, he broke the kiss and leaned over. He moved the paper on the bottom of the drawer and looked again. "Fuck. Where are the condoms?"

Eden's hand grasped the side of his neck. "I'm on birth control. Don't stop."

He slammed the drawer shut and moved over her again. They kissed in a searching, longing way that told him she was just as needy for him as he was for her. He entered her and stopped as his head breached her sex. The experience of sex without a condom was a first for him. He'd never not had protection, a lesson he learned from his father.

Eden curved her hips and moaned a deep throaty sound when he moved inside her. Her heat wasn't different and yet it was. Sex without condoms was a gigantic step for him. More than he could express, but perhaps he could show her through his touch.

With infinite care, he made slow, languorous love

to her, and yes, he was making *love* to her. Saying the words wouldn't change the actions. They shared the same breath as he finally entered her. He dropped his head to the bed just above her shoulder. Trying to mesh his body to hers, he rolled his hips, not lifting away from her. He wanted the contact, and by the way she wrapped around him, she did, too.

The sensations, the emotion of this act on this night, joined them in perfect harmony as he pushed them higher.

"Make love to me, please, Remi. Please."

Eden's whispered pleas undid him. He rose to kiss her. "I am, babe. I am." He caught her lips and drove them into a climax. Eden gasped and tightened like a bow string under him. He let himself go and his hips moved as if on their own accord. He pushed deep and came, his cock kicking deep within her several times before he could suck a lungful of air and drop his head to the bed beside hers.

There was a distinct ding from the kitchen, and she half-groaned, half-laughed. He shook his head when she gave him a gentle push. "It can burn. I'm enjoying this too much."

"You can enjoy this for five more minutes. I'm not burning dinner." She wrapped her arms around him and held him as he cradled her under him. "This is good. What we have." She spoke in a timid voice.

"This is great," he acknowledged.

"I..." She sighed and shook her head. "Never mind."

He lifted away from her and stared down at those beautiful blue eyes. "What?"

She cupped his face with her hands. "I have feelings for you."

He let a smirk slide across his face. "I should hope so."

She rolled her eyes. "I'm being serious here."

He laid down and brought her on top of him. "I'm not going to lie to you, Eden, I have feelings for you, too."

She dropped and rested her chin on her fist. "Doesn't bode well, though. You're only here for a few more months."

He dipped his head in a yes and no type of movement. "That's what's left for this contract. I'm pretty sure I can find a job for me somewhere in the Black Hills."

She lifted. "So, you're willing to stick around?"

"I would never go back. I just wasn't going to stay here. The citizens of Hollister have won me over. I'll call and make it official." He nodded and she pounced, kissing his face all over. He caught her and sat up in bed, stopping her. "Thank you."

She blinked at him. Happiness radiated off her. "For what?"

"For making that decision easy." The beeper sounded in the kitchen again. "You better go." He let go of her and she grabbed his t-shirt, pulling it on as she hustled out of the room. He laid back down and listened to her moving around in the kitchen. The decision *had* been easy. His clothes and his toiletry items had made the move to Eden's apartment one night at a time. He hadn't slept in Gen's guest room but a couple nights in the last weeks. Was it fast? Yes. Was he uncomfortable with the rapid development? He closed his eyes and searched. No. There was nothing about the relationship that gave him any pause. It was as if all the shards of a shattered image had found their way home and fused together seamlessly to complete a picture.

His phone vibrated and he opened one eye. Where had his jeans ended up? He sat up and groaned as he stood. Swooping down to grab them, he pulled the phone out of his back pocket.

> *Tank: Bike's done. Had some free time.*

> *Perfect. Will be there tomorrow to pick up and pay.*

>*Tank: Cool. Turned out pretty sweet. Even for a Royal.*

Jeremiah laughed and stepped into his jeans. He paused and hit Tank back up with one more request.

>*Tank: It will cost yah, man.*

>*I'm willing to pay.*

>*Tank: You should have asked the price first. Stupid Indie.*

He chuckled at the insult and headed into the kitchen.

Eden had just sat a huge cast iron pot on the little table. "Damn, that smells like heaven."

She stopped and looked up at him. "Do you know what heaven smells like?"

He stepped forward and pulled her into his arms. "Every time I'm with you, I'm in heaven, so yeah, I do."

She stared at him for a couple seconds before she smiled. "That is so cheesy, but I'll take it."

Jeremiah let her go and slapped a hand against his bare chest. "I'm wounded!"

Eden laughed and hit him with an oven mitt as she passed him. "I'm sure you'll survive."

He grabbed her again, lifting her up into the air. "Only if you kiss it better." He dropped her down and took his kiss. Her laughter made the connection messy, but it was as sweet as any they'd shared.

She slipped out of his arms. "Go sit down. I'm getting the bread." He did as he was ordered, and she came back with a loaf of the sourdough bread from Sanderson's tiny little market. It was more like a convenience store for items you couldn't get by without, but the homemade goods were a tremendous bonus.

She used the oven mitt to take the top off the dish and his stomach growled when he saw the inside. Roast beef, carrots, pearl onions, and potatoes. "Oh, man, extra everything, please." He lifted his plate and she scooped out enough food to feed an army... or him. He took a bite and moaned around the deep, rich flavor of a long, slow-cooked meal. "Heaven."

She finished serving herself and sat down. "What are the plans for this weekend? I haven't been to the root cellar you're digging for Gen all week. How is it coming along?"

He chewed a huge bite of beef before he responded. "Well, once Phil came over with his little bobcat, the hole was dug in an hour. I've got the support system in place, but I need to frame out the shelves, bins, and benches, put in the roof and a door, and then get Phil to help me bury the thing again."

She dipped a small piece of bread into a pool of gravy on her plate. "You made it big enough for all of us, right? Tornadoes around here are no joke."

"I made it big enough for all of Gen's dreams. When I finish the cellar, she wants me to rent a tiller and plow her a garden. Phil's backlot. He's letting her lease the land for like ten dollars a month and his fill of veggies in season." The community of Hollister was fantastic. He'd had no less than five of the local men stop by to give him input on the structure of the shelter and how to construct the entrance so it would be easier to open and close during high winds. Father Murphy stopped by every day and checked on the progress while he chatted. Ken Zorn, the deputy, also stopped by. He told Jeremiah the Klingler boys were out on bail but had a court date and that he shouldn't worry about them as their father had them shoveling shit until they went to court.

"Did Father Murphy stop by again?" She took a sip of her water.

"Yep. He's a great guy, but I keep telling him I'm not converting." He laughed when Eden almost choked on her drink.

"He's trying to convert you?"

"Nah, but it is fun messing with him." He waggled his eyebrows at her.

"Admit it. This town has grown on you."

He buttered a piece of bread as he spoke, "I like it here. I'm sure Hollister isn't everyone's cup of tea, but something about the vibe of this community is alluring." He smiled at her. "And, like I said earlier, a particular citizen has caught my interest. "

She looked up from her plate and wiggled her eyebrows up and down. "Who, me?"

He winked at her. "You'd be a reason to stay regardless of the town."

She smiled and batted her eyes. "Why, kind sir, are you trying to woo me?"

He shook his head. "No, the wooing comes tomorrow."

"Tomorrow?"

"Yep, we're going on a ride through the Hills." He bit into his bread and watched her.

"I'd love to! We just went last weekend, but if that is you wooing me, I'm all in."

"That's only part of it. I have a surprise for you."

She sat up straight and asked, "What?"

"If I told you, it wouldn't be a surprise."

She damn near vibrated on her chair. "But that's okay, I'll love it no matter what it is."

"Good." He took another bite of the beef and she deflated.

"You're not going to tell me, are you?"

He shook his head, and she narrowed her eyes at him. "For future reference, while growing up, I knew what every Christmas present was before I opened it. I don't like surprises; the need to know what it is drives me crazy."

"Well, good thing I'm certified in South Dakota now, isn't it? I'll be able to help you get over that issue." He laughed when she stuck her tongue out at him. God, tomorrow was going to be a great day.

CHAPTER 14

E den gripped onto Jeremiah's hard, muscled core as they rounded another corner, bringing them to the junction that would take them to Rapid City or the other direction further into the Hills. He turned left, which surprised her.

"Where are we going?" she shouted into his ear, her borrowed helmet clanking against his.

"It's a surprise!" She groaned, knowing that he wouldn't hear it, but by now he'd know she was doing it. Surprises were cool as long as she was the one surprising people. Not knowing what was in a package or what plans he'd put in place for the day drove her crazy. Surprises always had.

The sun baked her shoulders, and she thanked the SPF 50 she was wearing for doing its job. Jeremiah wore a t-shirt with a low scooped neck and no arms. On him... holy moly, the things that shirt did to his chest and abs defied logic. He'd applied sunscreen too because he didn't want his tattoos to fade.

They'd spent a lazy morning in bed last weekend talking about each of his tattoos. They were personal memorials to his grandparents, and the one that snaked around his arm and claimed a spot on his neck was a reminder. He'd downplayed the incident. She leaned against his back and recalled the conversation.

"What is this guy all about? He's pretty in a scaly reptile kind of way." Eden traced her finger over the snake's scales.

"He is my reminder, my warning to myself." Jeremiah shrugged as if it was no big deal.

"A reminder of what?" She lifted onto her elbow and stared down at him.

He drew a deep breath and let it out before he looked at her and answered, *"A handful of years back, an inmate attempted to kill me and an FBI agent while we were questioning him. That was a wake-up call for me, and this guy is my reminder that there are dangers lurking and I need to protect myself and those I care about."*

"He's important then."

"Very."

"What have you done to make sure you're never in that position again?" She laid down and he rolled to face her.

"Lots of things. I wasn't a ninety-pound weakling, but I put on about fifty pounds of muscle. I found an MMA gym and I've advanced enough that no one wants to spar with me." He smiled. "That is an accomplishment."

"So, you can kick butt and take names, huh?"

"I can. I won't be a victim again." He leaned in and kissed her. "But I don't want to talk about that anymore."

She sighed. He was a master at diverting her questions about his time working at the prison. And he usually diverted her with sex. She needed to stop letting him do that.

The ride into the small city had the usual problems such as idiot drivers that didn't look before they merged lanes, but Jeremiah handled the incursions with ease, although her heart still landed in her throat. She loved to ride, but she also knew it was a dangerous pastime, especially in the city.

They pulled into a business. A motorcycle repair shop. She got off the bike and took off her helmet as Jeremiah did the same. "Is something wrong with your bike?"

He nodded. "I thought I heard it missing." She

frowned. She had noticed nothing, but then again, she'd been daydreaming and enjoying the scenery until they entered city traffic. "Why don't you go look at the bikes and I'll be right back." He motioned to the display room off to the right. She ran her hand through her hair and shrugged. Why not, she didn't know anyone here, who cared that she had helmet head?

Jeremiah headed to the maintenance bay where he'd seen Tank sitting beside a Harley Panhead. He stood beside the man and looked at the bike. "I haven't seen a Panhead in this condition in a long time."

Tank glanced over at him. "She's my son's. Complete rebuild."

Jeremiah took in the lines of the bike. There was a simple, elegant beauty to the machine, nothing modified, no personal enhancements, just the Harley the way they built it. "Excellent craftsmanship. Looks like it just rolled off the showroom floor."

"That's the plan. I got what you wanted, but let's talk payment." Tank crossed his arms over his chest and glanced around.

"You got it." He pulled his wallet from his back pocket.

Tank shook his head and held up a hand. "You weren't joking about being a shrink?"

Well, hell, where did that come from? He nodded. "I'm a psychiatrist, yes."

"Can you see patients?" Tank rubbed the back of his neck. The cheeks under his silver beard turned a ruddy color.

Jeremiah glanced around, too, to make sure they were alone. "I can. Are you having problems?"

Tank shook his head in a sharp movement. "Not for me. My boy. He came back from the service fucked up physically. He got hooked on pain pills, you know, but he's kicked it."

"Okay…" Jeremiah prompted.

"Derek needs help. He ain't caved into the pills again, but he's been going to more and more NA meetings. Something's riding him hard. Won't talk about it to me or the old lady. Could you talk with him? You know bikes. You don't look like no button-down prep school graduate. He could relate to you."

"He'd have to agree to it, Tank. You can't force a person into therapy."

"He has. He won't talk to me about it, but he knows he needs help."

"I'm three hours away."

"Don't care. We'll ride up and see you. My son is more important than any damn distance."

Jeremiah nodded. "I'm going to caution you, Tank, I don't have a magic wand. If Derek wants help and will work, we can give it a shot. If he doesn't, then I won't string you along. What happens is up to your son and I cannot discuss a damn thing he says without his permission."

"Doc, I don't give a fuck what you talk about. Not my business, but I wouldn't be able to live with myself if I didn't at least try to get him help."

"Then I'll give you my address and telephone number and you have Derek call me. We'll set up times and dates to talk if he's willing."

Tank extended his hand. "Thank you. You don't know how much this means to me."

"It's what I do, man. Now, about paying for that bike and the helmet?"

"Nope. It's on me. Consider it trade for treatment. You let me know when you need more money. I've got capital, but no insurance."

"Tank, I can't. What if Derek refuses treatment?"

"Then we'll settle up the next time you're in the area. I'm not worried about it, I'm a fucking righteous judge of character." Tank slapped him on the arm. "Besides, you're giving me your telephone number and address. I'm the president of a motorcycle club that may or may not be civilized. Do the math, Doc."

Jeremiah chuffed out a laugh. So not what he expected when he walked into the shop. Trade wasn't exactly something he could report to his accountant, or at least he didn't think it was, but if Tank's kid needed help, he'd make it work. He followed Tank back into the showroom.

"Remi, look! They have a Royal, just like the one I used to have back in Alabama." She grabbed his hand and pulled him over to the small motorcycle. "Remember I told you about the one my dad and brothers fixed up for me?"

Remi dropped his arm over her shoulder. "I do. That's why I asked Tank here to fix this one up for you."

She spun to face him. "What?" Her eyes darted between him and Tank, who now held a blue helmet, her size.

"I can paint this to match this winter when you're not riding." Tank extended his hand toward her. "Doc here is doing me a favor by taking the thing off my hands. I'll go get your paperwork so you can register it." Tank meandered out of the showroom.

"Jeremiah Wheeler, you can't buy me a motorcycle!" Her hand not holding the helmet plopped onto her hip and she narrowed her eyes at him.

He shrugged and held up his hands. "I didn't actually *buy* the bike." Which was true at the moment.

That pinched stare grew tighter. "Explain that."

He glanced around and noticed a woman behind the counter. He took Eden's elbow and moved closer to the Royal before he leaned down and whispered, "I'm helping Tank out. His son needs to see someone."

She blinked up at him and shook her head. She glanced at the counter and lowered her voice to match his. "So, he's giving you the bike in exchange for therapy?"

He nodded and shrugged. "I can't ride it. Too damn small, so I guess you'll have to drive her home."

Eden sighed but looked back at the bike. Tank had done one hell of a job. The vibrant blue paint was flecked with silver and the same color pinstripes trimmed the gas tank and fenders. "But it's yours. You register it. I can't accept something so expensive."

"But you'll ride it?" He snuck his hand around her neck as she stared at the bike.

She glanced over at him and smiled. "Try to keep me off it." She pushed into him. "Thank you for this, I've never had anyone..." She shook her head. "You *listened*."

"I'm glad you're happy." He dropped a kiss on her lips but kept it PG because they were in public.

She stared up at him and whispered, "I haven't been this happy in a very long time. If you're not careful, those feelings I have are going to get bigger."

He pulled her into a hug and dropped a kiss on her head. "Remind me not to be careful, then."

"Here's the paperwork. You're responsible for the tag. I signed it over to you. Could you write that information down on this?" Tank handed him a small desk pad. He gave the paperwork to Eden and in precise letters put down his contact information and the address to Eden's clinic, although he hadn't asked her if he could use the office again. Actually, if he was going to build a business up north, he'd need to build a small office building up in Hollister. He wasn't sure if Eden had cleared his use of the property with the county and he didn't want to get her in any trouble.

Tank took the pad and slapped it against his

palm. "Expect a phone call tomorrow." He pointed at Eden. "You need to get that Royal out of my show-room before it brings down the property value."

Eden smiled and walked over to the fierce biker and hugged him tightly. To say the man looked shocked was an understatement. His eyes were enormous and his face behind that silver beard turned a wicked shade of violet-red. Finally, he patted her on the shoulder as if he wasn't sure what to do with the display of gratitude.

"Eden, let the nice man go before he has a heart attack."

Tank blinked over at him.

Eden laughed and stepped away from the biker. "Thank you so much. Jeremiah knows how much this means to me, I only wanted to let you know, too."

Tank stepped back and combed his beard with his hand. "Yeah, well, you be careful on those roads. Watch out for the assholes, you don't want to lay her down."

"I promise." Eden beamed and put on her new helmet. Jeremiah helped adjust the chin pad and made sure the fit was good. The one they'd borrowed from Doc Macy, the local vet, was ancient, which meant it wasn't as safe as it could be, plus it was too big.

Tank opened the double doors and Eden rolled the bike out onto the pavement of the parking area. She put her leg over the bike and started it. The sound was nothing less than perfection. He turned to Tank and extended his hand. "If your boy needs to talk, you have him call me tonight, otherwise, have him call tomorrow and I'll set up an appointment."

"Thanks, Doc." Tank nodded toward Eden. "Make sure that little one doesn't end up as a statistic."

"I have every intention of making sure of that." He headed to his bike, affixed the extra helmet, and put his on. Once he fired up his Hog, he extended his hand to Eden, giving her the lead. She released the clutch and eased into traffic, handling the smaller bike with ease. She signaled a left turn, and they made the corner together, riding side by side. As she worked them out of the city, his shoulders relaxed. Watching her handle the bike was a joy. She was a smart and safe rider. Eden took no unnecessary risks in traffic and she drove that bike like she'd grown up on one which, in reality, she had.

He followed her lead as they went into the Black

Hills and meandered through the tall pines. When they finally stopped for dinner in Spearfish, she was still brimming with excitement. "Hold on." She took a picture of the bike and darted over to him. "Take a picture of me with it, please?" He took her phone and snapped a couple pictures. "Thank you. I'm going to email these to my dad. He won't believe it. She runs like a charm. The balance is perfect, no pull whatsoever, and I know it doesn't have the horsepower your Harley has, but dang it, she can scoot, too."

He dropped his arm over her shoulders as they walked to the entrance of the restaurant just over the river. "This place is amazing. They have the most eclectic menu, but all the food is fantastic."

They sat down. Each ordered a beer and both of them chose the special. "What made you do that?" She leaned forward. The smile that had been on her face all day was still there, and he loved the fact that he'd put it there.

He shrugged. "I wanted someone to ride with. Don't get me wrong, I love you riding with me on my bike, but when you talked about the freedom of riding, the longing in your voice mimicked everything I felt about when I ride. I met Tank on one of my solo trips down to the Hills right after I got here. He mentioned he owned a custom bike shop, so I asked when I stopped in. They'd parked your bike out back in the bike graveyard. I think he wanted it out of the shop more than anything."

She leaned back as the server placed their meals. "You should set up a practice in Hollister. We don't have resources, of course, but you know there are people who could benefit from your help. I think your normal pay scale may have to be adjusted downward, though."

He snorted as he picked up his fork. "I worked for the state at my last position. I'm not in this profession to make money." He stopped and looked at her. "I have plenty of money. I inherited it from my grandparents, just like Gen." He had more money than he knew what to do with, and Gen and he had only received a quarter each of the inheritance. His father received the other half. They were required to sign documents stating Celest wouldn't receive any of the money. Grandma Wheeler's doing. She didn't like Jeremiah's mom, and according to the letter read by the lawyer at the reading of the will, unless Celest got a job or had any means of self-support, she'd never see a dime. That caused an epic scene and hissy fit in the lawyer's office. Thank God he could walk out—he did, and he kept walking. He was tired of his mother's overdramatic responses.

Eden blinked and then shrugged. "I figured, but neither of you seem pretentious, you know? I mean, if I met you hanging out at the Bit and Spur, I wouldn't peg you as someone with a big bank account. You're normal, not stuck-up." She lifted a bite of the speckled trout and tried it. "Oh, this is fantastic."

He laughed. "Well, I'm glad I don't come off as stuck-up. I work hard at my leather biker image, kink not included."

She snorted and started coughing. He moved to help her, but she held up a hand. After a moment she drew a stilted breath and released it.

She croaked, "Warn me next time."

"What fun is that?" He lifted her beer and gave it to her.

She took a sip and dabbed at her eyes. "Well, I guess there is that."

He took a bite and agreed with her, pre-coughing fit. The garlic butter sauce they had poached the fish in had enhanced not only the fish but the brown butter and sage spätzle served with it. A red cabbage and beet salad with a feta dressing had enough acid to cut through the richness and made the entire dish a home run.

"I didn't ask earlier if I could use your office

again. It wouldn't be after business hours this time. He'd be driving up for the meetings from Rapid."

"From a space perspective, I don't think it is an issue. The office is rarely used. I usually do my notes in the exam room right after the patient leaves. If Zeke moves his practice north it could get tight, though." Jeremiah lifted his eyebrow as he ate a bite of the fish. She waved a hand dismissively. "Zeke understands there will be nothing. Stop with the glowering."

He swallowed his food and lifted his beer. "You realize I will never forgive him for spoiling our first night together."

She reached her hand across the table and placed it on the one that wasn't holding the beer. "He didn't spoil it. Granted, he cut it short, but spoil? No, that night will always be a cherished memory. It was the night I started living again."

He lifted her hand and kissed the back of it just as his phone vibrated in his front pocket. He rolled his eyes. "Excuse me." He leaned back and pulled the phone out. The number was one he didn't recognize from California. He silenced it and shoved his phone back into his pocket. They were just getting on their bikes when it vibrated again. He put on his helmet and started his Harley. Whoever it was could wait. It was probably the administration from the prison. He'd emailed his boss today rendering his two weeks' notice and listed Eden's address to ship his personal effects left in his desk. It wasn't much and he didn't think they'd ship it out, but inmates had made some of the items in the wood and metal shop. He couldn't display them because they were potential weapons, but he kept them locked up in his desk drawer. Although, it was curious that they'd call on a Saturday. Whatever, he'd deal with it later.

The feel of the cooler night air was refreshing as they turned onto the highway. They had a lot of miles to travel. This time, he pulled out first and Eden fell into position beside him. They wouldn't be home before dark, but that was all right because, for the first time in one hell of a long time, he was at peace.

CHAPTER 15

Jeremiah rolled over and grabbed Eden, pulling her against him. He settled into the pillow and her warmth. He'd just faded into sleep when he heard his phone vibrating from wherever he'd dropped his pants. They'd barely made it up the stairs before their clothes were off. He opened one eye and glared at the clock. *Really? One o'clock in the morning?*

He woke with a jolt. Crap, it could be Tori or Tank's boy. He slid out of the bed, grabbed his boxers, and hopped into them on the way to find his pants. He grabbed his jeans by the leg and shook them. Keys, change, his wallet, and cell phone dropped to the floor. He leaned over and picked up his cell. Fifteen missed calls, and five of them were from Jamison.

"What the actual..." He opened the phone, disregarded the messages, and called his mentor.

"Where the fuck are you?" Jamison snapped.

"I was sleeping until someone woke my ass up. What the hell is the problem?" He ran his hand through his hair and noticed Eden, half-awake, wearing one of his t-shirts, standing at the door. He opened his arm and she shuffled over to him, dropping her head onto his chest in a zombie-like stupor. Damn, he hated that he'd woke her.

"Cyrus Macmillan escaped from custody."

The words tightened his gut and cut out his ability to move air in and out of his body. He belted his grip on Eden, almost crushing her against him. "When?" His heart was hammering in his ears.

Jamison bit out the answer, "This afternoon."

Cognitive reasoning tapped back in and he nodded to himself. "Okay. He doesn't know where I am, no big deal. The authorities will find him."

"He eluded capture for seven years before the FBI caught him last time, but that's not the important issue here."

"What is the issue, then?" He and Eden were

somehow sitting on the couch. He took the phone away from his ear and put it on speaker.

Jamison continued quickly, "He stole a laptop belonging to the warden. It updates from his desktop every day at noon."

"The prison has passwords and protections." He fisted his hands together. "Damn it, how did this happen? He should have been in restraints."

"I know, believe me, I know." Jamison cleared his throat. "Remi, he slaughtered fifteen people to get from the hospital ward to the administrative branch."

"How did he get out?"

"Guardian hasn't been asked to investigate."

"But?" he prompted.

"But they placed the prison on lockdown. Every guard moved to their assigned posts. He slaughtered those in his way. We believe a guard shot him once, but with the amount of blood covering him on the video we obtained, it was hard to determine."

"I still don't understand. How did he get out?"

"Every guard went to their assigned positions. There weren't enough to maintain coverage in the admin area. According to what we are getting out of the mess, the warden directed everyone to help with the lockdown. There weren't any guards in the admin area and there isn't camera coverage there, either. He killed the new warden, the one who came in to clean up the mess. They found his prison uniform in the office. The warden's body didn't have clothes, the computer was gone, and we have camera footage showing Cyrus walking out the main doors to the secure parking lot. He punched the warden's key fob and found his car. He drove out using the warden's keycard to unlock the barrier gates."

"Do we know what information is on that laptop?"

"Officially, no. Unofficially, the email you sent your supervisor was forwarded to the warden at ten-fifteen a.m. The laptop would have synced at noon."

Eden grabbed his hand. "What email? What does that mean."

He lifted her hand and kissed it. "I'll tell you in a minute."

"Jamison—" He left the word hanging. Not only was he fucked, but so was this tiny town. Cyrus would kill everyone to get to him.

"You don't have to say a word. Our main computer tech says the encryption would keep a normal person out and finding someone to open a computer would be his second priority, his wound would be his first. That being said, I've called in one of my many favors with the big guy. Guardian is going to track this and encourage the Governor of California to put us in charge of the investigation. Again."

"Do you know what was in that email?" He looked at Eden's bewildered expression and pulled her into him.

"I do. If we get wind Cyrus is heading your way, we'll send a security team out there. They'll be bunking close by and will deploy if we get any indication shit's heading your way."

"Jamison, even if I leave—"

"That's just it. My bosses don't want you to leave. There are a lot of variables in play in this situation. If he doesn't die of his wound, if he isn't captured, if he can crack that password and get into the computer, and if he looks through the warden's email, we will at least have a safety net for you at your current location. Right now, my boss is planning for a worst-case scenario and hoping none of the plans he is putting in place have to be used."

"So, I just sit here and wait?"

"Yes, there is nothing else to do at this point. Go about your life. I'll keep you updated. As soon as we know something, you'll know it."

"And if he is coming this way?"

"Then he will have made a critical error. Guardian isn't the government, they're private, agile, and damn good at what they do."

"All right." He glanced at Eden. "I need to explain this to Eden."

"I'll call every morning with updates. You have my word on that. By the way, I checked. South Dakota is an open carry and open concealed carry state. You don't need a permit."

Jamison's promise reassured him that his agency was engaged, but he'd seen what the man was capable of firsthand. There was no way he'd let him contaminate this town, his sister, or his lover.

"Understood. Thank you, Jamison. I appreciate you reaching out to me and letting me know."

"I believe the prison tried to contact you also. Your supervisor is an okay lady."

"She is. Until morning, then." He waited for Jamison to hang up before he locked his home screen on his phone.

"Tell me what's going on because not knowing the backstory here is freaking me out." Eden turned to face him on the couch, and he took her hand in his.

"Remember what I told you about my tattoo?"

She reached up with her free hand and cupped his neck where the snake was visible and nodded.

"The man who did that is also the man who drove me away from my prison practice." He cleared his throat and gave her the bare minimum to convey what he'd witnessed and what Cyrus had done.

She stared down at their linked hands for several minutes, and he gave her time to process what he'd revealed. She finally lifted her eyes to him. The expression wasn't one of fear; rather, what he saw in those beautiful blue eyes made his heart expand. "You've been living with this since it happened? Why haven't you told me? Does Gen know?"

"She knows."

"And you didn't tell me because…?" Eden cocked her head and held his gaze.

"Because it was over. I talk to Jamison once a week, a professional courtesy to me, and I've put it behind me. Or I thought I had until tonight. It isn't the type of conversation you just bring up. I would have told you eventually." He shrugged. "He had no place in this relationship and I didn't want to taint you with his deranged acts."

"Do you think he will come for you?"

"If he finds that email, he'll try. There is no doubt in my mind," he answered honestly. "The thing is if he comes and I'm not here, he'll still kill anyone he thinks is important to me. Any way he can hurt me, he will."

Eden nodded and moved across the space between them, hugging him. "I don't know what Guardian is and it's good that they are going to be around, but you've never seen this town close ranks." She sighed and then sat up. "We need to tell Ken so he can let the sheriff's department know. Then we need to get the word out. Every man and woman in this town owns weapons. If they know there is a risk, they'll arm themselves and watch out for strangers."

God, he didn't want that. He didn't want to disrupt the town in any way. "How about we tell the deputy but wait on informing the town until we get any sign he's making his way this direction? I'd hate to put the town up in arms only to cry false alarm when they capture him."

Eden blinked and then nodded. "Yeah, that makes sense. I guess I'm overreacting.

It is just such a shock."

Jeremiah shoved his hand through his hair. "Yeah, tell me about it."

Eden stood up. "Come on."

"Where are we going?" Jeremiah took her hand and stood up.

"We are going to go into the kitchen and make an early breakfast. Neither of us are going to go back to sleep, so we eat, we talk, and because those feelings we keep talking about are getting the better of me, we're going to work out a plan of what we're going to do if that batshit crazy person shows up here. I never want to lose you." She hit the kitchen light and turned into his arms. "I'm sorry if it is too soon to say that, but I can't..." Her eyes misted up. "I lost Riley and it tore my heart out. Losing you isn't something I think I'd survive."

He pulled her into him and held her tight as she cried. He kissed the top of her head and rocked back and forth while letting her vent her emotions. When she finally stopped, he reassured her, "I'm not going anywhere. If he is coming this way, I'll hire Guardian and get more protection for the town, for all of us." He had the money, and if he needed more, he'd contact his father. Taking care of this town—and of Eden—was his purpose now. He'd never let them become the victim that Cyrus had made him.

She nodded, and with her head still tucked against his shoulder, she asked, "Until then?"

Liquid steel in the form of resolve poured over him. "Until then we live. I won't let that bastard take anything else from me." She nodded against his shoulder but didn't release him from the embrace. He dropped his chin onto her hair and closed his eyes. He'd turned the corner from being Cyrus' victim. This wasn't a topic he'd discuss with Jamison, but he knew if he had the chance, he'd probably kill Cyrus. There wasn't a court in the land that would convict him. What he needed was a gun, a truckload of bullets, and a target. There was no way he'd be unarmed or unprotected. He'd talk to the deputy about what type of handgun to purchase. If it was time to make a stand against a psychotic killer, he'd be ready.

CHAPTER 16

Ken Zorn blinked at him and then looked away. Jeremiah could see the wheels turning in his mind. "Dude, we don't have the manpower." His gaze went down the small main street of Hollister. "The people here are tougher than nails and if need be we'll alert them, but I don't want word of this to leak before it needs to. Every one of these people has a slew of weapons. Hell, some of them order the parts from the internet and build the weapons themselves." Ken rubbed his hand on his chin for a minute. "We got to keep this quiet."

Eden squeezed his hand and Jeremiah agreed. "Eden and I are the only ones who know that his escape could have consequences for me. We aren't talking. Although Guardian Security is going to be staging some men close by. They didn't say where."

Zorn snapped his gaze back to him. "I don't know what Guardian is, but let me tell you, if they can help, we'll let them." He sighed and put his cowboy hat back on. "I'll take this back to the sheriff. If he needs any more information he'll call." Zorn extended his hand, shaking Jeremiah's before he nodded to Eden and walked out of the clinic's small office.

"What's next?" Eden asked.

His phone rang and he looked at the number. It wasn't one he recognized, but it had a South Dakota area code. Tank's kid. He winked at Eden and smiled. "We work and live our lives."

Jeremiah sat on the back porch he'd built, holding a beer. He propped his feet up on the rail and relaxed in the coolness of the shade cast by the building's roofline. Even in the heat of the summer, the little porch was an escape. He closed his eyes and relaxed in the quiet.

Eden had a patient downstairs and two more slated, but he'd finished for the day. Three weeks had passed with morning updates coming from Jamison or, when he was busy, from one of the staff members of Guardian. They'd found the warden's car abandoned. The authorities tested the blood on the seat and the DNA matched Cyrus'. According to Jamison, the amount was substantial. There had been no sight of the man since that point. The state placed Guardian in charge of the investigation. With what the security agency found at the supermax, the federal government oversight agencies directed a transfer of a third of the inmates to other facilities. The feds had authorized additional manning based on the antiquated systems which were now scheduled for updates.

He sipped his beer and closed his eyes. A damn shame good people had to die to get the political machine to pay attention. There had been no word on Cyrus, which was something of a Schrodinger's cat scenario. It could be good, or it could be bad; there was no way of knowing unless you opened the box. He didn't have a box, and the waiting––that was a bitch.

His phone vibrated and he lifted it off the small bistro table he'd bought Eden for the porch. He swiped the face and dropped his legs off the rail. Jamison's number. *Fuck.* "What do you have?"

"They found agent Docker this morning, dead."

"How?"

"We believe it was Cyrus. Docker was home alone. His family, thank God, were visiting her parents for two weeks while the kids were on summer vacation. When he didn't come into work this morning and they weren't able to reach him, his partner went out to his house."

He set the beer down on the table. "Where does Docker live?"

"Santa Maria, California, so he's still in the state. He used ropes. Our profiler believes that's because he's still weak. He'd never used ropes before, but the MO has enough markers that the FBI is pinning it on him. They are working with Guardian to pull any camera surveillance in the area."

"Docker's family?"

"In protective custody until he's caught."

"If only it were that simple." He couldn't put a whole damn town in protective custody.

"Not an option in your case," Jamison sighed. "We still don't know he's heading your way. Docker was low-hanging fruit. And yeah, it sounds like absolute rubbish to say that because we're talking about a man who had his life ahead of him. That bastard." He finished his rant with a snarl.

Jeremiah rubbed the back of his neck and asked, "Has your team arrived in the area?"

"They will be there in two days. My boss pulled them in from overseas and they're being briefed now. He also wanted me to reassure you that no one will see them if there isn't a threat."

"All right." He stared at the wood under his feet and absorbed the information.

"How are you doing?"

"I'm as jumpy as a herd of goats on a trampoline right now."

Jamison belted out a belly laugh. "You better watch it, Remi, you're sounding like a local."

He chuckled and leaned back into the shade again. "I'm staying here. I've told you that."

"Ah, yes, the lovely Eden. How is your lady?"

"She's worried. She tries hard not to show it, but the stress is evident." He drank the last of his beer.

"And you? Keeping busy?"

He grunted. "I now have three patients. Ms. Marshall, a young man with PTSD and addiction problems, and the guy I saved my first night here. He's having problems dealing with the incident."

"Not enough to pay the bills or stay busy," Jamison mused.

"I have enough money so that I'd never have to

work another day in my life. However, my sister is turning me into a farmer, whether or not I want to be one. We just tilled four acres and planted veggies that can produce in the growing time left. And when I say veggies, we're talking bulk wholesale quantities of veg."

"What's she going to do with it all?"

"What she can't serve at the cafe she'll can or freeze to use throughout the winter. She can squeeze a penny until it begs for air." That, and he'd figured out she was hell-bent on proving to their mother that she could be her own woman. That spun Celest off in episodes of dramatic dismay, at least according to his father.

"Sounds like an admirable trait. Is Eden within earshot?" Jamison asked.

"No, she has a couple more patients." He placed his empty on the little table. The low sound of thunder in the distance made him look up.

"The boss did a background check on you, your sister, and Eden. He doesn't work for or near people who have questionable backgrounds. Plus, he's been told you're making huge strides with Ms. Marshall. He liked what he heard and saw, and he wanted you to know there will always be a position here for you."

"I'm not leaving Hollister unless it's in a pine box. If he has people who want to come out here for treatment, I'm game."

"Ha, well, if I know him, he's thought about it. Guardian could keep you better protected here in D.C."

"I appreciate the thought, my friend." The town wouldn't be protected. His sister and Eden lived alone. No, it wouldn't happen.

Jamison sighed, "But you're not going to bite."

"Not even a nibble." He heard Phil's garage door go down and glanced at his watch. The man was punctual. Every night at five Phil closed that shop and went to the Bit and Spur for a cold beer before he walked home to his family. You could set your watch by the man. Routines that Cyrus would know and identify in an instant and use against the people who lived and loved in this small town. "There are so many lives here that he'd mess with just to get to me. I won't be responsible for any more—" A loud rumble of thunder vibrated the ground under him.

"Storming there?" Jamison asked.

"Yeah, the front's moving in. The storms are massive." The vast horizons filled with dark clouds and he could see lightning popping as the fronts advanced. He'd seen nothing quite like it. Not wanting to get caught in a sudden downpour, he picked up his bottle and went into the apartment.

"Do I need to address the fact that you were not responsible for their deaths?"

"No. Logically, I understand it. Emotionally, it will take time before I believe it." He went through the apartment and dropped his empty into the waste bin. Looking out the kitchen window, he saw another lightning strike. The thunder rolled from a distance about six seconds later, still powerful enough to vibrate the apartment.

"I'll call as soon as we know more. Until then."

"Thanks, bye." He hung up the phone and closed his eyes. Thank God Docker's family had been gone. He opened his eyes and stared at his hands. There were things he could do. He'd go to the pasture Ken Zorn had shown him and keep practicing his aim with his handgun. He was proficient, but he needed to be better.

Another rumble of thunder vibrated the foundations of the building. He turned on the oven and grabbed a take-out casserole courtesy of Gen. He put it on a sheet pan and shoved it in the oven, deciding not to keep tonight's information from Eden. Yes, it would do nothing but cause her more stress, and there was no indication Cyrus was heading his way, but she needed to know about the situation. He leaned against the door and stared sightlessly into the small living room. Dread slithered up and down his spine. *Cyrus would come. It was only a matter of when.* The next time Jamison called he was going to get contact information for the Guardians that were coming to South Dakota. He wouldn't be a victim this time. He'd be prepared.

Lightning flashed and thunder exploded nearly instantaneously, shaking the building. The power flickered and then died.

"Remi!" Eden's voice calling up the stairs sounded panicked. He jogged to the door and opened it.

"Are you okay?"

"Yeah, but we need to go to the root cellar, there is a tornado heading this way." She waved at him and he raced down the stairs. They were out the door seconds later and she locked it behind them. He grabbed her hand and they dashed across the street behind the cafe. Rain pelted them, stinging with the force of the wind. He glanced down the street. A funnel cloud at least a mile wide was heading right toward them. They dashed behind the cafe, soaked by the slashing rain. He bent down and opened the door for her. "Gen!" There was no response. "I'll be right back."

Eden's eyes said the words the wind whipped away. He nodded, shut the door, and raced to the cafe. He threw open the back door just as Gen moved to open it. "Get in the cellar!" she screamed at him as she fought the wind to close her back door. He pushed with her and she locked it before they both bolted toward the root cellar. He braced the door against the wind and Gen ducked in.

Moving his hands so he wouldn't lose hold of the heavy plank door, he fisted the handle and used all his strength and weight to fight the screaming wind shears, closing the door. Gen slid the bolt securing the middle of the door. He hit the other two bolts and sagged, gasping for breath.

Gen dropped her hands to her knees and looked up at him. "I wouldn't have been able to shut that door."

"It was a close one. What were you doing still in the cafe?"

"I didn't have my phone with me. I was washing pots and pans. When I finished, I grabbed my phone, read the text, and I bolted out the door, running into you."

Eden had the battery-powered lamps lit and was

sitting at the back corner of the cellar. Gen moved to the far side of the cellar and pulled a crank-operated radio out of a small plastic box. She cranked the handle and turned on the radio. Through the static, a tinny, robotic voice told the residents of the county to take cover.

He sat down by Eden and grabbed her hand. "How did you know there was a tornado coming?" Gen walked over and sat down right beside him.

"It touched down on the Marshall ranch and was heading this way. They called Phil, who started the phone tree."

"Where is your patient?"

"My last one canceled because of nasty weather where they live. Deloris was heading home, the other direction, so she should be fine."

A loud, trundling rumble vibrated the ground under them. "Man, I hate this part." Eden scooted closer to him and so did Gen. He wrapped an arm around both of them.

The rumble grew louder, almost a percussive thrum, and the ground continued to shake. "Was anyone hurt at the Marshall ranch?" Gen leaned against his chest and almost shouted the words to Eden.

"Fence lines and an outbuilding, nothing else," Eden shouted back.

The rumbling lessened and then stopped, although the wind continued to howl. "The twister lifted." Eden took a deep breath just before the rumbling started again. She dropped her head onto his chest, and he tightened his hug on both of the women. The sound ended and then started again, but the rumbling was further away. The wind subsided, and rain fell gently on the door.

Eden sat up. "Let's go see what's left or if there are any injuries." Standing, she straightened her soaking wet scrub top and headed to the door.

"Hold up." He hurried to get to the door first. "Be careful of any downed lines."

She nodded. "Not my first twister, but it is my first one in a new root cellar." She smiled back at Gen. "Thank you for having him build this."

Gen brushed off her jeans and smiled. "He's good for the grunt work. Not much on brains, though. Good thing he's pretty, huh?"

Eden laughed. "Right?"

"Hey!" He glanced back at them. "I'm right here."

Gen chortled and motioned to the door. "Open the door so we can get to work."

CHAPTER 17

The sense of community that flowed around him after the tornado was something to behold. The damage could have been so much worse. As people emerged from their shelters, everyone gathered on main street. Phil Granger waved him over. "We need to get them organized. You take the lead, and I'll make sure they do what they need to do."

"What?" He blinked at Phil, confused as to why he'd be the one to take charge.

"Look, Doc, we all have families and businesses to look after. We need someone to note who doesn't have insurance. I can help you with that. There are some that can't afford it, but some may have had to let it lapse because of a hard year. We figure that out and get the work crews going."

"Work crews?"

"Yep. The ranches here will send in who they can, but it will be a mess if we don't know who to help and how to prioritize. First thing is shelter. Roofs, doors, and windows. After that, we'll help to patch and rebuild if necessary."

Carson Schmidt walked up at the same time as Reverend Olsen and Father Murphy. "Where do we start?" Carson asked. He was clipping a work belt around his hips. "The hardware store has a bit of roof damage and a window broke out. I'm going to board that up and put a tarp on the roof, then I'm game to help. I'll put all the tarps and nails and hammers we have out front. Those that need them can have them."

"My sanctuary roof flew away," Father Murphy said.

"Looks from here like ours made it through with no major damage. We can move services an hour earlier and your congregation can use ours until the parsonage insurance comes through."

Father Murphy extended his hand. "As always, my friend, I appreciate the help."

Jeremiah blinked at the selflessness. He glanced

back at Carson, who was shielding his eyes from the drizzle and looking at roofs around him.

"You'll be out some serious money."

Carson shook his head. 'Nope, not an issue. The Hollisters have made it clear that we support this community any way we can, especially in times of need. I'll be back. Who's in charge?"

Phil nodded in Jeremiah's direction. "I'll set him up and then go take care of my issues. The business problems are minor like yours; the house lost the roof. I'll move Maude and the kids to the garage until we can get it closed up." He turned to Jeremiah. "I have insurance. You'll need to make a list."

Jeremiah watched Carson turn away and Phil grunted, "You'll need something to write with."

Jeremiah pulled out his phone, pulled up a document, and stopped Phil from moving away with a hand on the shoulder. "I'm ready."

Jeremiah lifted and wiped the sweat away from his brow. In the last ten days, he'd roofed five houses, learned how to install glass into windowpanes, reframed two more roofs, put down sheeting while awaiting more shingles, and worked fourteen-hour days. He worked with an alternating crew of people on every job. He met, sweat, cussed, and laughed with people he hadn't yet had the chance to meet. Neighbors taking care of neighbors with baked goods or a hammer and nail.

The weathered cowboys from the ranches were the hardest workers. There was no give in them. They put their heads down and worked until they finished the job. When Father Murphy worked with them, he kept them all entertained with his stories and jokes. Gen fed everyone and Eden took care of the occasional thumb smashing. Those usually occurred when someone wasn't paying attention, like when Father Murphy had them laughing so hard they couldn't concentrate.

"What's next?" Gregg Koehler stood on the roof with him, holstering his hammer in the tool belt he wore.

Jeremiah wiped his brow again and glanced around the town. "We're done until the last shipment of shingles comes in from Rapid the day after tomorrow."

Gregg nodded. "All right. I'm headed back then." He moved to the ladder.

"Hey, would you like to have a beer over at the

Bit and Spur? Declan is offering a free tap pour to anyone who volunteers."

The man shook his head. "Thank you, no. I have to get back. I have chores." Gregg descended the ladder, taking the last of the shingles with him.

Jeremiah assessed the rooftops. With his hands on his hips, he stared at the work the town had finished. Simply amazing. Some of the uninsured houses had mismatched shingles, donated by people who had excess or left over from outbuildings they'd constructed over the years. He'd bought what they needed to complete those projects. The patchwork wasn't beautiful, but the houses were watertight.

"Hey, are you coming down anytime tonight?" Eden shouted the words from the ground, and he whipped his head in her direction.

"Actually, I was thinking about camping out under the stars tonight."

She laughed. "Come on, I want a beer. Let's grab one from the Spur."

And damned if that didn't sound like a fine idea. He did a double-check of the roof and picked up a box of nails that had slipped down the far side. He scrambled down the ladder and wrapped his arm around Eden, pulling her in for a kiss. They'd had little time together recently. The hours he worked were backbreaking and when he'd finished for the day, he was bone tired.

"Hey, handsome." Eden reached up and moved his sweaty hair from his brow. "Let's go have a beer and then maybe I'll take you home and give you some TLC."

He growled and pulled her closer. "Let's skip the beer."

She laughed and spun out of his grasp. "Put away the nails and take me for a drink."

Jeremiah rolled his eyes but did what she said. He'd turned Gen's truck into a handyman vehicle. There were bits and pieces of just about everything organized in boxes and staged in the truck's bed. He put the nails back into the box he was taking back to the hardware store and unbuckled his belt, laying that and his gloves in another box.

"Let's walk. It isn't far and it will give us time to visit." She grabbed his hand.

He glanced at the scant city block he had to walk and nodded. He dropped his arm over her shoulder, and they ambled down the little town's street. "Have you heard from Jamison lately?"

"He called this morning. Nothing new." They'd lucked out and caught an ATM picture of Cyrus in

San Diego. He'd used Docker's card with the correct pin number. No doubt Cyrus forced the agent to tell him the number. That was five days ago.

"Well, that… sucks." Eden gave a half-hearted laugh. "But at least that means he probably hasn't killed anyone else."

That we know of. He hummed his agreement.

"Are you almost done with the repair work?"

"We are. It went faster than I thought it would that first night." He pulled her closer and kissed the top of her head as they walked. "You picked a damn good town."

"Right?" She smiled up at him. "They all love you."

He grimaced. He'd worked people hard, but he put in just as much effort. "I doubt that."

"It's true." They stepped off the blacktop into the pea gravel in front of the Spur as the locals called the Bit and Spur. "It's kind of hard to believe it's only been a few months since we met outside this door."

He stopped and pulled her into his arms. "Time is irrelevant when you know what's in your heart."

She smiled up at him. "I'm going to quote you on that. The scientific journals will have a field day. 'Psychiatrist who understands what a woman needs to hear.' That is banner news, Doctor Wheeler, but not exactly what the Freudian scholars would approve of, is it?"

He stepped to the side of the door and tugged her to him, staring into her eyes. "Screw the medical journals and anyone else who hasn't been in our shoes. I know what my heart wants and it's you. I'm in love with you, Eden Wade." He lowered, capturing her gasp in his kiss. She wound her arms around his neck while he claimed her. He hadn't planned on saying the words so soon, but he knew what he felt. It was fast, but he didn't care.

When he lifted away, she stared up at him. Her kiss-swollen lips were glossy as a smile spread across them. "I love you, too. And yes, it's fast, and no, I don't care."

He smiled as her words echoed his thoughts. Glancing at the door he suggested, "Let's just go home."

She blinked and stepped back. "Ah, no, let's just go in for a quick drink. We're here already. It will be a celebration."

He lifted an eyebrow at her. "What is going on?"

"Nothing. Come on." Grabbing his hand, she dragged him into the bar.

When they entered, close to a hundred people were there. Someone started a rendition about him being a jolly good fellow and the rest took it up. Eden beamed up at him. Just about everyone he'd worked with in the last ten days was present. Handshakes and congratulations on a job well done came from friends, new acquaintances, and the people he'd helped after the storm. He kept Eden by his side as he worked his way through the congratulations.

Gen hugged him. "You did well, big brother. Thank you."

"I just did what everyone else was doing."

Gen shook her head. "No, you did more. The only time you took away from the repair work was to see your patients. You're one in a million." She lifted her empty beer. "I'm having one more of these and then heading home." She kissed him on the cheek and headed toward the bar.

Phil stood up on a chair and whistled to get everyone's attention. "Someone get those two a drink while I talk. Now, Doc Wheeler here isn't a typical city slicker. We saw that fact with our own eyes as that man worked beside us. He's learning. Give him two or three more storms and he'll be able to roof a house by himself." The crowd laughed and

Jeremiah lifted his beer glass in acknowledgment of his deficiencies. "But I want to tell you things you didn't know. The Doc bought and paid for all those shingles that miraculously showed up to finish up the Johnson and Voight houses. He also bought the sheeting for all the non-insured houses."

A mumble of gratitude sounded around him. He shrugged. "I did what we needed and gave what I could. So did everyone here."

"Yeah, but Doc, most of us have grown up on this land. What you did wasn't just an act of kindness, it was the action of a true neighbor and friend." Phil lifted his beer. "To Doc Wheeler."

The cheer roused around him, and to his embarrassment, he blushed, not that anyone could notice with the amount of sun he'd gotten the last ten days, but it was humbling. He accepted some more thanks and congratulations on a job well done before he had a moment to pull Eden closer to him. "You knew."

She laughed. "I did, but you deserve the recognition. You were wonderful to everyone." She lifted on her toes and he bent down to kiss her. The crowd hooted and they broke apart, laughing. He scanned the faces of the people he considered friends. This was his home.

~

Eden watched as Jeremiah laughed with a group of men back by the dartboard. There were still dark marks under his eyes. His bad dreams had been worse since that maniac had escaped. She knew he roamed the house at night, that he was worried, and the nightmares terrorized him. Last week he'd screamed her name and jumped out of bed while still asleep. The long hours of physical labor knocked him out for a couple hours, then his dreams would strike. She knew he was working with Jamison, but she hated to see him suffer.

Zeke strolled over and leaned next to her barstool. "I hate to admit it, but he's a damn good guy."

Eden smiled and nodded. "He is." She glanced up at Zeke. "Any word on you moving north?"

He nodded. "The county has approved my move but..."

She turned to see him better. "But?"

"Eden, that would mean we would work together, sharing the clinic. Is that going to cause a problem with—" He nodded in Jeremiah's direction.

She frowned and tried to decipher what the question actually meant. "A problem? You mean will he have a problem with two professionals doing their job? No. I can't think of a reason... Wait, you know I'm with him, right?"

Zeke snorted. "Yeah, you'd have to be blind not to know that."

"Then I don't see any reason for problems. I let Jeremiah use the office if he has a patient."

Zeke's head snapped her direction. "He has a license to practice in South Dakota?"

She nodded. "He does."

"And he's staying here?"

"He is."

"Permanently?"

She nodded again. Zeke's eyes moved from her. She felt Jeremiah's hand slip around her waist. "Zeke." Jeremiah acknowledged the man. Zeke nodded at him in return.

Eden jumped off the stool. "Zeke got approval from the county to work out of the clinic. Isn't that great?" She bounced her gaze between the men.

Jeremiah straightened and extended his hand. "Damn happy for you. That drive is long on a good day. I can't imagine how you navigate it after a full day at work."

Zeke took his hand and shook it. "Thanks. Red Bull is the secret." The men released hands and Zeke looked between them. "I'm happy for you two." He lifted his beer and wandered off into the thinning crowd.

She turned to gaze up at Jeremiah. "How much longer do you think we need to stay?"

He smiled at her and then turned to assess the crowd. "As much as I hate to say it, let's stay for a while longer, I don't want to seem unappreciative. Then I believe you promised me some TLC." He bent down and kissed her before Doc Macy, the vet, called him over to a group of five or six men.

Allison slipped onto the barstool next to her. "Hey, stranger," her friend quipped and tossed her long red ponytail off her shoulder and signaled Declan for a beer.

Eden hopped back onto her stool. "Hey back. How are things at the store?"

Allison rolled her eyes. "The insurance agent is being a pain in the butt; however, we have it tarped up, waiting for them to release the money. I didn't see any damage to the clinic."

"Nope. Well, a couple shingles blew off, but Jeremiah fixed that the first morning. He boarded up Gen's picture window that shattered and then started working on everyone else's issues."

"Have I told you this week how sexy that man is?" Allison took her beer from Declan and thanked him.

"Not this week, but it has been insane lately." She took a sip of the beer in front of her as Allison drank half of her glass in one go. "Whoa, lady, what's with the power chugging?"

Allison sighed and shook her head. "How in the heck am I going to ever find a man? I'm thinking of moving south."

Eden sat down her glass. "What brought all of this on?"

Allison shrugged. "Guess I'm feeling sorry for myself." She smiled and waved a hand. "Never mind me. I'm pulling the party mood down."

She put her hand on Allison's arm. "Before you decide to move, maybe you should ask yourself if moving is going to help."

Allison snorted. "So, I'm undateable?"

Eden bumped her shoulder against her friend's. "No, I didn't say that. But there are options here." She pointed to Zeke. "Doctor number one. Trent Macy is Doctor number two. Carson from the hardware store, Kerry Ross out at the processing plant." She waited until Declan passed by and pointed at him. "Prime options. They have jobs and are good-looking."

Allison rolled her eyes. "They know me and have never looked twice in my direction."

Eden shrugged. "So, give them something to notice."

"How?"

Eden lifted an eyebrow. "You sure you want the answer to that?"

"Yeah, I do."

"Stop chasing after them." Her friend could scare away a man in two seconds flat. "Men enjoy the chase."

Allison turned to face her on the barstool. "Did Jeremiah chase you?"

Eden felt her face flame. "Well, he really didn't have to. But Zeke tried harder each time I said no. Think about it, at least."

Allison took another sip of her beer. "I don't know. I mean, what I've been doing hasn't worked, has it?"

"Just don't take it too far." Eden glanced over at Jeremiah, who seemed to know she was looking. He turned and winked at her, which sustained the blush that her conversation with Allison had caused.

"Geeze, Eden, I want to date, not balance on a tightrope." Allison's comment drew her back into the conversation.

"Moderation, Alli. Be yourself, how you are with me and Gen when we're having a girl's night. Be fun but don't crowd."

The woman snorted. "But I *am* an in-your-face person. Why should I change? You either like me or you don't."

Eden stared at her friend and digested her words. She put her arm around her friend. "Oh, crap, honey. You know what, you're absolutely right. Disregard everything I said. You be you. There *is* a man out there for you. I'm sure of it, and if these guys don't see how great you are, to hell with them."

Allison leaned her head against Eden's. "Thanks."

"Nothing to thank me about. Someday, some man is going to walk in and sweep you off your feet."

Allison lifted away and groaned, "Well, damn it. Now I have to lose twenty pounds."

Eden felt Jeremiah's hands on her shoulders. He leaned between them and spoke to Allison. "Bullshit. Never change for a man. If he doesn't love you for you, then he's the wrong guy."

Allison's eyes widened and her face flamed. "Yeah?"

Jeremiah nodded. "Definitely. Now, if you will excuse us, my woman made me a promise I intend to cash in on."

She watched Allison light up. Her friend looked directly at her. "Have I told you this week how lucky you are to have this guy?"

Eden laughed and jumped off the barstool. "You have, but feel free to remind me."

"You are *so* lucky to have this guy," Allison repeated.

"I agree. See you later." She grabbed Jeremiah's hand and they made their way to the door, saying their goodbyes.

They strolled out of the parking lot to the blacktop before he spoke. "I've experienced nothing like that. I mean, I've attended political rallies with my father, but the people there were plastic. They had their hands extended for one reason or another. Here, the only reason they extend a hand is for a handshake."

Eden hummed in agreement. "Life here isn't easy, but it is... fulfilling."

Jeremiah dropped her hand and placed his arm over her shoulder. "I'm not sure I'll be able to make a living as a doctor here." She glanced up at him and waited. "I don't need to. I've told you I have money, right?"

She nodded. "Your grandma and grandpa gave you some when they passed."

He toggled his head back and forth. "Some is a slight understatement."

She lifted her eyebrows. "Slight?"

"Okay, massive understatement. Anyway, all of this is to tell you that even if I don't have a full practice, I'm staying here in Hollister. I can find things to occupy my time if I'm not busy. Maybe I'll buy some land, get a couple head of cows to raise organic like the ranchers around here are doing. You know, for meat for Gen's cafe and us. Till up a garden. Build us a house, and maybe a small office building for me if my practice actually grows."

Eden stopped him and stared at the man she loved. "You are the most amazing person. Your ideas for the future sound like heaven. Now, take me home, Doctor Wheeler."

"Your wish is my command." He swept her off her feet, and despite her protest carried her the last bit to the clinic entrance where he had to let her down to get the keys to open the door.

She led him up the stairs through the apartment and into the bathroom. "I seem to remember a promise of some tender loving care. So, first, I'm going to wash every part of this sexy body, then I'm going to give you a back rub."

Jeremiah lifted his eyebrows and smirked down at her. "And a front rub?"

She chuckled and lifted his t-shirt. He took the hint and pulled it off. "If you're a good boy."

"Oh, woman, I might not always be the best, but I'm always good."

She unfastened his jeans and belt after he toed off his boots. She pushed him back into the shower under the water. He stood there, a solid mass of shifting muscles and gorgeous inked skin, and he was watching her as she removed her clothes. She joined him in the shower. His erection was hard and ready for her, which was what she wanted, but first, she adjusted the showerhead and then moved him closer to the back of the shower. He steadied her as she stood on the bench seat. Her breasts were now at eye level and he moved to capture one. She pulled away. "Be good," she chastised him before she reached for the shampoo.

Lather streamed down over his shoulders and down his back and chest. When she finished washing his hair she stepped back down and lathered a cloth to wash his body. Methodical, slow, and sensual were her goals. She hid a smile when he groaned and bucked into her hand while she lathered his shaft. His balls were tight and full as she pulled the cloth over them. His fists clenched at his side. She moved him to rinse the suds before she dropped the washcloth on the floor by the bench. "Sit down."

He huffed, "You don't need to wash my feet. In case you missed my rather obvious predicament, I'm dying here."

"Be good and sit down." When he arranged himself on the bench seat, she knelt and placed her hands on his knees and moved his legs further apart. Jeremiah stared at her; the heat in his eyes could have evaporated the water in the shower. She smiled and ran her hands up his inner thighs. The springy dark hair under her hands thinned as she went higher. In all the times they'd had sex, she'd never taken the time to leisurely admire him, and he was something to behold. She positioned herself between his legs and moved the washcloth to pad her knees. She leaned in and kissed his chest, taking time to circle each flat disk of copper and flick the taut nipple with her tongue. His hands went to her hair, but he didn't move her or rush her. She smiled against his skin and licked lower, trailing the beads of water that trickled over his abs. She spent time Frenching his belly button, a tactic she'd learned from him. A pleasure to be sure, but in his state, she wanted the slow tease to pitch him into a fiery need.

Licking down lower, she tongued the very base of his cock and the hands in her hair tightened. She looked up and caught the intense fire in his eyes. He was letting her have her way, but she could tell it wasn't easy for him. She smiled up at him and palmed his balls before she lowered her head and opened her mouth to take his shaft. His size prevented any attempt at a deep throat, but what she couldn't do didn't matter. She used one hand to stroke that velvet skin up to her mouth as she lowered on his cockhead, and when she pulled off her hand moved down. It was a slow, sensual pace. Her tongue teased and circled, moving faster as she sped up. His thighs trembled beside her and she slowed. A long, agonizing groan from Jeremiah was music to her ears. She pushed until he peaked and she tasted precum, only to slow and back off the stimulation. His groans and panted breath filled the small shower enclosure. Finally, that stoic man whispered a plea.

"God, Eden, please…"

She sped up. It took less than a minute for him to arch up, barking out a shout as he released into her mouth. She swallowed as much as she could and licked up what she couldn't. He shivered and grabbed her shoulders. "Sensitive."

Trailing small kisses up his torso, she reached his lips and kissed him. Her man was languid, loose muscled, and relaxed in his response. He had to be exhausted. He'd been pushing himself, working hard in the summer sun all day, sometimes with only necessary breaks.

Standing up, she repositioned the showerhead and washed them both quickly. Jeremiah caught her as she turned off the water. "Your turn." He dropped to kiss her.

She sidestepped and looked back at him. "No. I still owe you a backrub." She handed him a towel and wrapped her towel around herself. "When you're dry, go lay down on the bed." She moved to the small cabinet where she stored toiletry items and reached down to the bottom shelf. She removed two bottles of massage oil and followed him out of the bathroom. He pulled the comforter down to the foot of the bed. "Lay on your stomach, please."

He did as she asked, and she climbed onto the bed, straddling him while still wrapped in a towel. Warming oil between her hands, she leaned forward and started with his shoulders. He released a low moan of pleasure. "Does that feel good?"

He mumbled something; the tone let her know it did. Falling into a rhythm, she made small circles with her hands, enlarging them and constricting them as she made her way down his back. She'd been working on his lower back for about three minutes when she heard the first snore. Slowly reducing the pressure, she listened as he fell into a deep sleep before she stopped and carefully got off the bed.

She prayed he'd sleep for more than a couple hours. One of his clean t-shirts was on the dresser so she helped herself and left the bedroom after closing the door. With a quick glance at the clock, she realized she hadn't eaten and neither had Jeremiah. She popped one of Gen's take-and-bake casseroles into the oven. If he woke, at least there'd be something for him to eat.

While she waited for the food to cook, she dropped onto her comfy couch and curled up in the corner. She smiled into the darkness. The man she loved and who loved her was sleeping peacefully—for now—in her bed. He had plans for a future. With her. Her eyes lifted to the picture of her and Riley. The smile held. "I found someone, Riley. He is so good to me, and as much as I didn't think I could, I love him as much as I loved you." She sighed and closed her eyes. Life was almost perfect. A sliver of dread tickled through her thoughts, and she batted it away. She wouldn't taint this night with fear of what might be. Tonight, she'd reflect on the love she'd found in the most unlikely place: the aftermath of a knife fight.

CHAPTER 18

Jeremiah laughed at Father Murphy's story; granted, it was one he'd heard before, but the Father's embellishments, voice accents, and inventive non-curse curse words made the story hysterical. He hammered down another shingle as the men on Phil Granger's roof laughed and worked. His phone vibrated in his back pocket. He dropped his hammer and took off his well-worn leather gloves, the ones he'd picked up after the splinter incident at Eden's.

The sun was directly overhead, so he couldn't see who the call was from. He swiped it and answered, "Hello?"

"Jeremiah, where are you?" Jamison's voice jolted him out of the good humor he'd been in.

"Hollister, why?" He turned around and sat down on the shingles. The men around him stopped working. Obviously, the way he'd tensed up wasn't lost on them.

"We have evidence indicating Cyrus was in Montana. A camping site. He took out a family."

"Which means he's coming here."

"He left the computer opened to the email from you when the park rangers found the crime scene." Jamison confirmed his worst fears.

"That team here yet?" He hadn't pursued the meet and greet with the men because he'd been so damn busy working to clean up storm damage.

"They are. The boss is having them come into town tonight. Where do you want to talk to them?"

"My sister's cafe will have enough room and privacy. What time?" He glanced in the direction of the cafe. Gen wouldn't mind. She was only open for breakfast and lunch, and takeouts had to be picked up by noon.

"Seven your time. My boss will call in for the meeting. He'll discuss Guardian's plans."

"How long do you think we have?" He glanced at the other men who'd stopped working and were making no pretense about listening to his conversation.

"He could be there now, or he could play cat and mouse with you. You know his MO the same way I do."

"All right. Thanks for the call."

"You be safe, you hear me? We'll catch this bastard before he gets to you."

He knew Jamison couldn't guarantee that, but it was nice that the man tried to reassure him. "I'll do my best. You take care, too." He hung up before Jamison could say more. He didn't want to say goodbye to his friend, and that was probably selfish on his part.

"What's wrong?" Phil asked from about ten feet away where he was working his line of shingles.

"My past is catching up to me, and unfortunately, it is going to endanger everyone in this town."

Phil dropped his hammer and sat down. "Well now, my friend, I think you need to explain that in a bit more detail." The other men followed suit.

Jeremiah nodded but held up a finger. "I need to make this call first."

Eden answered the phone. "Hi! Are you done early?"

"No." His tone said it all. He didn't need to say another word.

"He's coming."

"Yes. You know what to do."

Eden drew a shaky breath but answered, "We'll get through this. We have to."

He nodded, although she couldn't see him. He sighed, "I'll be home soon. I love you."

"I love you, too. Be careful."

He disconnected the line and dropped the phone to the rooftop. Turning, he looked at the men. He started at the beginning and told them everything, not leaving a single detail out. He watched as they blanched, as their eyes widened, and then as they hardened when he told them that Cyrus was heading to Hollister and may already be close. "So, I need you to take your families and leave for a week or so. I'll pay for hotels, travel costs, whatever you need, but you have to let everyone know and get them out of town by nightfall. Eden has my credit card information for anyone who needs help to evacuate."

Phil nodded and stood at the same time he did. "What are you going to do?"

"I'm going to get Eden and Gen out of here, and then I'm going to wait for him to show. I have a team from Guardian Security meeting me at Gen's cafe tonight. We'll talk tactics then. Gentlemen, I can't apologize enough for bringing this to your doorstep."

Carson Schmidt snorted. "Sounds like this killer is the one that needs to apologize, not you, but I get your drift. Phil, you start the phone tree and keep the information to the basics, or by the time the last person hears what is going on the story will be so exaggerated there will be vampires invading the town."

Phil nodded as a bolt of lightning flashed in the distance. "Rough weather coming this way. Guys, let's pull everything down and deal with the business at hand."

Jeremiah pulled his hand through his hair for the five millionth time since he'd received that call from Jamison. He knew the telephone tree for the town had worked because businesses were closed and truck after truck loaded with families pulled out of town. There were only two who called to ask for financial assistance and he was happy to help the families out. The last tornado had hit both families hard. He had Eden call in advance and pay for rooms for them in Belle Fourche. He'd give her his debit card and have her make sure they had cash for food when she headed south—if he could get her to leave.

"I'm not going until I know what these Guardian people say." Eden crossed her arms and stared at him, her jaw set and angled up at him in a defiant challenge.

Gen stuck her head out from the kitchen where she was busy making sure her supplies were stored properly for a prolonged closure. "What *she* said."

"For God's sake, he could be somewhere in this town right this minute!"

"And he could still be in Montana! You know no more than we do!" Eden snapped right back at him. "I'll go but only when I know those Guardian people are competent and you've got a chance of surviving this." Lightning lit up the sky, illuminating the small cafe with a brilliant flash.

Jeremiah started counting, a habit he'd formed when he was a child to tell how far away the lightning had struck. He reached fifteen before the thunder rumbled over the town. He glanced at his watch. The Guardian people would be there soon. "I don't like it." He shook his head.

"Tough," Gen said as she came out to the front with bottles of water for each of them. "You're wearing a gun. I have a shotgun behind the counter. If he shows up, he's toast."

Eden blinked and gaped at Gen. "You'd shoot someone?"

"In a heartbeat," they both said at the same time. Eden's eyes swung to him and then flashed to the door. He spun, his hand on his handgun.

Phil opened the door and was followed into the cafe by Zeke, Trent Macy, Carson Schmidt, Kerry Ross, the man who ran the meat processing plant, Dutch Patterson, the barber, Declan Howard, and several others.

"What are you doing here?" Jeremiah scanned the crowd of men. Each one of them wore a sidearm and carried a rifle.

"The families are out of town, they're safe. In this part of the woods, we protect ourselves and we protect each other." Trent Macy sat down at the counter. "What's the plan?"

"I'd like to know, too." Zeke leaned against one of the highback benches.

The door opened and everyone turned, weapons leveled and pointing at the man who entered and raised his hands. "I'm looking for Jeremiah Wheeler?"

Phil grunted. "Yeah, and who are you?"

Red dots flashed across the room, landing on

chests before moving on. "Guardian Bravo Team Leader. You can call me Ace."

Jeremiah stepped forward. "I'm Jeremiah. Guys, lower your weapons. These are the specialists that Guardian sent in."

"I'll lower my weapons when those red dots disappear, *and* I see who had me in their sights," Kerry Ross growled in response.

The man at the door made several sharp hand signals. "They'll be here in a minute." The red dots disappeared, and Ace glanced at Jeremiah. "The plan was that you would be the only one left in the town." A blinding strike of lightning flashed, brightening the evening sky into daylight for a few seconds. Four other men entered the cafe. The hardware they were carrying was impressive. One of the men gave Ace a rifle then dropped a hook and loop flap on his tac vest and handed Ace a handgun, too. The leader of Bravo Team slung the rifle over his shoulder and holstered his handgun.

"I know that was the plan, but these hardheaded people think they know better."

Ace leveled a stare and scanned the entire room. "We appreciate your offer, gentleman, but we can't do our job if we are worried about you or worried that this murdering son of a bitch will take you hostage. Believe me, we have a trap set for that asshole. If you're here, you're only hindering us."

Nobody said a word for a long moment. Then Jeremiah heard a sound he'd never wanted to hear again. An unmistakable, ominous, long, rolling sound that grew louder.

Every resident of Hollister snapped their attention to the window. "Fuck, not again." Phil was the first to push himself through the men and race outside. He turned around and yelled, "Take cover!"

"What the fuck?" Ace and his crew flattened against the wall as the men flew out of the cafe and headed toward their shelters. Zeke grabbed Phil's arm and pulled him toward the garage. They'd use the oil-changing pit as a shelter. Several others went with him.

Kerry Ross was running across the street when a board flew through the air and knocked him down. The man didn't move. Jeremiah bellowed, "Get to the root cellar! I'll be right there." Gen and Eden flew out through the kitchen. He grabbed Ace. "Follow the women!"

"Fuck that! Keys, go after the women." One of the team peeled off and bolted through the kitchen.

Jeremiah raced out the door and the team followed. He glanced up and saw the tornado as it moved along the ground, winding debris around the center funnel. There were three funnel clouds. Two hadn't touched the ground yet.

Dirt and rain lashed his face by the time he made it to Kerry. The man was out cold. He motioned for Ace to help him. He glanced down the street. Carson Schmidt was about a block away when the windows of his store exploded.

Ace motioned and his remaining men sprinted down the street. Jeremiah yelled, "They need to find cover!"

"They know!" Ace called back, and they headed back toward the cafe.

They never made it. Cyrus Macmillan stepped onto the walkway, half-dragging Eden with him.

The tornado's percussive roar reverberated around them. Cyrus' mouth moved, but Jeremiah couldn't hear anything. They could barely stand against the wind. The overhang of the cafe lifted and flew into the air. Jeremiah screamed as Macmillan dragged Eden back into the alley. Ace grabbed his shirt and yelled, but he couldn't hear a word. Ace started moving, and because he was helping to hold Kerry, Jeremiah moved, too. He glanced to his right then pushed Kerry into Ace, sending them both to the ground and diving after them. An exterior wall screamed past them, exploding into the side of Phil's garage.

He and Ace crawled toward the cafe, dragging Kerry with them. More debris flew above them, smashing into the cafe. The windows exploded outward. Hundreds of shards nipped at his skin, but they kept going, pulling Kerry's dead weight behind them. They crawled under the boardwalk. It wouldn't protect them against the tornado if it took the building, but it would protect them from flying building parts. He put his mouth by Ace's ear and yelled, "I have to go!"

Ace cupped his neck and pulled him back. "You'll be killed! What good will you be to her then?"

Jeremiah jerked away and stared at the man. If he didn't go now, Cyrus would kill her. What had happened to Gen, to the guard? No, Cyrus needed to be stopped. He shook his head, turned as best as he could in the limited amount of room, and scurried under the boards, pushing against the torturous wind. He pulled himself forward on his elbows, blindly heading toward the alley where Cyrus had disappeared.

CHAPTER 19

His eyes were irritated with dirt so he couldn't see shit, but he knew when he'd reached the end of the boardwalk. The sheets of rain hit him as he made his way out and flattened himself against the side of Gen's cafe. Carefully, he wiped his eyes and blinked the world back into focus.

The wrenching screech of metal grinding against metal rent the surrounding air, penetrating the almost untenable decibels of the tornado's destructive roar. He shifted enough to see Phil Granger's garage door fly into the sky like a piece of paper. Jeremiah pushed back and crawled along the side of Gen's cafe, the siding on the building grating against his arm like sandpaper.

When he reached the end of the building, he took

in the damage. The wild wind had flipped Gen's truck on its side and over the root cellar door. There was debris everywhere. There was no sign of Eden, Gen, the man from Guardian—or Cyrus. He grabbed the corner of the building as the wind screamed. He pinned himself and prayed like he'd never prayed before. Explosions punctuated the never-ending roar as he let the wind crush him against the side of the building.

Almost as suddenly as it had started, the storm abated. The wind buffeted still, but he could peel himself off the exterior of Gen's building. Rain pelted him as he took in the mounds of debris. "Eden! Gen!"

"Remi! In here!" He heard Gen's yell from the root cellar.

"Gen, are you all right?" He weaved through the debris, searching for any signs of Eden or that fucker Cyrus.

"I am. The Guardian guy pushed me in and went after Cyrus. He took Eden!"

"Gen, your truck's blocking the door. It's going to be a while before we can get you out."

"I'm fine! Find Eden!"

He stopped and turned around. The totality of the devastation resembled the hurricanes the south had gone through when he was growing up. *Where the hell to start?* Cyrus couldn't have made it through the storm. They had to be under the debris.

He lurched forward and peeled back boards, yelling for Eden over and over. Ace appeared by his side and grabbed his arm. "Any sign of that son of a bitch?"

He pitched boards as he answered. "No. Gen is in the root cellar. Your man pushed her in and went after Cyrus."

Ace let out a string of curse words. "We have thermal imagers. I'll get one of my men on top of a building." A low call snapped their attention to the right. They raced to the spot and started pulling off debris. Shingles, boards, window frames, some with the glass still intact.

They worked together and hefted a large piece of corrugated tin. Remi braced it as high as he could as Ace ducked under and chucked smaller pieces of wood off his man. Remi could see the man's head and chest. Blood trickled from his ear and nose. The buried Guardian grabbed Ace. "The target, he's got the other woman."

"Okay, we'll find them. Hold on, man, we're going to prop this shit up and get Coaster over here to look at you."

"Leg's done for, man. I'm looking at the sole of my boot. Something hit me and sent me flying."

"Zeke is with the group in the garage next door. He's a doctor, too." Remi strained under the weight of the tin and the debris that remained on top of it. "Go get him. I'll hold this up."

Ace flew out of the hole they'd dug. Remi adjusted his grip and talked to the man. "So, sleeping on the job, huh? What's your name?"

A huff came from the man. "Keys.... I mean Mark, and I'd tell you to fuck off, but it might get me in some serious shit with Ace."

"Nah, dude, didn't you know when you're injured nothing you say can be used against you?" Jeremiah glanced over his shoulder and stared at the debris. He had to find Eden. Had to make sure Cyrus couldn't hurt anyone. He adjusted his grip again.

"I tried, man. I had her, I put that bastard on the ground with one punch. Next thing I know I'm flying with part of a building at my back." The man moved and groaned. "Damn it. My wife is going to kill me."

"A tough one, huh?" Jeremiah scanned the debris he could see without shifting and sending more crap down toward Mark.

"Dude, she's not even five feet tall, but she's

strong." The man shifted again and sucked a sharp breath in.

"Try not to move. They'll be here in a minute." Remi focused his attention on the man. He couldn't tell how bad the injuries were from his position.

"Jeremiah?"

"Here!" he responded to Zeke's yell.

Zeke appeared on the far side of the cafe, carrying Eden's medical bag. Two of the Guardians followed him.

One took over bracing the tin and the other went to work building a temporary hold for the metal. "Ace is getting to a place to use the thermal," the one holding the metal spoke.

Jeremiah nodded and headed away toward the piles nearer the alley where they'd disappeared.

"Eden?" He called her name over and over as he pulled material off the pile. The rain had stopped. He threw a 2x4 off the pile and stopped to listen after he called her name again. "Eden!"

He cocked his head. Had he heard something? He glanced over at the propped-up metal. Zeke and the two Guardians were removing the other man using a mylar blanket wrapped around two boards as a makeshift stretcher.

He filled his lungs and called again, "Eden!" Nothing.

"Wheeler!" Jeremiah whipped his head around and looked up. Ace was standing on the porch he'd built for Gen. "About two hundred feet to your left, just past whatever is sticking straight up."

He moved as fast as humanly possible through the jagged edges and shards of wood. "Here?"

"Up about ten feet," Ace yelled back at him. "Now to your right about three feet."

He moved up and halted when Ace shouted for him to stop. He pulled crap off the pile. His hands were bleeding; the cuts didn't matter. The only thing that mattered was finding Eden. Another set of hands joined him, and then another. Phil and Doc Macy worked alongside another Guardian. Carson Schmidt joined them, handing out gloves. Jeremiah didn't stop to put them on. The person under the rubble was either Eden or Cyrus. He'd kill that bastard with his bare hands, nothing between them, and if it was Eden, he needed to touch her.

Phil lifted a piece of siding and Jeremiah dropped to his knees. With shaking hands, he felt for a pulse. He found it, and it was steady. "Get Zeke back here. Tell him we need a neck collar and a backboard." He picked the smaller pieces of debris off her. Eden laid on her stomach, one of her arms bent at an angle that could only mean it was broken, but there was no blood he could see so the bone hadn't gone through the skin. He examined her as he pulled rubble off her and talked to her, letting her know he was there. She had numerous cuts and abrasions. A wicked lump on the side of her head had bled and clotted her blonde hair to her skull. Caked blood and dirt under her nose could be from being hit with something, or it could be from the blow to the head. Either way, he wasn't taking any risks.

Zeke crested the top of the pile and sat Eden's bag down. "We don't have a backboard. Most of the clinic is somewhere in the next county. We'll use a piece of plywood. I have a collar." He moved down to where Jeremiah was. "Status?"

"Pulse is regular. The arm is broken, but no signs of an exposed fracture. I'm worried about the contusion to the head and the blood from the nose."

"All right." Zeke twisted and looked around. "Carson, we need that board." Zeke pointed to a large piece of plywood. Carson and Phil made their way through the rubble and worked the board out. "Bring it over here. This side." Zeke moved and put the board next to her. "Jeremiah, you have her head. Phil, over here. You're going to help me roll her.

Smooth, no sudden movements. Carson, that arm is going to drag when we roll her. I want you to keep it in line, don't let it drag. Like this. Now, slip your hands under her elbow and wrist and move with her body. Everything is slow, got it?" Zeke looked at all of them as they took their positions. "All right, Jeremiah, on your count, we go at three."

Jeremiah placed his hands in position and counted it down. "One, two, three, and slowly now…"

They rolled her over and he winced. She'd been torn up in the storm. Minor cuts and swelling contusions littered her body. He and Zeke put the spinal collar on her and the four of them carried her out of the tornado's refuse.

Ace was there to help as they moved to uncluttered ground. "We have no more heat signatures in this mess."

"We're taking her to the garage. It still has a roof." Zeke coordinated movements, which he was thankful for because his mind was on overload. He wanted to stay with Eden, yet they needed to find Cyrus.

When they moved through the small space between the cafe and the garage, Jeremiah got the full extent of the devastation. It looked as if the tornado had skipped several buildings and then wiped out three or four and jumped over the cafe and the garage on one side of the street. The clinic and Eden's apartment were gone; only framing and the exam table remained.

They moved her inside. Phil handed his side off to a Guardian and rushed to grab two sawhorses for them to place the plywood that Eden was lying on.

Jeremiah kneeled beside her and stroked her cheek. "Wheeler, our objective is still out there." At Ace's statement, he closed his eyes and said a prayer for Eden.

He stood, still holding her hand. "Phil, do we have a count on the people still here?"

Phil nodded. "Yeah, we're unburying my tractor and then pulling Gen's truck off that door to get her out. We have ambulances coming for these three." He nodded at Eden, Mark, and Kerry.

"I don't need an ambulance," Kerry grumbled, although he was still laying on the concrete floor.

"You took a crack to that brain of yours. Don't damage it any more by declining treatment," Phil grumped right back at him.

"Zeke?" Jeremiah glanced down at the doctor who was examining Eden.

"I've got this." He looked up at Jeremiah. "You

know I'll take care of her." The silent conversation between them said so much more. He nodded and placed her hand back down. "I'll be back." He leaned down and kissed her forehead.

As he straightened, he rolled his shoulders back. He had a fucking psychopath to catch.

They emerged from the garage and Ace took charge. "Hondo, you're watching this position. If that fucker shows up here, take him out. Those people are your mission, copy?"

"Roger that." The man nodded and spun away from the rest of them.

Ace placed his hands on his hips and stared at the damage. "If you were a serial killer, where would you go?"

Jeremiah sent his eyes down the street to the meat processing plant. "There."

Ace followed his gaze. "What's that?"

"A meat processing plant. If I wanted to kill someone, I'd go there, lure whoever I wanted to kill in. He could string up his prey and work on them without hurrying. That's what he enjoys. Taking the time to make his victims suffer."

"Jesus. What are we dealing with?" one of the other Guardians spoke up.

"A man that has no remorse," Jeremiah answered.

"Stud, get up on the top of the cafe and see what you can see." Ace slapped the thermal imaging device in the guy's hands.

"Roger that." The man took off.

"He knows we're here now."

Jeremiah shook his head. "He knows *you're* here. He doesn't how many others." Ace was the only one with him when Kerry was knocked out. They stood in silence and he scanned the darkened street of the small town he loved. They'd have to rebuild again. For some, it would be too much. The ones without insurance would probably move on, find another place in another small town.

A short whistle caught their attention. Ace put his earpiece in. "Shit. All right. The main door is open. Everything else is shut tight. He's not close enough to get a heat signature from the building, but other than us, he can't see anything else in this part of the town. Nothing is moving."

"Then we go to him." That's what Cyrus wanted, after all. What he'd wanted in the prison. For Jeremiah to give himself over.

Ace nodded. "We're going to put you on the end of a hook and use you for bait, Wheeler."

He sent a sideways glance at the Guardian. "Under one condition."

"And that is?"

Jeremiah crossed his arms. "If I get a bite, I get first shot at taking that bastard down."

"No way, man. You pull him out into the open and we'll take the shot."

"Have you ever craved revenge, Ace?" Jeremiah stared down the street.

"On more than one occasion, but that isn't what this is about. This is about taking down a serial killer. You put revenge into the equation and that bastard has an edge."

Jeremiah cocked his head. Ace was right. He needed to go in emotionless. A tick of a smile tweaked the side of his mouth. That would infuriate Cyrus. So be it. "If you get a shot, take it. If I get a shot, I'll do the same." He took his weapon from his holster and handed it to Ace. "I won't need this if you have my back."

"Thank God. Civilians with weapons scare the fuck out of me." Ace chuckled and checked the safety before he inserted it into loops on his vest. "All right, here's the plan. The three of us are going first. Give us ten minutes to get set up. Then you walk down the middle of the street and call to him. Distract him so we can enter the building. We'll locate him, take him out if possible. If not, we'll always have one sight on you while the others move through the facility and try to find him. Now, tell me as much about the inside of that building as you can."

Jeremiah told him as much as he remembered of the building. He'd been in there twice and it was a basic design, but he went into as much detail as he could remember.

"All right. Ten minutes, Wheeler." Ace slapped his arm, and he and his men filtered into the darkness.

CHAPTER 20

Jeremiah stepped back into the garage. Zeke looked up at him and smiled. "Come see who's awake."

He was at her side in three strides. She grasped his hand. "Cyrus is here."

"I know. We've got a plan and Guardian is setting up near where we believe he is." He lifted her hand and kissed the back of it. "Are you in much pain?"

She closed her eyes and opened them again. "Not much. Zeke gave me some happy juice."

He glanced over at the doctor. Zeke shrugged. "I'm not setting that arm without an x-ray and we want a CT on her just to make sure that head injury won't cause any further problems. I gave her something to help the pain, but not enough to knock her out."

The Guardian with the broken leg was hooked up to an IV and out cold. Kerry was still laying down and wasn't talking. "How long before the ambulances get here?"

"Guardian made calls and has an air medevac coming up from Rapid City. Shouldn't be long."

Eden grabbed his hand. "I didn't see him. We were running toward the root cellar and the next thing I knew, he had me. The Guardian who came after me. Is he okay? A wall hit him." She swallowed and tears pooled in her eyes.

"He's in the bed next to you. He's busted up, but he was talking when they dug him out." Jeremiah kissed the back of her hand again.

"What happened to your hands?" She looked down at the blood-stained skin.

"Debris. We had to go through a lot to get down to where you were."

"I should have been crushed." She swallowed hard again.

"You weren't. You're here and you're safe."

"I tried to get away. He had a knife. Then the tornado. I could see it coming behind you. He must have realized he was going to die, too, if he stayed there. He dragged me back to Gen's truck, but it had already flipped over. Something hit me." She lifted her hand to her head. "The next thing I saw was that light." She flicked her eyes up at the old bare bulb that hung over her.

"You're safe now. That's the only thing that's important." He glanced down at his watch and closed his eyes. He needed to go. Placing her hand back on the plywood, he leaned up and kissed her lips. "I have to go help the people from Guardian with a few things. Zeke will get you on that helicopter and I'll be down to see you as soon as we get Gen out of the cellar. I love you, and I'll see you soon."

Eden grabbed his wrist. "You're going after him?"

He stared down at her and nodded. "I am."

She took a breath and spoke, "Watch out for the knife. He pulled it from behind his neck." She squeezed his hand. "Come back to me."

He would not promise something he couldn't deliver. Instead, he leaned down and kissed her again. "I love you." He whispered the words against her lips and

lifted quickly, forcing himself to walk out onto the main street and head to the meat processing plant.

Phil ran after him. "Doc, hold up." He held out a long blade. "This hunting knife is razor-sharp. If that man has a knife, you need one, too. Do you know how to handle one of these things?"

Jeremiah took it and nodded. "To a degree."

Phil held his hand up, mimicking holding the knife. "Grasp it like this. You don't need to get close to the man. Flick him with the blade. You might hit clothes the first couple times but be quick, don't get in close to him, and don't lunge. Believe me, Doc, this technique will take him down. You'll have him on his knees in three minutes. Quick, snake-like flicks."

He put the knife between his belt and jeans behind him and then held out his hand. "Take care of them for me."

Phil nodded. "Until you get your ass back here. We got the tractor uncovered and we're going to get Gen out of that cellar."

"Thank you, Phil, for everything."

Jeremiah started toward the other side of town. The walk toward the processing plant would take about five minutes, and that was due to the debris he had to circumvent. The only light came from sporadic glimpses of the moon through the fast-moving clouds that trailed the main front.

As he neared the hardware store, the debris piles forced him to veer toward the side of the street in front of the store. His boot hit the step and he froze when Cyrus stepped out of the shadows.

"Well, Doctor Wheeler. We meet again." The sound of the man's voice was a wide-awake nightmare come to life. Cyrus crossed his arms and leaned back against the wall of the hardware store. Jeremiah knew the man wasn't relaxing; no, he was trying to control the event.

Jeremiah mimicked the man's relaxed lean against the storefront. "Cyrus. I see the bullet wound is healing." The man's shirt was torn to shreds, exposing a red, puffy, vicious-looking scar.

His tormentor's head cocked, and Cyrus studied him for several long seconds before he smiled. "You've changed."

"Change is inevitable." The moon broke out from the cloud cover and illuminated the area. Jeremiah could see the strap around Cyrus' neck, probably the device that held the knife. "The storm got in your way tonight."

Cyrus flinched as if someone had slapped him, which was exactly what Jeremiah wanted to happen. He wanted to keep the man off-balance, not behave as a victim would. No, he wouldn't get mad; no begging this time. This time he was going to treat Cyrus as a normal human and watch the man go mad trying to figure out his endgame. But his endgame needed time to move into position. From where he was leaning, he saw someone dart across the street. They were aware something had happened, and they were adapting.

"What is different about you?" Cyrus lifted away from the wall and took two steps toward him. "Why aren't you afraid?"

Jeremiah shrugged. "Fear won't change your plans." He moved off the wall and took a stabilizing breath before he leveled his weight evenly on his feet. He'd have to move fast if Cyrus struck.

The man closed the space, but Jeremiah held his ground. When Cyrus was within three feet of him, the man slowed and stopped. "When I finish with you, I'm going to skin your woman and anyone else I can find in this Godforsaken hovel. You said you weren't afraid, but only fear would drive someone to hide way out here." Cyrus laughed and it took all his willpower not to cringe. The man was unhinged. Cyrus smiled widely. "I know what! I'll take her your heart. That's a romantic gesture, isn't it?" Cyrus lifted his arm to go for his knife.

Jeremiah took a quick step with his right foot

and snapped his right palm out, pushing Cyrus' arm back farther and faster than he'd want. He slid back and pulled his knife, having it out before Cyrus. The surprise on the man's face lasted only a split second before evil invaded the stare. Cyrus lunged, holding his knife in an icepick, overhand hold. Jeremiah moved out of the way and flicked the knife as Phil had instructed.

A long red line formed over the man's ribs. Blood welled from the cut. Cyrus glanced down. Enraged, he lunged again. Jeremiah used his MMA training to avoid the frontal attack. As he moved away and then past Cyrus when he stumbled forward, he slashed the man's back. Another long, angry gash opened across his skin.

Cyrus screamed and ran toward him. Jeremiah waited and dropped just as Cyrus swung the knife in a downward motion. He caught Jeremiah on the shoulder, slicing the skin.

Jeremiah spun and sliced at Cyrus' legs with a strong motion. He launched to his feet and backed up.

Cyrus followed. His movements were less intense, but the man's fury was palpable. Jeremiah dipped and weaved, moving away from the knife while slicing the man with every forward advance

Cyrus made. Blood covered what remained of Cyrus' clothes. Jeremiah slipped and went down on one knee.

Red dots suddenly illuminated Cyrus' chest. Jeremiah shoved himself upright and yelled, "No! Don't shoot him. He's going back to jail. He'll die *there!*"

Cyrus growled like an animal and searched the darkness unable to see the men who held guns on him. A wild scream ripped from him, "I'll never go back!"

Jeremiah's eyes narrowed. "Yes, you will." His chest heaved in heavy pulls, but he controlled his physical responses whereas Cyrus' actions were crazed. Cyrus screamed and pushed forward, slicing in wide arcs. Out of instinct more than training, he caught Cyrus' arm. Jeremiah moved forward and jabbed with the hunting knife. Once, twice, and a third time. Cyrus collapsed forward toward him. Against every instinct, Jeremiah stepped away and let the man fall.

Ace stepped onto the porch. He held a gun on the man and turned him over. Cyrus' eyes were open wide, but he wasn't seeing a thing. The madman's own knife protruded from the middle of his chest.

Ace stood up and extended his hand. Jeremiah gave him the knife Phil had loaned him, only then noticing how his hands shook. "Wheeler, next time tell your security detail you can handle a knife."

Jeremiah blinked and shook his head. "I can't. I've taken MMA lessons. Phil just gave this to me and told me how to use it."

Ace's eyebrow rose. "Well, then you're either a natural talent or you've been touched by an angel tonight. We had him in our sights the entire fight." Jeremiah moved his gaze from the dead man at his feet to the Guardian. The question was obvious without saying a word. Ace shrugged. "You wanted revenge, Doc. How's that feel?" Jeremiah opened his mouth to answer, but he couldn't. He felt horrible. He'd taken a life. Something he'd sworn he'd never do. Do no harm. He'd ripped apart the vows to his professional creed. Ace handed him back the knife. "Just FYI. You didn't kill him. That knife he fell on did. Look at your cuts, Doc. Superficial except for those last three, and believe me, they wouldn't have done him in. This one, over the hip, is nothing. The other two aren't deep enough to finish him, either. The reason he's dead is that he killed himself. He wouldn't give you the satisfaction of taking him back to jail. We watched it happen. He realized he was falling forward and turned his knife to kill himself, and that's the God's honest truth."

KRIS MICHAELS

The sound of a helicopter in the distance sent everyone's eyes heavenward. "Get down to your people, Doc. We'll clean this up." Ace motioned to one of his men with signals Jeremiah couldn't comprehend. The man nodded and knelt, taking off his pack.

"We've got a body bag. He's going with us. That is if we have a ride."

"Thank you." Jeremiah extended his hand.

"No worries, this is what we do. Granted, it is usually somewhere where they don't speak English, but taking care of good people is where our company excels." Ace grabbed his hand and nodded down the street. "Get out of here, Doc. We got this."

Jeremiah started at a walk but ended up jogging down the street. He wasn't sure Ace was right in his assessment of the injuries. He'd wait for the autopsy to relieve himself of any guilt, but one thing he knew was that Cyrus Macmillan would not kill another person. His vicious walk on the planet was over.

CHAPTER 21

J eremiah jogged up to the edge of town where the helicopter had landed. He weaved through the men to get to where Eden was laying. It was then that he noticed Zeke had applied a tourniquet to the Guardian man's leg just below the knee. He glanced at his watch. Far too much time had elapsed. He hated the man was going to lose his leg. Better that than his life, though.

Jeremiah knelt beside the stretcher that they had transferred her onto and pushed her hair back from her face. Her eyes fluttered open. She smiled at him softly and then jolted. "What happened?"

"Cyrus is gone. He'll never hurt anyone again."

"Gone? Back to jail?" Eden licked her chapped lips.

Jeremiah shook his head. "No. He's dead. He attacked me with a knife. Phil gave me one and showed me how to use it. We fought. I walked away, he didn't."

She tried to move and gasped in pain. He grabbed her hand. She nodded to his shoulder. "You're bleeding, fresh blood." She gripped his hand tighter and asked, "Are you sure he's dead?"

"It's nothing, just a small cut. I'm sure, Cyrus is dead." And he wasn't responsible, at least according to what Ace saw. However, there was no way for him to know if it was his actions that killed the man or if Cyrus had purposefully fallen on his knife. He'd leave it to the law to sort out. At the very minimum, it was self-defense. He'd hire a damn good lawyer. After what Cyrus had put him through, no jury in the world would convict him. Which did nothing to ease the remorse and guilt that stood on the center of his chest.

Eden closed her eyes and whispered, "Thank you, Jesus." Those blue eyes opened, and she stared up at him. "We're going to rebuild. The clinic is gone."

Jeremiah glanced back down the street. "You saw that, did you?"

"Or didn't see it," Eden chuckled softly. "I don't know if the county has the resources to rebuild."

Jeremiah kissed the back of her hand. "I do."

She narrowed her eyes. "What?"

"I can build us offices. Enough room for us both to work from. Then maybe we can look for some property not too far away and build that house we've been whispering about at night."

"Even after all of this, you're willing to stay?" A tear slipped from her eye and he caught it as it trickled down toward her ear.

"Under two conditions." He rubbed the tear between his fingers.

"Only two?" She lifted an eyebrow at him.

"First condition. We build proper tornado shelters. I'm ordering at least two from people who build them for a living and burying them within ten feet from the office and wherever we end up living."

Eden moved her eyes to look at him because the hard plastic collar wouldn't let her turn her head. "I won't argue that point."

He leaned forward and swept her lips with his. " The second condition is that you love me for the rest of your life."

"I won't argue that point either. I love you."

"Time to load up." Zeke made to drop his hand on Jeremiah's shoulder but stopped and pulled his shirt away from the wound. "That cut needs to be cleaned and there are at least five or six stitches in your future."

Eden narrowed her eyes. "A small cut, huh?"

Jeremiah shrugged and stood up, still holding her good hand. "Zeke is overreacting."

Zeke grabbed the head of the stretcher while a member of the helicopter flight crew grabbed the foot. "Zeke is not overreacting, although he is now speaking in third person."

Jeremiah stood at the door to the helicopter as they strapped her in and waved as the crew closed the door. Zeke slapped him on his good arm and nodded away from the helicopter. He gave Eden one last wave even though he doubted she could see him and then cleared out of the way of the massive rotors on the aircraft.

When the engine powered up, they had to turn away. The powerful whoop of the long blades spit dirt and small debris outward as the bird lifted into the air and then swooped to the south.

"I wasn't joking about that shoulder. Let me take care of that before we assess what's going on here. Then we can find a truck to drive down to Rapid. I want to check on all of them." They walked in silence to the garage. Phil had a portable generator running and the lights on.

Gen saw him and stood up to give him a hug. "How's Eden?"

"Her arm's broken, we're worried about the blow she took to the head. She's tough, but we'll deal with what happened together." Jeremiah released his sister and sat down, suddenly exhausted.

"Any other injuries?" he asked Zeke as the man sat Eden's medical bag on the bench. The makeshift seating he was using was constructed out of broken boards and a couple of turned-over five-gallon buckets.

"Cuts, bruises, scrapes. I'm trying to keep these macho S.O.B.s here. I don't need one of them stepping on downed power lines." He took off his shirt at Zeke's demand and spent the time it took Zeke to clean and suture his knife wound talking to Phil and the rest of the men about the damage. Gen leaned on his good side, and he could tell when she fell asleep. The events of the night over, everyone would start to crash sooner rather than later.

Zeke took off his gloves. "You know the drill. Keep it clean, keep water out of the wound until it closes, any redness or heat…"

"I got it." Remi nodded. "Gen's building is still in one piece. What say we all head up there and find a nice, clean, protected place and get some sleep.

None of us are fit to drive to Rapid even if we had a truck."

"My truck is fine." Gen sat up and yawned. "I started it right after Phil pulled it back onto four wheels. The passenger side looks like crap, but it can make the trip."

"Fine, we'll go in the morning. As much as I want to see Eden, wrecking because I fall asleep at the wheel isn't ideal, either."

"I agree. We all need sleep." Phil nodded. "Has everyone contacted their family?"

"I got word out via my CB to the Hollister Ranch. They're making calls for us. Everyone will be here at daylight to clean up," Carson Schmidt spoke as they all rose, and Phil turned off the generator.

They scaled the stairs to Gen's apartment, cleaned up as best as possible, and bunked out. He slept with his sister and let the other men duke it out for the guest bed, the couch, or the floor. He took off his clothes down to his boxers and pulled the blanket at the foot of the bed around him.

Gen stepped out of the bathroom in her pajamas of an oversized t-shirt and silk bottoms. She slid under the covers he was lying on top of and turned away from him. "You okay, Remi? I heard the guys talking. They said you took out the serial killer."

He thought hard about his response, searching the corners of his mind for emotions he wasn't feeling, for thoughts that fleeted through his mind, but he couldn't find any extraneous clouding of his thoughts. "If I killed him, it was in self-defense and defense of others. He threatened to kill each of you, and I know for a fact he would have followed through with that threat. Ace said he believed the man killed himself. I guess we'll wait to see what law enforcement says."

Gen turned over and looked at him. "Yeah, but are you okay?"

He flicked a quick look her way. "I'll be fine. Either way, I know I'll be okay. I did what I needed to do. I wouldn't change a thing about what happened against that man tonight. Other than, you know... the tornado."

Gen snorted. "I missed it all. Thank God. Night, Remi."

"Night, Gen." He closed his eyes and rolled through his memories of the night from start to finish. It could have ended so much worse. If one thing had happened out of order, the night's tragedies would be tenfold. He turned to his side and stared out the window. He'd never been one to believe too much in a higher power, but tonight had changed his mind. There was a God, and He was merciful tonight.

Eden blinked awake and listened to the machines in her room. She glanced over at the walls and sighed. Surgery, that's right. She remembered glimpses of the nurse in the surgical recovery area but not much more. They had to use hardware to secure her fracture and the orthopedic doctor explained in detail how he would repair the bones that had broken. She was looking at a minimum of six weeks in a cast and then a month or so building the strength back up in her arm.

A nurse walked in and smiled. "Well, there you are. How are you feeling?"

Eden blinked several times and rolled her head to the side. She stopped. "No collar?"

She'd had it on when the surgeon was talking to her. Hadn't she?

The nurse flipped open her chart. "That's right. Doctor Frederickson said you were very lucky. Although that bump on the side of your head did a number on your eye. You've got a serious shiner."

Eden sighed. "No, a serial killer punched me in the face. That's how I got the shiner."

The nurse stopped what she was doing and looked at her. "Okay. Can you tell me your name?"

Eden snorted. "Eden Wade. I'm a nurse practitioner up in Hollister, and I'm not insane. Ask anyone else that came in with me last night. Speaking of which, how are they? The Guardian and Kerry?"

Her nurse nodded and smiled. It was the type of smile you give a child that is trying their hardest but not quite getting it right. "The guardian." She shut the lid of the chart and smiled again. "I'll just be a minute."

Eden rolled her eyes and stared at the frosted plastic over the fluorescent lighting. Just what she needed, a psych eval.

A soft clearing of a throat to her right startled her. She glanced over and smiled. "Mr. Marshall, what are you doing down here?"

"I'm here checking on someone for a friend and I heard you were down here. They cleared Kerry almost as soon as he arrived, and his cousin picked him up earlier."

"What about the Guardian? He risked his life to get me away from that madman."

Frank shifted his feet and stared down at his cowboy hat he held in his hands. "He's lost a leg. He's got a long road ahead of him, but he'll get the help he needs."

Eden frowned. "How do you know that?"

"My friend is with Guardian." The man nodded at her. "How long is your wing out of commission?"

She glanced down at her arm. "At least six weeks. Did the ranch suffer any losses?"

Frank Marshall shook his head. "Went north and east of us. Tori tells me your man is helping her. Would you tell him I appreciate what he's done?"

Eden's heart softened. Those girls and that ranch were Frank Marshall's world. "I will. Jeremiah will be here shortly." Or she assumed he would be. She glanced at the clock. "You must have been on the road early."

"Before sunlight. We're packing up supplies and heading into Hollister."

"Thank you so much. You don't know how much that means to the town." For some reason, she started crying. She wiped at the tears and chuckled, "I do not know why I'm crying."

"You've been through one hell of a lot in the last twenty-four hours, I reckon." He walked forward and popped two tissues out of the small box on her bedside table, handing them to her. She dabbed at her eyes.

"Thank you."

There was a knock at her door and the nurse who'd stepped out came back in with another person. "Hi, I'm Doctor Frasier. I understand you were looking for a guardian?"

Eden snorted. "No, I was looking for the people who came in with me, one of which is a Guardian."

Frank grunted. "He's next door. Works for Guardian Security."

Doctor Frasier lifted an eyebrow. "I see. And the serial killer?"

"Killed last night after he took her hostage." Frank crossed his arms and stared at the man. "Seems you don't know much about what's going on. Homework before knee jerk."

Eden tried to snuff out the laugh from Frank's gruff response, but it was impossible. The Doctor spun and looked at the nurse. "Words to live by in my book."

The nurse, flushing from her toes to her hairline, followed him out of the room. Eden let the laugh she'd been suppressing out. "Mr. Marshall, you are the best."

"Nah, just don't suffer fools. I'll get out of here

and let you rest. If you need anything, you got our number out to the ranch." He nodded and stepped out of the door.

She chuckled and closed her eyes. Her arm ached, but from what she remembered, the nurses in recovery said everything went well. When the doctor showed up for rounds, she'd find out when she could go home. Her thoughts stopped right there. Everything else swirling in her mind slammed into the back of that thought, but she couldn't get past the blaring issue. She didn't have a home anymore. The clinic was gone. Some broken 2x4 studs still stood around the exam table, but there was nothing else. Her possessions were easy to replace. Oh, God. Except for the pictures of her and Riley. She'd have to contact Riley's parents to see if she could get copies of the ones they had.

A soft knock at the door drew her attention. "Ready for visitors?" Jeremiah stepped into the room holding a small paper bag. She reached out with her good arm, screw the IV. He was beside her in an instant and hugging her a moment later. The tears showed up again. It wasn't because she was weak; rather, she was so relieved to see him, to hold him. His handsome face was the confirmation that they'd made it through the long, dark night. His big, hard body filled her arms while his presence healed her soul. He was her touchstone, the only stable place amongst the chaos that swirled around them.

Jeremiah held her until she pulled away. The smile on his face was tentative. "I hated not being able to be here when you went through surgery."

She reached up and touched his face. "You're here now, that's all that matters. How is it? In the daylight, I mean?"

He sighed and shrugged. "Pretty much what it was in the dark. The clinic is gone. I walked through what was left this morning as the sun was coming up. I could follow the debris trail for about three hundred feet, which is where I found this."

He lifted the paper bag and pulled out the frame holding her and Riley's wedding picture. She reached for it, her hand shaking as she held it. Jeremiah cleared his throat. "I took the glass out, it shattered. Gen is in town with me. She's taking her truck to the insurance agent's office to give us some time alone. When I leave, I'll find another frame for it."

She placed it on her chest and closed her eyes, whispering, "Thank you for understanding."

Jeremiah pushed her hair off her brow. "He was your first love. You'll always have special feelings for him. I'm not jealous of your love for Riley. It doesn't threaten what we have."

She left the picture on her chest and reached up, placing her hand on his cheek. "It doesn't and it never will. I love you."

"I love you, too." Jeremiah leaned down to kiss her.

"I guess I should come back." Zeke's happy declaration made her laugh and Jeremiah groan.

"Dude, if you don't quit interrupting my quality time with my woman, I'm going to start hating you again." Jeremiah lifted but winked at her as he chastised the other man.

"Admit it, my timing is impeccable." Zeke crossed the room and picked up her chart. "And you, young lady, have made a laughingstock of one of the hospital's nurses. I got the scuttlebutt as soon as I walked out of the locker room just now." He pulled a pen from the pocket of his light blue scrubs and scribbled something on the paper sheets inside her chart.

She snorted. "I didn't, Frank Marshall did." Both Zeke and Jeremiah shot her a questioning look. "He was here to check up on someone for a friend and stopped in. The nurse, bless her heart, thought I was a little loose in the noodle."

Jeremiah snorted a laugh. "Loose in the noodle?"

She opened her eyes wide and lifted her good arm. "I asked where the Guardian was and told her the shiner I'm sporting wasn't from the tornado but from a serial killer who clocked me. She heard guardian and serial killer and thought I was the crazy one." She flicked her hand dismissively. "Serves her right for not believing me."

Jeremiah looked at Zeke and then they both busted up laughing. She reached up and gently pushed Jeremiah. "Stop it. Both of you."

Zeke shut her chart while still chuckling. "The surgery went well. You'll probably be released tomorrow morning."

She rolled her eyes. "I want to go home today." She stopped and glanced at Remi. "Except there is no home."

"We're staying with Gen until we remedy that situation. Her building is missing shingles, but it was almost as if the tornado skipped some buildings and wiped out others."

"Usual." Zeke nodded. "I'm heading next door to check on our friend. I'll be back north as soon as I can, but with the clinic being gone, I need to talk to the hospital administrators and see if they can put me on a month-by-month contract until I can figure out what I'm going to do."

Jeremiah glanced at her and she smiled, seeing the question in his eyes. She nodded and mouthed the word 'yes'.

Jeremiah cleared his throat. "Zeke, I'm going to build a professional space for Eden and me. Adding exam rooms and an office for you wouldn't be a problem. I made calls on the way down. I can get a construction company from Wyoming to come in and build it after I buy the land from the Hollisters."

Both she and Zeke shook their heads. "They won't let you buy it," Eden spoke for both of them. "They will give you a hundred-year lease on the land for a song, but they won't sell the land. It's theirs and they want to keep it."

"Who would I contact?"

"Andrew Hollister the fifth," Eden spoke, but she looked to Zeke for confirmation.

He nodded and added, "Andrew the sixth is overseas. He's in the service. I don't remember what branch. Depending on the rent for that office space, I'm in."

"I'm sure we'll come to some agreement, and if you agree to quit cock-blocking me, I'll even consider lowering it."

She gasped at Jeremiah's words and felt the blush rise from her toes to her cheeks. Zeke chuckled and rubbed his neck. "How about I'll try to stop? I mean, with my perfect sense of timing, talent like this is hard to keep in check."

"Deal. Now, go away." Jeremiah turned his back on Zeke and smiled at her, waggling his eyebrows. She peeked around him and waved at Zeke, who took no offense to the dismissal and laughed as he walked out of the room.

"Now, where were we?" He leaned down and swiped his lips over hers. "Oh, that's right. You were telling me you loved me."

CHAPTER 22

E den sat on Gen's back porch and rubbed her arm. The cast had come off yesterday. Eight weeks after the tornado, and what a difference that time had made to her little town. The debris behind Gen's cafe and Phil's garage was carted off to either landfills, burn barrels, or metal recycling shops. Jeremiah was down tinkering with his new four-wheel-drive king cab truck. Gen came out of the apartment and handed her a frosty glass of sweet tea, a delicacy that the South Dakotans of Hollister hadn't adopted.

She took a sip and sighed. "Thank you again for letting us stay here, Gen."

"No worries. I enjoy having someone around to visit with and you've been so much help getting the cafe back together."

"I've been doing paperwork." She lifted her arm. "This prevented me from doing anything else."

"If you only knew how much I loved saying, 'Eden, could you please order this or that?' and boom, I knew it was done. Plus, you helped me pick out a new counter and booths. I'm going to put one of those roll-down awnings out front, too, so people don't melt at lunch. That sun gets boiling hot in August. Hey, did I hear Remi say he hired a contractor for the house?"

She nodded. "Yes, hopefully, they can get everything done before the first snowfall, which means October."

Gen nodded. "I think it's awesome. The work across the street is moving along."

"I'm surprised, but Jeremiah is over there almost every day helping. Or getting in the way, I'm not sure which. His version and the contractors are polar opposites."

A soft chuckle filled the air. "Remi has to see how things work. That's why he's such a good psychiatrist. He digs until he knows the why of things."

"I've noticed that." The trait made him dynamic and fun, but melded with his profession, it made him an outstanding provider.

"Hey, just FYI, I'm saying good on you guys for putting in offices and exam rooms for Zeke, too."

"It only makes sense. Remi has a few clients with the promise of more when the county completes the paperwork. He wants his own space with his own entrance for people to come and go, so we'll have parking in the rear for them, out of the eyes of wagging tongues. Plus, the county is going to rent the spaces for both of us. It's a win/win for everyone."

Gen nodded as she stared out over the distance. "You know, if Jeremiah hadn't sent everyone away that night, there could have been so many more injuries and—God forbid—even deaths." Gen leaned back in her chair. "As much as I hate to say it, that crazy man did this town a favor when he showed up. At least to some degree."

Eden nodded and relaxed against the cushion of the deck chair. She and Jeremiah had discussed the coincidences while they whispered to each other after Gen turned in at night. The woman woke at four every morning, so she was usually in bed asleep by nine. That was the time that Eden and Jeremiah would whisper dreams, hopes, and plans for their future. He hadn't mentioned marriage, and that was okay with her—for now.

They'd both talked to Jamison about what happened the night the tornado hit. She could see why Jeremiah liked Jamison so much. He was irreverent but caring. Simple questions he posed could stand her on her head and make her see a fresh perspective and way of looking at what happened. She'd moved on from victim to survivor and so had Jeremiah. His fears about being the cause of that man's death had ridden him hard for a week, until he got his hands on a copy of the autopsy, thanks to Jamison. There were annotations of the wounds Jeremiah had inflicted, but the coroner found they were not the cause of death.

Gen roused her out of her daydreaming when she excused herself to go downstairs, probably to triple-check something she'd already triple-checked. The cafe was her life.

The sun felt good, but it was going to be a hot one. In the shade it was warm and lovely, in the sun it would soon be miserable. Listening to the world around her, she heard Jeremiah close the hood of his new truck. Opening her eyes, she swept the small yard and found him as he wiped his hands. She watched the way he moved when he placed his tools in the bed of his truck. Then he took the stairs two at a time, heading toward her. He leaned down and kissed her before he dropped into the chair Gen had just vacated. She handed him her iced tea and watched as he drained it.

"Feel up to going for a drive?" He grabbed her hand and brought it to his mouth, kissing the back of it.

"Where to?"

"The Hills. Let's pack a lunch and make a day of it."

"That sounds lovely. I'll go settle our lunch."

"Perfect. I'll let Gen know we're leaving for the day. I'm sure she'd love to have a day to run around naked in her own home."

She swatted at him. "I so did not need to hear that."

He laughed and stood up. "Be back in a second to help." He loped down the stairs and jogged into the cafe. Eden bypassed the kitchen and changed into a nice pair of shorts, a light cotton top, and slipped on a pair of sandals.

Jeremiah was back in the kitchen shoving little white boxes into a picnic basket when she returned. "What is that?"

"Gen had some stuff she's been working on. She wanted us to taste test it today and let her know which ones she should keep."

"And she had them ready to go?" Eden opened the fridge and pulled out four bottles of water, handing them to him.

"Yeah, she was going to bring them upstairs, so I asked if we could make a picnic out of them. Grab that bottle of wine, too, would you?"

"You don't like white wine." She pulled the bottle out anyway and handed it to him.

"True, but you do, and Gen said there were a couple dishes that paired well with white wine." He flipped the basket shut. "Ready?"

She laughed at him. "Where's the fire?"

He grabbed the basket and opened the door for her. "No fire, I'm just looking forward to having uninterrupted alone time with my woman. Come on." She watched him as he jogged down the stairs with the basket.

She made sure the apartment door was closed before she walked down the stairs. Jeremiah opened the passenger side door and helped her step up into his truck. He'd special-ordered a bench seat for the front. She slid over to the middle and he got into the truck. She'd barely strapped on her seatbelt before they were on the interstate.

Talks of the plans for the house they were building consumed most of the drive down to the

Hills. Remi pulled off the main road near Horse Thief Lake. The towering ponderosa mixed with densely populated lodgepole pines, crowding the road as they wound through what was obviously an unimproved gravel trail into the national forest.

Eden leaned forward to look up at the sky. "Where are we going?"

"I found this spot the day after the bar fight." Jeremiah pointed. "About another half mile up is a nice place for a picnic."

"God, that seems like a long time ago, doesn't it?" Eden leaned against his arm and rested her head on his shoulder.

"Sometimes it seems like years, sometimes like yesterday."

She hummed in agreement. "Life can be that way, can't it? Funny how time, consistent and precise, can be perceived as slow or fast."

"The human condition is such that one is always reaching toward something. Maslow's hierarchy of needs dictates when the basics of life are provided for a person will move toward love, esteem, and self-actualization. We move up and down that scale all the time. I guess our perception of how hard the route is to the next goal could skew our remembrance of how quickly we get it."

She turned and stared at him. "You know, sometimes I forget how brilliant you are."

He snorted a laugh as he put the truck in park. "I'm not sure if that is a compliment or not."

She laughed too and shook her head. "It was a compliment. Most of the time I feel like your equal and then you pop off with something deep and utterly compelling and I have to take a step back and realize that you're extraordinary."

He twisted in his seat and smiled at her. "You are my equal in all things. Never forget that."

She smiled and glanced out at where they'd stopped. "Oh, this is lovely."

He grinned from ear to ear and opened his door after taking off his seatbelt. "Come see." He jumped down from the truck and offered his hand. She took it and scooted out to where he could put his hands on her waist and help her down.

She walked a few steps from the truck and stared at the massive granite boulder to her right. Soft, wild grasses bowed in subjugation to the whispers of wind that wound through the trees. The pines provided enough shade that the heat of the summer day was muted. "Beautiful."

"I agree."

She turned. Jeremiah stood watching her with

two blankets in one hand and the picnic basket in the other. She reached for the blankets. "You are very good for my ego, sir."

"I only speak the truth." He nodded in the direction he wanted them to go, and she fell into step with him. They walked behind the boulder and he put down the basket to help her spread the blankets.

She slipped off her sandals and walked to the center of the throw, waiting for him. He toed out of his boots and carried the basket to where she was kneeling.

They emptied the basket of the small white containers and he reached for the bottle of wine. "There's one more." Eden reached for the small white box in the basket's corner.

"No, that's for dessert." His words were rushed, stilling her reach. "Wine?"

"Ah, sure. Thank you."

Gen had outdone herself. Each box held two servings of wonderful bites of heaven. Only appetizers, but the quantity of each offering filled her long before Jeremiah reached the end of the samples. "Wow, that was fantastic." She laid down and put her hand over her stomach. "Gen has missed her calling. She should be a caterer in a big city. She'd make money hand over fist."

Jeremiah broke down the empty boxes, placing them in the basket first before he carefully closed those that still contained food. "Did you save room for one last box?" He picked up the small white box, moved the picnic basket out of the way, and laid down on his stomach, propped up by his elbows as he held it in his hand.

She hummed her acknowledgement and closed her eyes, enjoying the warmth and happiness of the moment.

He bopped her nose with a finger. "You have to stay awake for this part."

She opened one eye. "Are you sure?"

He nodded and handed her the box. "You open it."

She sat up and reached for the box. He held it in his fist and beckoned her down for a kiss. Laughing, she agreed and leaned, kissing him. The laughter stopped as the heat of their connection ramped up. She was breathing hard by the time they separated. He rolled onto his back and she dropped into the hollow of his arm. She lifted the box up and opened it. Another smaller white box was inside. She chuckled and opened that one. It nestled another, even smaller box inside.

"Okay, I take it back. Gen is making me work too hard for a bit of sweet."

"Just keep going."

Two more boxes fell beside her. When she opened the last one, a square-cut diamond solitaire ring was nestled in a red velvet ring holder. She gasped and sat up. Jeremiah was beside her in the same instant. He took the ring from her hand and pulled it out of the velvet and foam holder. "This stone was my grandmother's engagement ring. I had it reset and added a few more diamonds, hoping that you'd say yes."

She popped her eyes up to his. "Yes?"

"Eden, I love you. Will you marry me?"

Her entire body shook as she nodded and then squeaked out, "Yes, oh, my, yes." Jeremiah held her hand to stop her shaking and slid it onto her finger. "You planned the entire day." She straddled his lap and wrapped her arms around his neck.

"I did, and I've been sweating bullets for a week. Gen knew and fixed the food. The woman teased me all week. I owe her payback."

She held her fingers out and stared at the ring over his shoulder. "I don't think I've ever seen a diamond that big."

He chuckled. "That isn't big. You should see the rocks Celest wears."

She brought her gaze back to him. "Where are we going to get married? Alabama or here?"

He laid down and brought her with him. She wiggled her legs between his and propped herself upon his chest. "I think we get married in Alabama and have a reception up here at the Bit and Spur. Invite everyone in the county and have an open bar with free rides home." Jeremiah chuckled, "And no knives allowed."

"Well, the Klinglers are still on probation, so I don't think they'll be showing up. How about next month? I don't need anything big, just us and our families at the justice of the peace." She leaned down and kissed him again. His hand snaked up her back to her hair. With ease, he rolled her over and devoured her, and she was more than willing to be consumed by this man. His hands knew where to caress her, how to touch her, to make her boil, and how to edge her along that point of no return and the building bliss that throbbed for freedom.

The songs of the birds in the trees and the quiet whoosh of air over the wild grasses serenaded a long, slow, sensuous build. The clothes they wore disappeared with kisses, touches and sensations replacing the feel of fabric.

Eden ran her hands over the cut muscles of his shoulders. Her hand skimmed along the scar that he'd suffered at the hands of a lunatic. She lifted and kissed his neck, skimmed the skin with her teeth, and held him as a shudder raced through his body.

They joined in complete silence. Their breathing and the sounds of their lovemaking melded with the beauty and silence of the moment. Knowing she was close, she whispered, "I will love you for the rest of my life."

He lifted away and stared down at her. "For the rest of our lives. You are my love, my heart." He dropped for a kiss and held it as her body crested. The rhythmic pulsing constricted her muscles, and she moaned into his kiss. His hips sped up until he, too, climaxed and pushed deep inside of her, his shaft kicking as he released. Eden held him as he pulled away and they both gasped for air.

She held him until he rolled off her and tucked her up against him. With a smile, she held up her hand and stared at the ring. "It's beautiful."

He reached up and took her hand in his, tilting the ring so it glittered in the sun. "My grandmother left a note with this ring when I inherited it. I'll let you read it. I have it in the same safe deposit box in Alabama where I stored her ring. It says that she would come back from the dead and tan my hide if I didn't find a woman that would stick with me through the good times and the bad. She said, 'Life isn't easy; don't go looking for a woman who won't lean forward when you're pulling hard.'"

Eden sighed, "Life isn't easy, but it is a glorious bundle of excitement, stress, and happiness. I'll share every day with you, together, by your side. I'll be there with you, pulling hard.'

He kissed her temple and sighed. "For the rest of our lives."

CHAPTER 23

A *year and a half later:*

"Are you all right?" Eden waddled up to him and he wrapped his arm around her. She was eight months pregnant with their son and he was a big boy who would be delivered via C-section in twenty-eight days—if he didn't make his appearance sooner.

"I'll be okay. I wish he'd told me before it came to this." Jamison's calls had lessened over the last year, but he and Eden had been so busy with their life that he hadn't noticed. It turned out that his friend had been fighting a brain tumor and his wife called this afternoon, letting him know Jamison had entered hospice.

"You're going to see him, right?" She sat down in his office chair and propped her swollen ankles up on his waste bin.

He sighed and shook his head. "Not with you being this close..."

Eden rubbed her stomach and eyed him. "Nope, not happening. You will go and say goodbye to your friend. I'll be fine, Gen is here, and so is Zeke if anything goes wrong."

"Zeke is not an OB doc." Jeremiah crossed his arms.

"Look, you know and I know you will regret not seeing Jamison one last time. Go, tell him how much he has meant to you and then come home to me and... Galen?"

Jeremiah made an exaggerated shudder, "God, no. Veto."

Eden sighed and patted her very round belly. "Don't worry, baby. We'll figure it out before you come. Your daddy is going to get online and buy plane tickets right now. Yes, he is." She looked up at him. "Don't make me a liar, go." She shooed him toward his computer that he kept on another desk so he could talk to his patients without looking around a monitor.

"I don't like it."

"We don't care. It is the right thing to do and you're going to do it." Eden lifted an eyebrow at him.

"Fine, but I'm making sure you have someone at the house with you at all times. Zeke can watch you at the clinic where you shouldn't be working."

Eden lifted her hands in exasperation. "I work half-days. I'd go out of my head sitting at the house watching the chickens all day. Babe, we'll be fine. Please, go and see your friend."

Jeremiah went to her and leaned over her, giving her a kiss before he dipped down and kissed her belly. "Your momma is the best woman in the world."

Eden chuckled and extended a hand to him. "Doubtful, but the one thing that is certain is she needs to use the bathroom again."

Jeremiah helped her out of the chair and watched as his beautiful wife and son toddled out of the office. He glanced at the computer and closed his eyes. The brunt of the problem was he really didn't want to say goodbye to Jamison. He didn't want to think of a world where his friend wasn't there to talk to and to laugh with, but he'd go and, as Eden said, let the man know what his friendship had meant.

The man lying in the hospital bed wasn't the man he remembered. Skin and bone, bald, and no eyebrows or eyelashes, he was pale against the white sheets. Jeremiah steeled himself and went into the room. He sat down beside the head of the bed on a small stool and put his hand over Jamison's. He could tell Jamison's wife spent a lot of time here. There were books, magazines, and needlepoint scattered around the comfortable chair beside his bed.

Memories of the time he'd spent with Jamison rolled through his mind. The indelible impact the man had made on his life was so much greater than the memories could represent.

Jamison jerked and opened his eyes, immediately looking to the chair where Marge usually sat.

Jeremiah applied light pressure to his hand. "It's all right. I'm here."

Jamison turned his head only the smallest degree as if the movement was too much. Jeremiah leaned in so Jamison could see him. "Not supposed to tell you."

Jeremiah nodded. "I'm glad she did. You don't get to cheat me out of saying goodbye, you old pain in my ass."

The man chuckled softly. "That's you."

"Maybe. I wish you would have told me. I could have been here for you."

With effort, Jamison moved his head back and forth, once. "No. Dying is a solitary event."

"The people who love you will beg to differ." He held Jamison's cold, bone-thin hand in his. "You've meant the world to me. From the first day we met we gelled. I have a father I love, but I picked you to help me grow, and in that process, I was honored to acknowledge that I had two fathers. I'm going to be straight with you. I love you and I don't want to say goodbye to you, I don't want you to leave." Jeremiah let a tear run down his cheek. Fuck it, his emotions were valid, and Jamison was a second father to him.

The frail body on the bed closed his eyes and then reopened them. "You are my son." His skeletal hand skimmed his body and landed on his chest. "Here. Be happy. Be good to yourself."

Jeremiah nodded. "I am happy."

Jamison took a shaky breath. "Talk to my boss. Promise me."

"Sure. Anything. I promise."

Jamison gave a ghost of a smile and closed his eyes. "Good. So tired."

"I know. Rest now. I'll come back later." He stared at the face of his mentor, friend, and yes, second father. The stress of talking dissolved as Jamison's body rested. He stood up and leaned forward, kissing the skeletal forehead. "Sleep in peace, my friend. You're loved."

He stepped outside the room and nearly walked into a man. "Sorry."

"Not a problem. Is he sleeping?"

Jeremiah looked at the man. He recognized the expensive cut of his suit and the hand-tailoring. The man was three inches taller than he was, which made him six feet five or six inches tall. "Yeah. I think our visit wore him out."

"The toll of talking is getting harder for him to recover from. I'm Gabriel, his boss."

Jeremiah shook the hand that was extended. "Jeremiah Wheeler."

"Jeremiah, thank you so much for sitting with him for a while. I needed a quick break." Jamison's wife, Marge, hustled back down the hallway. "He's sleeping?"

He nodded as Gabriel gave Marge a quick hug and then held her away as he spoke, "I told you you don't have to do this by yourself."

"Oh, the night nurses you provided are wonderful, but I can take care of him during the day. He put me through nursing school all those years ago, it is only right I take care of him now." She misted up as she spoke and shook her head. "I don't have many moments left with him and I'm going to be here for the ones we have. Now if you'll excuse me, I'll go check on him. He's due his pain meds soon." Marge slipped into the room.

Gabriel cocked his head in Jeremiah's direction. "You're the one that helped Victoria."

Jeremiah's eyebrows jumped. "How do you know Ms. Marshall?"

"It's a long story. You're located in Hollister now, right?"

Jeremiah nodded. "How do you know that?"

"Ah, Jamison is very proud of you." Gabriel motioned toward a set of chairs in the small sitting area outside the bedroom where the hospital bed was now set up. "Are you busy with your practice?"

Jeremiah sat down and chuckled. "Busy? No. I have a couple cases from the county, and believe it or not, a motorcycle gang has been referring me. I worked with the president's son, and they all sing my praises. It makes a rag-tag clientele list, to be sure."

Gabriel nodded and leaned forward. "I have a proposition for you."

Jeremiah waited, not drawing any conclusions on

what type of proposition Jamison's boss could toss his way. There was no way he was leaving Hollister.

"In conjunction with Frank Marshall, I'm building a small rehab center on his ranch. In our line of work, injuries happen, usually in battlefield conditions. My people deserve the very best chance at recovery I can give them. I'd like to put you on retainer to work with my people as they transition through the facility."

He leaned forward, putting his elbows on his knees. "What type of caseload are we talking about?"

Gabriel sighed and shook his head. "We're expanding quickly because of the current events around the world. I couldn't give you a number. That will depend on operations. There will be other clients that I'd like assessed to make sure they are competent to continue work. Jamison used to handle those." The man glanced at the shut door and sighed. "He told me you were the man for the job."

Jeremiah sat back. "What you propose sounds interesting. When would you like to start?"

"The contractors are putting the finishing touches on several structures. They should finish the clinic by spring."

"Send me the contract. I can give you my address."

KRIS MICHAELS

Gabriel lifted a hand. "I can get it. I'll send you the contract and the compensation package. Congratulations, by the way. You and Eden are having a boy, right?"

Jeremiah blinked and sat back. "How did you know that? We've told no one the sex of the baby."

Gabriel stood and buttoned his suit jacket. "I work for the world's largest security firm. You were vetted and so was your wife. I don't hire people I can't trust or those who have secrets that could be used against them."

Jeremiah stood. "Rather intrusive, isn't it?"

Gabriel smiled. "Perhaps, but in the long run, it pays off." He turned and walked to the closed door where Jamison rested. "I look forward to working with you, Jeremiah." He opened the door and walked in.

Jeremiah leaned back and stared at the shut door. The man's confidence should probably put him off but didn't. If he was honest, he was running out of things to do to fill the days between patients. He had plenty of money. That had never been an issue, but the desire to work, to help, had been getting stronger. So, yeah, unless this Gabriel sent him a hack of a contract, he'd take on the patients that went through the little rehab center on the Marshall ranch.

He'd let Jamison know, too. For some reason, the man had wanted him to talk to Gabriel. He was glad now he could put Jamison's worry to rest.

The door opened again, and Gabriel came out. He motioned toward Jeremiah. "He'd like to see you again. I don't think…" Gabriel shook his head and swallowed hard.

Jeremiah bolted into the room. Marge sat on one side of the bed. Tears streamed down her face as she held Jamison's hand. He moved up to the bed and took the man's other hand.

"Jay, honey, Jeremiah's here." Marge tapped his hand softly.

Jamison opened his eyes partially. "Take care. The Shadows. Promise."

He looked at Marge and she shook her head. She did not know what he was talking about. Jeremiah leaned forward and gently squeezed Jamison's hand. "You have my word. I'll take care of all of your shadows. I promise."

Jamison's body relaxed. He reached back and pulled the small stool over so he could sit down. Marge spoke to him. "He loves you. To him, you are the son we never had."

"I love him the same way," Jeremiah admitted.

Marge's eyes filled with tears as Jamison's labored breath lifted his chest. "Rest now, sweetheart. Everything's done. You don't have to worry about anything or anyone."

They sat silently in the room together, holding Jamison's hands for the next twenty minutes. When he stopped breathing, Marge reached up and kissed him tenderly. "I will always love you."

Jeremiah stood and moved over to her, hugging her as her heart broke and their tears fell.

CHAPTER 24

E *ight months later:*

"This is a big step for you." Jeremiah sat across from Doctor Adam Cassidy. The man had been a challenge to engage as a patient, but he was willing to start, and they'd had their first productive session. Adam had a long way to go. Admitting you need help, especially as a medical professional, was damn hard. The idea of being able to heal yourself was a byproduct of their training. It was also wrong. Self-diagnosis was always skewed.

"Th-thanks." The man dipped his head and nodded to the door. "R-ready?"

Jeremiah glanced down at the folder in front of him. His first Shadow. Jamison had extensive case notes on the man, and Gabriel provided more information. Information that, in his opinion, put the man in the same category as Cyrus Macmillan, and yet the man was free and working for Guardian. Taking a bolstering deep breath, he nodded. He'd do the evaluation, and unless something miraculous happened, he'd stamp a No Go on the man's file and move on.

Jeremiah stood up and limped over to the door. Adam pointed at his leg. Jeremiah understood the question. "I twisted it getting out of Phil Granger's tractor. Wasn't watching what I was doing."

Adam nodded and pointed at the door. He opened it and let Adam leave first and smiled ear to ear. Damn it, he knew there couldn't be two Ember Harrises in the world. He knew this woman.

"Good morning, sunshine! How the hell are you?"

The redhead squeaked and then jumped up. "Oh, my God! Remi Wheeler! What are you doing here?"

She launched into his arms and he laughed. "I could ask you the same question, Red." He pulled her tight and twirled her around before setting her down and planting a completely innocent kiss on her upturned lips.

Ember laughed and turned to the man she'd been sitting with while still hugging him. "Joey, this is

Remi Wheeler. He and I were on the same rotations during medical school. We put up with the same doddering old doctors and dealt with the same hospital politics and med school bureaucracy before we went our different ways."

He released Ember and held out his hand. Ah, so this was Joseph, aka Fury. "Dr. Jeremiah Wheeler. I take it you two are friends."

Joseph extended a hand and grasped his. The power behind the shake was an obvious warning. "No, she is more than a friend. In the interest of full disclosure, if you kiss her like that again, I'll kill you." Aggression rolled off the man in waves. Jeremiah had dealt with people of his ilk before, but usually, they were behind bars. Thank God after signing iron-clad NDAs they had briefed him on exactly what these... assassins could and couldn't do. It took him months to wrap his head around the fact that Guardian employed assassins to perform horrendous acts which were sanctioned by a worldwide council.

He gripped the man's hand harder and stared straight into his eyes. "Yeah? Well, if you kill me, it won't be sanctioned."

The assassin wrapped his arm around Ember's

shoulders and tucked her close to his side. Another possessive move, bordering on abusive.

"True, but the idea of an off-the-books hit doesn't bother me right now. Make an informed decision, Doc. It may be your last."

Jeremiah threw back his head and laughed. If the man wasn't a psychotic killer, he could like the guy. " Fair enough. You have no worries. I have a woman in Hollister that will string me up by the balls if I stray. Now, since I sense absolutely zero trust from you, big guy, why don't we do our session first, and if Ember agrees, you can sit in when I talk to her about last week?"

Ember rushed to agree. "That's fine. I think I'd actually prefer Joey to be with me." He nodded. He could read the room, and he could see that this man didn't want him to be alone with Ember. Fine, he'd adapt.

Jeremiah sat down and pulled out a pad of paper and a pen. He drew a deep breath and released it, clearing his mind of everything but the evaluation at hand. He watched the assassin scan him up and down with those cold-as-fuck eyes. "Done measuring me?"

"Yes." Well, no attempt to obscure the facts at

hand. Straightforward was a demeanor with which he could work.

"Tell me. What do you see?"

"Clarify the question," Joseph snapped the response.

Ah... this was going to be a tough nut to crack. This man would never open up. What he needed to know would be obtained with the word equivalent of a crowbar. "You sized me up. What do you see?" He leaned back to relax the conversation, but the information that Gabriel had provided him yesterday was still in the forefront of his mind.

Joseph's facial expression didn't change one iota as he replied, "You appear relaxed. You're not. You limp slightly on your left leg. I would exploit that weakness should I decide to kill you. Your heart rate is elevated. Your repetitive clicking of that pen indicates you're nervous. Smart man. You've read my file, and my relationship with an old friend of yours has upset you. Most likely because of what you've learned from that data. You've been around hard people. You're comfortable in that environment. You're not comfortable around me. Probably because what I do upsets your morals."

To say he was astounded at the clarity of the man's mind—and to a degree, his ability to read him,

KRIS MICHAELS

even with his professional armor on—would be an understatement. He placed the pen and paper down. Okay, so it was time to find Joseph's edges. "You're very astute, Joey."

The man's eyes narrowed. "If I weren't, I wouldn't be alive. Knowing my environment and my enemy is essential. My name is Joseph."

Jeremiah smiled. One point for him. Joseph considered him an enemy, and he didn't like the use of Joey, at least not from him. "I'm not your enemy, and Ember called you Joey."

"You're not my friend. Therefore, you're a potential enemy. She is the only one who calls me Joey."

Ah. Point number two. There was no in-between with the man. You were one or the other. Friend or foe. Straight lines and structure-based reasoning. He needed to push farther. "The fact you limit your friends isn't surprising. Why is Red the only one who calls you Joey?"

A sneer appeared on Joseph's face for a nanosecond. "I allow her to do so."

Interesting. Jeremiah knew the answer to the next question, but he asked it anyway. "Do you have to control everything? Even what people call you?"

"Yes." Joseph's expression revealed nothing.

"Why?"

The man focused somewhere over his shoulder and answered. "I want to live."

Jeremiah went through all the documentation they had provided him. The recent wounds that the man was recovering from were a testament to that will. "You almost didn't live. Your last assignment almost killed you."

"Yes."

Again, no eye contact and one-word answers. So, he prompted, "Tell me about it."

"Clarify the question." Again, the assassin's quick comeback zinged his way.

Jeremiah referred back to the verbal crowbar and expounded, "Tell me what happened after your cover was blown." He leaned back in his chair and waited.

"I was taken."

"And then?"

"I woke in a dungeon with my hands tied to a wooden pole. They didn't secure my legs. That was their second mistake."

Jeremiah jotted that down. Interesting, leading off with a second mistake instead of a first. Something to circle back and address. "Go on."

The man shrugged. "Things got uncomfortable. You read my file. You know very well what happened."

He dug deeper as he needed to determine if this man could perform for the company, and what he'd received so far was minimal. He turned the verbal sparring corner and asked a harder question. "How did you endure the pain?"

Joseph blinked and looked at him. "Clarify the question."

Jeremiah did. "According to the medical records, they peeled your skin off your back. The pain must have been excruciating. How did you deal with the pain?"

The man's expression didn't change. "I focused."

Jeremiah waited a minute before he asked, "On what?"

That sneer came back in full force, and Joseph spoke with a growl, "Killing the motherfucker."

"And did you?"

"Yes."

"How?"

Joseph lifted his hand and replied, "I freed my left hand and severed his carotid artery with a scalpel."

Jeremiah had read that account. He'd thrown the scalpel. He continued through the incident. "How did you escape?"

"I ran."

Jeremiah lifted an eyebrow, "Just ran? Nobody

said anything to you about the strips of skin hanging off you? The blood? That must have been obvious."

"An old woman saved my life. She hid me underneath the floor in the kitchen of the compound where I was held. Two days after she moved me out of the crawl space, they found it. She refused to tell them where the women of the village had hidden me. They pulled her into the town square and raped her––broke every bone in her body and then eviscerated her alive as a warning to others never to help the enemy again."

That bit of information wasn't in his briefing. The atrocities of war were impossible to understand unless you've been there. He knew that from working with people who'd returned from combat. The world did not reserve depravity for the Cyrus Macmillans of the world, proof in point. "Intelligence reports indicate all the men in that compound were mutilated and dismembered."

"Do they?"

He nodded. This was the money question, the one thing that would stop this man from going back out to the field. If he went off script, it would end his career. "Yes. Did you do that, Joseph?"

The man met his eyes. "No."

"Then who did?"

"I don't speculate."

Jeremiah snorted. He would not let this one go, and the assassin in front of him had to know that fact. "Ah heck, just this once, give it a try. It'll stay between us."

Joseph gave him the full weight of his icy stare.

"I killed who I had to, Doc. Clean, quiet. When I finished, I opened the compound gates and drove one of the guard's trucks away. The women must have done what is indicated in the reports."

There was no way in hell. He shook his head, not trying to hide the disbelief. The man had to be lying now. "Women? You believe old women committed this… this atrocity?"

"Aside from the fact that it takes a fair degree of strength to dismember a body and I was not at my best, those men took everything from that village. They murdered husbands and sons. Daughters as young as eight vanished into the compound, never to return. The women spoke of the screams they heard at night, the helplessness and guilt they lived with. Those bastards kept them alive to be servants, and the dogs were treated better than they were. I'm an assassin, Doctor. They were victims. I made it safe for them. What they or anyone else did after I left isn't my concern."

332

Jeremiah absorbed the words and the simple way this man dealt with the horror that he'd read in the report. "You're very matter of fact about this abomination."

Joseph laughed and Jeremiah flinched at the outburst. Jeremiah drew a breath and pushed his focus back onto the man in front of him. "I don't fabricate drama or surround myself in fantasies, Doctor. You asked for the facts, then you asked me to speculate. I provided you both. How you process the information isn't my concern. Your outrage is your baggage. You deal with it."

Jeremiah counted to seven slowly. The assassin in front of him was blunt and, in fact, correct. He cleared his throat twice and glanced down at his pad. Time to circle back to the points he still needed to address. "Okay, let's backtrack for just a second. You said leaving your legs untied was the enemy's second mistake. What was the first?"

This time that sneer almost appeared as a smile. "They didn't kill me immediately. Rank amateurs."

Jeremiah leaned back. Time to take off the gloves and make a determination. "Tell me, do you care about the lives you took?"

"Bingo. The money question sprung after a distraction. Do they teach that in Shrink 101? Every fucking one of you have the technique down. I don't have sociopathic tendencies, Doctor. Why don't I save us both some time and effort? Do I value human life? Yes, I do. Would I have taken those lives if it were not for the requirements of my job, for my safety, or to protect those women? No. Did I have average family attachments growing up? Yes, I love my family. They're big, noisy, and messed up, but they are mine. Do I have healthy relationships with women? If you asked me before Ember came back into my life, I would say no. I used women for sex. Do I have problems dealing with what I do for a living? Absolutely not. I have never had a sleepless night. I trust my handlers at Guardian implicitly."

Jeremiah narrowed his eyes and picked out the slice of that diatribe that clunked. Everything else was smooth, almost practiced. Something a sociopath would say in order to make themselves sound normal. "Since Ember came back into your life? You knew her before?"

"Yes."

He had to stop himself from chuckling. One-word answers again. "Would you care to elaborate?"

"No."

This wasn't getting easier. The man was slick, but he'd yet to provide any information that he could grasp onto to prove or disprove his diagnosis. "You threatened to kill me if I kissed Ember again. That is territorial and in direct conflict to your stated reasons for killing—your job and safety."

"Yes."

Jeremiah leaned forward. "Please explain."

"Ember is a part of me, and you threatened that part."

He scoffed. "With a simple kiss?"

"Yes."

He pushed on. "Don't you trust her?"

"Of course, I do, but I don't trust you."

Ah, back to the straight lines and structure. Friends and foes. "Why not? Guardian does. Gabriel does. He directed you to talk to me."

Joseph cocked his head. "If a complete stranger did the same to your woman in Hollister, would you trust him?"

He smiled. "No. Can't say that I would. But I don't think I would threaten to kill him."

The assassin looked bored. "No, you'd just think it. The difference between me and your polite society? I act."

Jeremiah lifted an eyebrow. Directly challenging the man in front of him, he asked, "And still you maintain you have no sociopathic tendencies?"

Joseph chuckled and shrugged. "I've been tested. The results are in the records you hold. Now, can we cut the hypothetical bullshit about what I would or wouldn't do?"

"All right, let's talk about this past week. How many people have you killed in the last seven days?"

"Three."

"How many were sanctioned kills?"

"One."

"The other two?"

"Had the intent, opportunity, and capability of killing Ember. I prevented that."

"And why would they want to kill Ember?"

"If you needed that information, it would have been provided to you. Not my place to fill you in on the specifics, Doc."

"You act as if this is a game, Joseph. How many of these evaluations have you gone through?"

"Is that a roundabout way of asking how many people I've killed?"

It was. He was curious as to how this man had reached this point. "Yes."

The assassin deadpanned, "If you needed to know, it would have been provided to you."

Damn, he'd expected more out of the man. He blinked and then shook his head. "Pat answer and a complete cop-out. How many lives have you taken Joseph?"

"It doesn't really matter. What matters is that I need to be cleared to take at least one more."

Ah, this was new. Joseph wanted to be cleared again. "Why? What is so relevant about your next kill?" He leaned forward.

"It'll be my last mission." Joseph leaned back in the chair. "Clear me for this last mission, Doc. After it's over, I'll never have to be cleared again."

Jeremiah smirked at the verbal maneuvering. It would not be productive. "That's not how this works."

"Sure, it is. You and I both know I passed every objective of this interview. Do your job and let me do mine."

He steepled his fingers together. No, he hadn't passed every objective. Not yet. "Tell me how many people you have murdered or assassinated, Joseph."

"Two different topics. Murdered? One. Assassinated at my country's request? Fifty-three."

Unbelievable. The number was staggering. He thought of Cyrus, who'd killed over sixty people they knew of, and all the people he'd killed just because they were in the way of the person he wanted dead. Finally, he asked, "Fifty-three assassinations. How many more were collateral damage?"

Joseph shrugged. "None that were innocent civilians."

A technical difference to Cyrus, but it was a difference. He changed tactics. "All right. Who did you murder?"

"The piece of shit that killed my father. I was sixteen. And yes, if I had to do it again, I would."

So, no remorse. He moved forward using a different attack. "Have you asked yourself if you can walk away from this? Turn your back on the massive adrenaline spike? Will you be able to leave this life and power behind?"

"Leaving it behind won't be an issue. There's little likelihood I'll return from this mission. Next to zero. This is the end of the road for me."

Well, shit, that was not what he expected to hear. He needed clarification. "Then why are you going?"

The man leaned forward and talked to his loosely clasped hands. "If I don't, they'll find Ember and they'll kill her. If the choice is her or me? The answer will always be her. I'm willing to die so she can live."

Well, that statement just turned his anticipated diagnosis on its ear. "Does she know?"

"That I'm leaving? Yeah. She knows I won't contact her again. I've told her from the start our relationship ends when I leave. She doesn't know this is my last mission. She doesn't know I don't expect to come back alive. She doesn't need to know the choices I made to keep her safe and give her a future. If you know her, then you know such knowledge would eat her alive. So, those sociopathic tendencies you think I have? They aren't too much of a concern any longer, are they?"

He blew the air out of his lungs and answered honestly, "No. Loving someone so deeply would eliminate that concern."

"Huh. You don't say." Jeremiah stared at the man. Joseph's comment was the equivalent of a huge 'fuck you'. He'd take it. The man had finally opened up and given him the answers he needed. He was going to get his Go on the evaluation.

Realizing he'd passed the evaluation, Joseph rose and went to the door. Jeremiah drew a deep breath and got ready to deal with his old friend with her overprotective assassin boyfriend in the room. Yay. He put his pen and paper down and rubbed his face. He was going to renegotiate his contract. Gabriel wasn't paying him enough.

CHAPTER 25

P*resent Day*:

Eden sat on the porch rocking Carmen even though she'd fallen asleep a half-hour ago. The sun was warm, and the house blocked the cool spring breeze. She watched as Jay helped his father by handing him tools from the toolbox. It would have taken half the time to work on the old thing if Jeremiah had gone at it alone.

She couldn't hear what was being said, but Jeremiah's low rumble as he pointed and talked made her smile. He was so patient with Jamison, who wanted to know everything about everything. She glanced down at their daughter and smiled. She was blessed. With Jeremiah's practice at full capacity thanks to Guardian, she'd followed her heart and quit her full-time job with the county. She still worked one day a week to give Zeke a day off. It was the best of both worlds for her. Phil Granger's wife watched Jay and Carmen until Auntie Gen was done at the cafe. The children loved Gen, and the woman doted on each of them.

Speaking of which, she smiled as Gen's truck came into view. Auntie Gen was going to take the kids for the night. She did it once a month, which gave Mom and Dad some quality time together.

When Jay saw her truck, he took off running down the dirt road, his arms waving wildly. Jeremiah shouted, "Jamison Riley Wheeler, you be careful!" She stood up and watched. Gen stopped the truck and got out, going to her knees for a hug. They climbed back into the truck, and although she couldn't see it, she knew Jay was driving the truck the rest of the way down the drive.

Jeremiah walked back to the house and leaned down to kiss her and then brush his lips on Carmen's dark hair. "I'll have to fix that tractor tomorrow; he wants to help."

She leaned into him when he wrapped his arm around her. "He's grown up when we weren't looking."

KRIS MICHAELS

"When did he get so big?" Jeremiah chuckled and waved when his sister's truck came to a stop and Jay put it in gear. His smile was bigger than the South Dakota sky.

"Mom, Dad! Gen said she got a new superhero movie and we're having popcorn. I'll go get my bag. Be right back, Auntie Gen!"

Gen laughed as she walked up to the house. "Ah, there's my little sweetheart. Come to Auntie Gen." Gen took Carmen and kissed her as she started rocking back and forth. "I love the smell of babies."

Jeremiah snorted. "Some smells I could do without."

Eden laughed and led them into the house. "I'll get her bag."

"I got it, Mom. Come on, Auntie Gen, we got to go." Jay raced back through the house, his backpack and the diaper bag bouncing as he ran.

"Whoa there, mister." Jeremiah lifted the diaper bag. "Trying to put me out of work?"

"Nope, but it's the latest release, dad."

Jeremiah leaned down. "See if she'll let us borrow it so I can watch it, too."

Jay put out his fist and Jeremiah bumped it with his own. They were out the door a moment later.

Eden chuckled at their antics. "Thanks, Gen." She

342

kissed Carmen one more time and gave Gen a baby quilt to keep the cool wind off Carmen.

"I love this. I plan for it all month. Besides, I want to see that new movie. Jay has me hooked on those damn superheroes. I'll have them back about noon tomorrow, then I'll head into Rapid for my monthly run. Do you need anything?"

"Let me grab the bottles out of the fridge and yeah, actually, I do have a list. I'll give it to you tomorrow along with the cash for it." She put the bottles into a thermal tote, and they walked out to where Jeremiah was putting the car seat into the truck.

Gen handed the baby to Jeremiah when he turned to her and nudged Eden. "I'm not worried about the money. I know where you live."

"I'll have it, anyway. You're coming out for dinner when you get back?"

"God, yes. I'll drop off all the orders from Hollister and my stuff and head out here. Hey, did you hear Andrew Hollister is coming home? According to Phil, he was hurt pretty bad overseas."

"No, I hadn't heard. I expect his father is glad to get his boy home." Now that she knew the bond between a parent and a child, she was positive of the fact.

"Yeah, not what I heard." Gen glanced at Jay, who was strapping into his seatbelt. She added, "But that's a story for another time."

"I look forward to it." Eden watched as Gen got into her truck, did a wide turn, and headed back into Hollister, ten minutes away.

Jeremiah dropped his arm over her shoulder. "I miss them already."

She chuckled; she did too. "How about I promise to take your mind off them for a minute or two?"

Jeremiah turned her and wrapped both hands around her waist. "Only a minute or two?"

She shrugged. "I could try harder."

He lowered and spoke a few millimeters from her lips, "You never have to try for me."

The kiss was slow and sweet, perfect in every way. They walked into the house and headed to the bedroom. Their time together was precious, and the stresses of a practice, the children, and day-to-day life fell away like autumn leaves in a soft wind.

After Carmen, she'd kept a little of the baby weight. She wasn't as toned, was softer, and most definitely self-conscious of the changes to her body, yet Jeremiah's passion for her hadn't changed. She undressed as he did, and they slipped under the sheets.

He pulled her to him. Not in a hurry. They touched, teased, and reconnected. A far cry from the rushed love making they caught through the month, this night was special; it grounded her as his lover, not just the mother of his children but something more. This connection was a foundation to all the rest.

Since she'd given birth, he'd taken extra care to excite and entice her. The feel of his fingers and lips on her skin as he went lower and lower pushed a shiver through her. As his lips found her core, she grabbed his hair and arched. The deliciousness of that gripping feeling low in her belly rolled with the passion his touch and kisses created.

She pulled his hair and beckoned him back up to her mouth. He obliged and situated himself between her legs. She wrapped her legs around his waist and reached down to guide his shaft to her center.

He entered her and stared down at her. "You are so beautiful."

She smiled and reached up, wrapping her arms around his neck. "Only to you, but that's all I ever wanted."

They rose to the crest slowly, in no hurry or rush. He found a rhythm that grew the tension and excitement but would draw out their pleasure. Eden kissed his shoulder and chest, sucking up a hickey where it wouldn't be seen, and used her hands to once again memorize every muscled ridge of the man she loved.

When they climaxed, she floated on the remnants of the lovemaking, closing her eyes and just being with her husband, the peace in the house amplified by the sounds of his breaths as he lay beside her. The utter contentment was perfection.

Until it wasn't.

Jeremiah's phone vibrated from somewhere on the floor. "Don't answer it." Gen would call her first, not Jeremiah, so the call wasn't about the children.

He sighed and rolled over. "Not really a choice."

She knew it, and the interruption shouldn't have bothered her as much as it did. However, a feeling of dread overtook her. She sat up in the bed as he stretched to reach his jeans.

"Wheeler." His eyes darted over to hers and then he raced to the window facing east. "When?"

"Who?" He ran his hand through his hair. "Do you need me?"

He sent her another look, this one scared her. "All right. I'll be on standby." He ended the connection.

She immediately asked, "What is it? What's happened?"

"There was an incident. A plane crashed just before landing at the Marshall ranch."

Eden untangled from the bed and went to him. "Do they know who was on board?"

He shook his head and wrapped his arms around her. "Not yet. This isn't good, babe. This isn't good at all."

Click here to read the next in the <u>Kings of Guardian Series</u>, The Siege Part One, Book Fifteen and The Siege Part Two, Book Sixteen.

Do you want a hint as to what's going to happen? Read Reaper's book for a small glimpse!

Reaper, Guardian Shadow World, Book Seven

This is not the end. It is just the beginning.

ALSO BY KRIS MICHAELS

Kings of the Guardian Series

Jacob: Kings of the Guardian Book 1

Joseph: Kings of the Guardian Book 2

Adam: Kings of the Guardian Book 3

Jason: Kings of the Guardian Book 4

Jared: Kings of the Guardian Book 5

Jasmine: Kings of the Guardian Book 6

Chief: The Kings of Guardian Book 7

Jewell: Kings of the Guardian Book 8

Jade: Kings of the Guardian Book 9

Justin: Kings of the Guardian Book 10

Christmas with the Kings

Drake: Kings of the Guardian Book 11

Dixon: Kings of the Guardian Book 12

Passages: The Kings of Guardian Book 13

Promises: The Kings of Guardian Book 14

The Siege: Book One, The Kings of Guardian Book 15

The Siege: Book Two, The Kings of Guardian Book 16

A Backwater Blessing: A Kings of Guardian Crossover Novella

Montana Guardian: A Kings of Guardian Novella

Guardian Defenders Series

Gabriel

Maliki

John

Jeremiah

Frank

Creed

Sage

Bear

Billy

Elliot

Guardian Security Shadow World

Anubis (Guardian Shadow World Book 1)

Asp (Guardian Shadow World Book 2)

Lycos (Guardian Shadow World Book 3)

Thanatos (Guardian Shadow World Book 4)

Tempest (Guardian Shadow World Book 5)

Smoke (Guardian Shadow World Book 6)

Reaper (Guardian Shadow World Book 7)

Phoenix (Guardian Shadow World Book 8)

Valkyrie (Guardian Shadow World Book 9)

Flack (Guardian Shadow World Book 10)

Ice (Guardian Shadow World Book 11)

Malice (Guardian Shadow World Book 12)

Harbinger (Guardian Shadow World Book 13)

Centurion (Guardian Shadow World Book 14)

Maximus (Guardian Shadow World Book 15)

Hollister (A Guardian Crossover Series)

Andrew (Hollister-Book 1)

Searching for Home (A Hollister-Guardian Crossover Novel)

Zeke (Hollister-Book 2)

Declan (Hollister- Book 3)

A Home for Love (A Hollister Crossover Novel)

Ken (Hollister - Book 4)

Finally Home (A Hollister Crossover Novel)

Barry (Hollister - Book 5)

Hope City

Hope City - Brock

HOPE CITY - Brody- Book 3

Hope City - Ryker - Book 5

Hope City - Killian - Book 8

Hope City - Blayze - Book 10

The Long Road Home

Season One:

My Heart's Home

Season Two:

Searching for Home (A Hollister-Guardian Crossover Novel)

Season Three:

A Home for Love (A Hollister Crossover Novel)

Season Four:

Finally Home (A Hollister Crossover Novel)

STAND-ALONE NOVELS

A Heart's Desire - Stand Alone

Hot SEAL, Single Malt (SEALs in Paradise)

Hot SEAL, Savannah Nights (SEALs in Paradise)

Hot SEAL, Silent Knight (SEALs in Paradise)

Join my newsletter for fun updates and release information!

>>>Kris' Newsletter<<<

ABOUT THE AUTHOR

USA Today and Amazon Bestselling Author, Kris Michaels is the alter ego of a happily married wife and mother. She writes romance, usually with characters from military and law enforcement backgrounds.

Made in the USA
Middletown, DE
31 August 2025

13425713R00199